A

Julian St. Aubyn's good looks and winning charm were such that Chloe found herself baring her secret heart to him. "Grandmama has informed me that I am to accept Lord Twisdale, and I simply cannot like the man," she confided.

"As to that, my pater has informed me that I must marry properly or risk my funds being greatly reduced," St. Aubyn countered.

"And a gentleman needs his funds to live in this world, does he not?" Chloe replied. She studied him, remembering him but a short while ago with his latest conquest, the ravishing Elinor Hadlow. "Are you truly a scoundrel?" she asked.

"I am," St. Aubyn affirmed. He let this innocent chit of a girl absorb this before he continued. "It seems we both have serious problems. But there is a possible solution." He looked into Chloe's eyes. "We might help each other," he suggested softly.

Chloe trembled at what this unrepentant libertine was about to propose—and at the terribly tantalizing temptation to whisper yes. . . .

SIGNET REGENCY ROMANCE
COMING IN JULY 1994

---•---

Barbara Allister
An Amiable Arrangement

Carla Kelly
Miss Whittier Makes A List

Gail Eastwood
A Perilous Journey

---•---

The Scoundrel's Bride

by

Emily Hendrickson

A SIGNET BOOK

SIGNET
Published by the Penguin Group
Penguin Books USA Inc., 375 Hudson Street,
New York, New York 10014, U.S.A.
Penguin Books Ltd, 27 Wrights Lane,
London W8 5TZ, England
Penguin Books Australia Ltd, Ringwood,
Victoria, Australia
Penguin Books Canada Ltd, 10 Alcorn Avenue,
Toronto, Ontario, Canada M4V 3B2
Penguin Books (N.Z.) Ltd, 182–190 Wairau Road,
Auckland 10, New Zealand

Penguin Books Ltd, Registered Offices:
Harmondsworth, Middlesex, England

First published by Signet,
an imprint of Dutton Signet,
a division of Penguin Books USA Inc.

First Printing, June, 1994
10 9 8 7 6 5 4 3 2 1

Dedicated to Laura Watson,
my Canadian lawyer friend,
whose expertise in Old English law,
especially regarding annulments,
proved most valuable.

Chapter 1

*F*rom a quiet, uninhabited corner in Lady Purcell's ballroom behind a convenient potted palm tree, Lady Chloe Maitland sketched the man who so fascinated her. Secure in her niche, she executed the clever little drawing with amazing skill for one untutored. Deft, swift lines captured the essence of the man as she perceived him.

He stood at ease in his starched collar and elegant cravat and the dark gray coat that fit his broad shoulders so admirably. He seemed wickedly handsome to Chloe, even after viewing nearly all the unattached, eligible men in London. Perhaps it was the dark hair that curled so appealingly about his well-shaped head, or maybe it was the insouciant smile that seemed to flit frequently across that lightly tanned and sharply chiseled face. He used a cane—not as a fashion accessory as most men—but because he appeared to require it. Then Chloe wondered if that was a flash of pain she glimpsed just now from across the room and her curiosity—and compassion—grew.

She studied him more intently. He chatted with her very beautiful and quite young aunt. Elinor Maitland Hadlow was the child of her late great-uncle's second wife and thus but a few years older than Chloe. Beautiful, willful, and not a particularly comfortable relative, Chloe tended to avoid contact with her.

There was something about that conversation that intrigued Chloe. Aunt Elinor looked furious, although she concealed it well. Chloe respected anyone who could make her aunt angry and survive. What do you suppose they discussed? A rather unpleasant smell assailed her nose, irritating it. She hastily smothered a sneeze.

"So this is where you are, Lady Chloe," Lord Twisdale

complained as he drew up beside her, huffing slightly in his haste. He peered at her with disfavor, most likely not appreciating her sneeze. Since the untimely death of his wife and subsequent search for a successor, he proclaimed the need for health in a second wife.

"Indeed," she said, keeping her face and voice carefully neutral. Quickly putting her sketch pad down along the folds of her gown, she rose to face him while waving her handkerchief about in the air. When one spoke with Lord Twisdale it was well to be upwind of the man. He drenched himself in a strong scent of musk that irritated her nose.

Chloe could not prevent a certain stiffening when he took a propitiatory grasp of her arm to remove her from her pleasant seclusion. For a few moments she had managed to set aside her feeling of impending doom; now he intruded.

"Come now, you promised me the next cotillion." There was no courtly coaxing in his voice, but rather a cold command.

"My grandmama did, I believe," Chloe said in a quiet voice. She cast her gaze downward lest she reveal her inner response to this man. Oh, but she found it difficult to be obedient as a girl ought when it came to Lord Twisdale.

"Same thing, my girl," said the somewhat—to Chloe's youthful eyes—elderly Lord Twisdale. His being thirty years senior to her made him seem ancient. But, it must be admitted, his being slightly plump with graying hair not to mention his air of worldly fatigue added to her belief.

Having quickly managed to conceal her pencil and pad in her reticule, Chloe walked at his lordship's side until they reached the polished floor where other couples congregated. She tried valiantly to join in the gaiety. As the dance involved frequent whirling about without his clasp on her person, she felt sufficiently free to enjoy it a little without a sense of dread.

But for a girl who had discovered she was basically shy, the London Season proved to be a great trial. Facing the gentlemen of the ton was not the least like bantering with a neighbor boy back home in Wiltshire. There she knew most everyone and felt most comfortable with them. In London she found elegant gentlemen and awesome dandies.

She and Lord Twisdale joined the same set as her aunt

and Sir Augustus Dabney, so Chloe had a chance to observe the lady more closely. Aunt Elinor was up to something; Chloe recognized that devious look in her eyes. Might her scheming have something to do with the handsome gentleman who had so infuriated her not so long ago? What *had* he said?

Chloe's gaze again sought the stranger who had been talking with her aunt until she caught sight of him across the room. He stood out from all the other men. She was disappointed to see him stroll toward the hall, a faint limp marring his progress. How sad he must leave, for she was intrigued with him and longed to watch him—from a safe distance, of course—a while longer.

Lord Twisdale claimed her hand and she must pay attention to the steps of the dance once again. She was a good dancer, if a quiet one. No bubbling laughter or flirting came from her. She had felt too hesitant about fluttering her lashes or bantering with the men she had met while in London. Pure and simple, they intimidated her with their polished airs and terribly civilized conversation. Wiltshire boys were far easier to converse with, she had decided.

As soon as the dance ended, she turned to face her aunt. "Good evening, Aunt Elinor." Elinor always hated to be called aunt—she said it made her feel ancient. "Lovely to see you again." Chloe had learned all the polite lies, the ones she must utter whether she liked to or not. In this instance she found it almost easy.

"I do not believe we have met before," Lord Twisdale said, intruding on the greetings of the not-very-friendly relatives.

Chloe performed the introductions with commendable grace, considering she disliked both people. She flashed an angry look at Lord Twisdale when he clasped her arm in a more-than-paternal grip, and tried to ease away from his side. "I believe Grandmama . . ." she began at last, breaking into their conversation when possible.

"Certainly, certainly, my dear girl. At once." With an appraising, all-encompassing look at Elinor, Lord Twisdale escorted Chloe back to her grandmother, as proper, then left immediately to wander in Elinor's direction. Chloe could only view that as a blessing.

"You had best make up your mind to marry him," the dowager said. "And do not try to nudge him in the direction of your aunt. It will not do in the least."

Quite unable to respond to this threat—or was it more serious than that?—Chloe mumbled something about a torn flounce and nearly ran in her flight to escape the room and the odious Lord Twisdale. He had made his objective quite clear—he looked for a second wife. He wished a biddable, innocent girl.

Just because Chloe had rejected the offer from Mr. Fane, the younger son of a wealthy viscount, Grandmama had decreed that henceforth Chloe was to accept Lord Twisdale's attentions. No protestation from her could shake that determination. Grandmama Dancy was a dragon of the first water.

What Chloe hesitated to reveal was that she had discovered that the Honorable Thomas Fane was head over heels in love with pretty little Mary Walsham. The very notion of marrying a man who loved another he was forbidden to wed because of her lack of fortune did not appeal to the romantic and tender-hearted Chloe. Not in the least. To tell the truth she was not all that pleased that he would wed her for her fortune rather than her person, although she knew that was the way things were done.

If only she might explain *why* she had refused. Her Tartar of a grandmama would hear no excuses and Chloe did not have the ability to forcibly communicate her point of view. Her dearest mama was far away on a honeymoon trip with her second husband. *She* would have understood, had she been here. But that was the rub—she was not.

Chloe felt a little betrayal at the desertion. Were Mama present, Chloe just knew she would have felt more courageous. She also knew that her mother would not have dressed her in dull gray as did Grandmama Dancy. Proper color for a shy girl, bah. Chloe felt a stir of rebellion.

She was an heiress—albeit a modest one. She also was from the Dancy family and that was no humble claim. Just because she was as timid as a dormouse did not mean that she might not aspire to greater heights, like her more daring and outgoing cousins had.

But Chloe's Grandmama Dancy had been given control over Chloe and her future while Mama was gone. Until she returned, when the power over Chloe and her fortune would become the responsibility of Mama's new husband, the Earl of Crompton, Grandmama's word was law. And now the pressure to obey that "law" was being applied every day. Chloe wished she had the strength to defy her grandmama, but she tried to be properly dutiful.

Tonight she must dance with Lord Twisdale, tomorrow she was to accept a drive in the park with the man. As she hurried along the hall, she again considered the means of her punishment.

He was a trifle over average in height and sported graying sideburns. They gave Lord Twisdale a menacing appearance, she thought. He creaked a touch when he bowed over her hand—his corset, no doubt. Quite a few elderly gentlemen had adopted them following the Prince Regent's obvious need and use of the restrictive device.

Chloe could not like his lordship. That he would pursue a young girl not long out of the schoolroom alarmed her, although she knew it was not unusual. However, she had heard stories whispered about him when ladies thought she was not listening. He was rumored to be cruel, and his wife had died not long ago under odd circumstances, or so it was said. It seemed quite strange to Chloe that his lordship would disregard the conventions of society to consider marrying so soon. Perhaps that promised a long engagement? Were she to be compelled to wed the man, she prayed that was the case. She had no desire to wed him, however, not *any* man unless she cared for him.

Rounding the corner from the hall into a pretty little room, she ran to the window to survey the lighted gardens behind the Purcell house, hoping to catch her breath and deliberate a bit. What was she to do? Was there any way at all that she might escape her dilemma? Her sigh was from the bottom of her distressed heart and she just barely fought back the tears that longed to flow.

The pretty colored lanterns that hung in the Purcell gardens swayed in a gentle breeze unseen by her tightly shut eyes.

* * *

Julian St. Aubyn had retreated to the shadows of a pleasant little anteroom where Elinor promised to meet him later on. Promise? It was more like a threat. He found himself in an unaccustomed predicament. That a man labeled a scoundrel by Society should have been trapped—no, almost trapped—by a widow was unthinkable. Yet here he was, considering how best to extricate himself from an entanglement.

A most lovely and delicate creature, Elinor Hadlow had enticed him while she was still wife to the elderly Mr. Hadlow. Julian ought to have known he should turn his attentions elsewhere once Hadlow went aloft.

Instead, he stupidly consoled the new widow. Was ever a more dangerous pursuit conceived? But . . . her dark auburn hair curled pleasingly about her face, setting off a fine pair of blue eyes, not to mention soft cheeks that held a luscious dimple next to her highly kissable mouth. Ah, she was a delight to gladden the heart of any scoundrel. And she was so available.

But he had erred, he scolded himself. *That* was how bachelors became trapped, he reminded himself. And *that* he had vowed to avoid, he concluded—at least for the time being, until absolutely necessary. He was having far too good a time in London to settle down in the country!

He was, he confessed, a scoundrel, just as he had been labeled. But it proved to be an amusing life . . . or had until this moment. Somehow he would gracefully disengage himself from the liaison. And, he also decided, he would inveigle Elinor into the position where she would be the one to make the break. He smothered a grin at this masterly notion.

Ah, the life of a scoundrel was not all so bad. His mother would have said he was merely mischievous but then, she had always been partial to him. He had no intention of marrying, at least not for some years.

Pity his time with Elinor had come to an end, for she had offered such promise. She came from an excellent family. Although—lately her tongue had been a trifle sharp, shrewish, almost. It was indeed a shame.

He might give her a disgust of him, or perhaps he could

flirt with another woman, to make Elinor annoyed. It might serve to force her to be the one who cried off. For Julian strongly suspected that lovely Elinor Hadlow desired more than a flirtation. She wished to become a wife. His wife. And that he would not allow.

His quiet contemplation and strategy planning came to an abrupt end when his little room was invaded by a young woman who appeared to be escaping a demon. She was a little dab of a girl dressed in a dreadful gown of gray sarcenet suitable for a dowager. However, he observed, her pretty curls that someone had tried to subdue now curled prettily about her face. And she had a pleasing figure, from what he could detect considering the lamentable cut of her gown.

Really, someone had much to answer for—decking a young woman out like a widow. At the thought of a widow, he drew up a trifle straighter and looked more sharply at her.

"Surely a pretty little thing like you cannot possibly be that troubled. What is it? A torn flounce? Too many beaux?" The teasing, flirtatious voice stopped Chloe in midthought.

She whirled about to see the man she had hastily sketched earlier leaning against the wall, his mocking eyes echoing the chuckle he now made at her alarm.

"Who are you?" she dared to ask, her threatened tears forgotten. Although normally shy, she did not pause to question her unusual temerity in confronting this man.

"Your mother has not warned you to keep a distance from me?" he said with feigned consternation. "I am Julian St. Aubyn, premier scoundrel of London at your service, dear child."

"I am Lady Chloe Maitland and I am no longer a child," she said with a frown, completely forgetting that they ought to be properly introduced—if at all. "And why do you mock yourself in such a way? Surely you do not seek to perpetuate that displeasing image."

"My image is of my own making," he snapped back at her with a frown as marked as hers. He shifted away from the wall and crossed the room to confront her, his ebony cane held in front of him as though to assure a distance be kept.

"At least you are not compelled into an odious marriage because of it." Chloe turned away from this entrancing man to again contemplate what her future would be if Grandmama had her way.

"And you are?"

His voice was so terribly sympathetic that Chloe found herself replying, "Indeed, I am. Grandmama Dancy has informed me that I am to accept the particular attentions of Lord Twisdale and I simply cannot like the man." There, she had said it out loud. She had told someone precisely how she felt about the coming attachment. It was infamous.

"As to that, my pater has informed me that *I* must marry properly or risk my funds being greatly reduced," Mr. St. Aubyn countered with an attempt at humor, joining her at the window to sightlessly contemplate the swaying lanterns.

"And a gentleman needs his funds to live in this world, does he not?" Chloe replied with a sage nod. She gave Mr. St. Aubyn a sympathetic look and a rueful smile. "It would seem we both have dilemmas." She studied him a bit, then added, "Are you truly a scoundrel?"

"I am." Julian experienced a twinge in acknowledging his status in the ton to this ingenuous girl with her trusting blue-green eyes. He turned again to look at her. That somewhat plain, heart-shaped face had worn a pert expression when she dared to ask her impetuous question. Yet he sensed that within her was a character entirely different from that of Elinor Hadlow, for example. Lady Chloe revealed a spirit of sympathy he did not find very often. Most of the women he flirted with played their own game and cared little for what he might feel.

This shy young miss revealed an odd sort of maturity beyond her years, along with surprisingly delightful common sense. Pity she was the virginal, marriageable sort of girl with whom he dare not flirt. Flirting with her might prove to be a charming adventure of a sort; he could envision teaching her all manner of interesting things. However, she was precisely the type of miss his father envisaged as the future Mrs. St. Aubyn. Julian barely suppressed a flinch at the thought of a wife—of any sort.

"I could not bear to wed a man who loved another so

now I shall most likely be compelled to marry a man I detest," Chloe confessed in a low voice. One trembling hand smoothed the glove on her other, gently stroking out the delicate wrinkles.

"I say . . . " Mr. St. Aubyn began, sounding most compassionate.

"There is nothing you could do, short of whisking me away from here." She laughed, but it had the sound of a cry. How she wished that some magic might help her escape this dilemma.

"As to that, there is a possible solution," Julian offered hesitantly. "We might help each other." He stopped abruptly, aghast at what he had been about to suggest.

"It has to do with more than the money from your father, does it not?" she said, suspecting this man would not permit mere money to upset him so much.

"You *are* wise beyond your years."

"My cousins tumble into the most interesting scrapes and I have picked up a thing or two," she said quietly. There was no trace evident of the wistful envy she had sometimes felt at the daring and spirit displayed by her more adventuresome relatives.

Chloe glanced at the strange man at her side. She ought to run from this room instead of confiding to a confessed scoundrel. Mention of her dashing cousins reminded her of her own shortcomings. When confronted with the sophistication of the members of Society, that select group of the ton, her previous enthusiasm for London had faded little by little. Without her mother at her side to support her, her cousins to encourage her, and only her Tartar of a grandmother to scold and fuss at her, Chloe had been frightened.

How strange that this particular gentleman frightened her not the least. Perhaps it was because she knew that he was not one bit interested in her or her fortune.

"Your cousins being?" the diverted gentleman inquired.

"The Dancys," she replied simply, for she had learned that most of London knew of her illustrious relatives and the splendid marriages all had contracted. How could she, a mere dab of a girl with no special talents to recommend her, hope to do half as well? For the moment she had overlooked her more than presentable fortune.

"Indeed," he murmured and looked at the young woman by his side with increased interest. If she was related to *that* family, she must have something special concealed behind that composed exterior. Shy and plain, she most likely found London and Society a somewhat painful experience. For once, Julian did not view a woman as a potential conquest, but rather as another fellow being who was also in trouble.

"What would you do if you were me?" Chloe blurted out and wondered where those bold words had come from.

He studied her for some minutes until Chloe feared she had exceeded the bounds of propriety beyond what was acceptable even to this man.

"Well, I would *not* marry Twisdale, that is certain." Julian detested the man. He had seen Twisdale fleece young chaps at cards too often to think it accidental. The man was a cheat and not to be trusted.

Julian mulled over the girl's dilemma, denouncing interfering grandmothers and parents in general. Were his own father to leave him alone, Julian would eventually find a woman to marry, for he well knew what was due his name and fortune. He hated being pressured; in this he could sympathize with the sweet child at his side. Child? He glanced at her once more.

She was not all that much younger than himself, although there was a vast disparity of experience existing between them. Yet few women he had met revealed their inner being so openly and with such devastating effect, for within her was a virtuous and trustworthy person. In short, she ought to have nothing to do with a scoundrel like himself.

How could he advise this irreproachable young woman on her course of action? He had not come to any conclusion regarding his own difficulty . . . although he eventually would, he knew. Besides, he had no experience with one such as Lady Chloe. None at all, more's the pity.

"Perhaps were you to flirt with someone else your grandmama might find acceptable, she would stop pushing you at this man you detest. I cannot imagine why your grandmama thinks Twisdale is a catch. I suspect he would relish your fortune more than you, if truth were revealed. I take it that you do have a fortune?" he inquired in an afterthought. Plain girls who could command a title and moved in the highest spheres usually did.

"Indeed, I do possess a modest fortune. If my dearest brother does not return from the Continent I shall have a rather vast fortune. Grandmama thinks he has been killed by brigands. I believe he is alive and merely biding his time before coming home to settle down. But I would like to receive a letter from him at least once," she concluded.

"To return to the matter at hand," Julian inserted, not wishing to become involved in the subject of erring sons, "is that you must learn to flirt."

"Impossible," Chloe said with a shrug, daring to laugh up at him.

"I believe you show potential; that was a fetching chuckle just now," Julian observed with a considering tilt of his head.

"That is merely because I am chatting with you. When I know that I need not please a man—you know, to attract him as a marriage partner—I do not feel the anxiety I do when faced with a peer of the realm and know I must capture his interest or risk displeasure from Grandmama," Chloe said in a burst of speech quite unlike herself.

"Hm," Julian said, while deliberating on the matter. At last he concluded, "I shall give you lessons."

"What? Lessons in flirting? I never heard the like of it," Chloe said, smiling with delight at the mere thought of a scoundrel giving lessons in flirting to a green girl.

"If you pause to think about it, who better? I have been flirted with by experts, I will have you know." Julian took her hand and raised it to his mouth to place a whisper kiss on it. "Now flutter those long dark lashes at me and coo with delight—something along the lines of: 'La, sir, you must not toy with my affections.' You *can* think of something along those lines, can you not?" He had uttered her words in a falsetto and sounded quite droll.

Chloe burst out in pleased laughter. "Absurd man! What a complete hand you are at this nonsense. I declare, you ought to be kept on a leash, so to protect the women of England."

Julian smiled, that devilishly winning smile that easily captured a woman's heart before she knew it.

"By Jove, I said you had promise. Your eyes are sparkling with your delight and I do believe you have an incipient dimple near your mouth. It is very fetching, my dear." His eyes twinkled down at her with a devilish gleam in them that created most peculiar sensations in her heart.

"I vow you have said that hundreds of times," Chloe scolded, but she did not stop smiling at him.

"It begs to be kissed," he teased, rather liking his plain little student.

Chloe blushed a particularly lovely shade of pink that made her look like delicate apple blossoms. "Sir, I protest. You ought not speak to me thus." She raised her hand in a gesture of objection and Julian caught it in his.

"Now, I am teaching you, and while I admit you are an excellent pupil, you have much more to learn," he admonished.

"I must agree with you on that score," Chloe handsomely admitted with a sigh, tugging her hand free of his.

Seeing she had a handkerchief in one hand, Julian pulled it from her and drew it across his lips. A hint of heliotrope reached his nose and he sharpened his gaze, surprised. Not the usual lavender scent? Bravo, he silently applauded.

"Sir?" She frowned up at him with her hand outstretched for the handkerchief to be returned.

"To draw the handkerchief across your lips is to signal you desire an acquaintance with a gentleman you espy across the room." He showed her the movement again, inhaling the aroma of heliotrope as he did. "You may have observed a woman trailing her handkerchief over her shoulder." He followed suit to demonstrate and was rewarded with an infectious giggle from Lady Chloe. "She is sending the message to follow her."

"Indeed!" Chloe took the handkerchief from him to duplicate his movement and shook her head in amazement. "I shall be watching the arrangement of handkerchiefs closely from now on. What a fascinating man you are, sir." She deliberately fluttered her lashes at him.

Julian stared down at her plain little face now alive with amusement. Those charming blue eyes with the hint of green danced with her delight in the situation, and he thought the grandmother a total fool for this girl showed great promise. Indeed, with that bone structure, she would grow in appeal as she grew older. That is, if she grew older, for he suddenly recalled a vicious rumor he had overheard about Twisdale. Lady Chloe ought not be subjected to such a man.

"Sir?" she said in inquiry, placing her hand trustingly on his arm. "You thought of something unpleasant just now. I hope it had nothing to do with your problems."

"We must do something about your dilemma," he said with a serious note in his voice that had been absent heretofore. Then he cleared his throat, reminding himself that he must not get serious about anything. "If you fold your handkerchief, it sends the message you wish to speak with the gentleman. Allowing it to rest against your right cheek indicates that your answer is yes, this in case he has asked you a question you dare not answer aloud."

"Goodness," Chloe murmured with a smile, touching her handkerchief to her right cheek as instructed. She raised her gaze to meet his and suddenly the foolishness faded away. She became aware of alien emotions within her that she'd not experienced before this. There was a fluttering sensation near her heart that almost frightened her. She swallowed with care, then brazened a grin. "Did I do it correctly?"

"You are rapidly becoming a little baggage, my girl," Mr. St. Aubyn teased, taking her handkerchief away from her. "Had you a fan in your hand, you might raise the handle to your lips," he said while watching her expression carefully.

She slipped her fan from her wrist, then did as he had suggested. "Like so?"

Julian felt an odd sort of stirring within him at the sight of those innocent eyes peeping at him from over the top of the pearl handle of the fan. Her rosy lips were pursed in imitation of a kiss and he knew the strongest urge to kiss her in turn.

"It is a signal that you wished to be kissed," he said, aware that his voice had dropped to a husky whisper.

"Gracious!" said a sharp voice from the doorway. "I did not suspect that your talents extended to lessons in love to infants. Not at all the thing, my dear," Elinor said in a silky voice that held a note of waspishness in it that Julian had come to abhor.

Chapter 2

*J*ulian did not miss the horrified gasp from the young woman at his side. He wracked his brain to think of a reason why he should have been in secluded conversation with this miss. He suspected what Elinor was capable of doing to the girl, and it was not pleasant to contemplate.

"Aunt Elinor," Lady Chloe said with more composure than Julian would have thought she could summon. She performed a commendable curtsy to her aunt. "I am not in the least surprised to see you here."

Julian barely refrained from a shocked gasp of his own. They were related? Incredible. He darted glances between the two women and waited, deciding it might be better to see what they said before jumping in with some comment of his own that might make things worse.

That Elinor Hadlow found Lady Chloe's remark startling was an understatement to say the least. Her eyes narrowed briefly, then a thin smile formed on her dainty lips.

"Lady Chloe," she purred with apparent censure, "it *is* a surprise to see you closeted with a scoundrel such as Mr. St. Aubyn. What will your grandmama say to this?" Although her voice teased, the look in her eyes implied that Chloe had better watch her step most carefully.

"Nothing. For I have not been closeted with this gentleman. We merely exchanged a few words when I ventured in here—and this is an open area—to look at the pretty lights hanging in the garden. I fancy that is why you are here as well. Lady Purcell is famous for her lovely display of lights, or so I have been told." Lady Chloe turned to face Julian and curtsied again. "I thank you for your kindness in sparing a few words for a green girl."

Julian watched the young woman glide with amazing

composure from the room. He sensed she was badly shaken, but you would never guess it from her outward behavior. He must try to see her again, continue what they had begun. He felt it important to assist her in avoiding marriage to Twisdale. That this was the first time in a good many years that his interest in a woman was one of sympathy and support without a romantic connection escaped him completely. He felt a kinship to one who was as intent on avoiding marriage as he was.

"Raiding the nursery, Julian?" Elinor jibed as she swiftly crossed the room to confront him. "Even if my silly niece has forgotten the dangers of being alone with a gentleman, you ought to remember. You usually take great care to avoid a situation where you might be compromised." She smiled archly up at him, baring her teeth in a charming smile.

"You ought to know better than to think I could be charmed by an innocent," he said in reply. Julian wrinkled his nose at the musky scent Elinor wore, contrasting it with the delightful heliotrope perfuming Lady Chloe's handkerchief.

Elinor quickly relented, apparently deciding that it was far better to cajole than scold. "Forgive me, Julian. Since Hadlow breathed his last my nerves have been overset. Lawyers are so dreadfully tedious with all their talk of jointures and allowances and dower houses." She formed a moue with her dainty lips, then said, "I fear that I will be required to move from Hadlow House quite soon. My husband's son writes that he wishes to take possession of the house before long. One would think he might wait a while," she grumbled.

Then she caught herself up and smiled at Julian. "However, you may have the pleasure of assisting me to locate a suitable house of my own, for I have no wish to share a roof with my stepson and his family." She trailed a finger along Julian's sleeve, smiling up into his eyes with a look that promised everything he might want. "I shall insist upon a place with a spacious bedroom."

Julian gave her a knowing look. Did she think him so foolish? She cast out lures to more than one gentleman of the ton. Julian did not care for the notion of being one

among many, particularly if he was expected to assist in fi-
nancing the dwelling.

"I would be pleased to oblige, although I suggest your
man of business would have a better knowledge of what
might suit you than I would."

"But Julian''—she pouted adorably—"I value your excellent taste."

What a baggage, he thought ruefully. She had not ceased
to hope that he would suggest she become his wife and
move into the grand St. Aubyn town house. Then he recalled her many talents and offered his arm. Between ap-
peasing her to keep Lady Chloe safe from recriminations
and maintaining his bachelorhood, he would have his hands
full.

Chloe sank down onto a padded bench along the edge of
the ballroom. Her heart slowly calmed to a normal pace and
she unclasped her fingers from the death grip they'd held
on her fan. Foolish girl! She might have suspected that St.
Aubyn would have had an assignation with her beautiful
aunt.

Head bowed, Chloe considered the delightful interlude
before her aunt had appeared. He had been so very kind and
concerned. At least, he had appeared so. It was most likely
a performance, for who would expect a scoundrel of his position to concern himself with her dilemma? But, she decided, perhaps she might assert herself a trifle.

"Ah, here you are," the Dowager Baroness Dancy cried.
"Lord Twisdale has been searching for you, my girl. He is
promised a second dance with you."

"I apologize. I had not looked at my card, Grandmama."
Chloe rose from the bench, resigned to her fate. As her
legal guardian in her parents' absence, her grandmother had
the right to control her marriage. Grandmama could well
command Chloe to marry a man regardless how she felt
about him. That she might have had help in avoiding marriage to the odious Twisdale had been nothing more than an
illusion. Mr. St. Aubyn would rightfully be occupied with
his own troubles. It was too much to hope a gentleman of
the ton would concern himself with a mere green girl.

"I meant what I told you about Lord Twisdale. He will

call for you at four of the clock tomorrow afternoon to go for a drive in the park. In the meantime you are to think about your future. It will be a trifle different from what you envisioned, but I fancy you will adjust."

Chloe murmured a word of protest, then pressed her lips into silence.

"You will marry better than I did. I had to content myself with a baron," Grandmama Dancy said. "Although never forget he came of impeccable lineage. I managed to capture a marquis for your mama. Cannot hope the same for such a dab of a girl as you, even if one were available. But Lord Twisdale is a viscount, so you will be decently elevated in this world."

"I would wait to marry until Mama and Lord Crompton return to London," Chloe daringly ventured to say with a rare, mutinous compression of her lips for a moment.

"Your mama has complete faith in my ability to align you with the best family available this Season. Twisdale is from fine stock, has an acceptable fortune, an excellent country house, and a town house with a good address. My man of business has investigated him for me and I am satisfied with the report."

Chloe longed to ask if the lawyer had also reported on the questionable death of Lord Twisdale's first wife, but knew she would be punished for being impertinent if she dared to say anything to that effect, so she kept silent.

Swept along at her imperious grandmother's side, Chloe curtsied to Lord Twisdale, joining in the country dance with little enthusiasm.

"It is good to see a young woman who can keep a civil tongue in her head," Lord Twisdale said to her grandmother when he returned Chloe at the conclusion of the dance. "You have done excellently well at schooling your grand-daughter, madam."

"She is an obedient girl, I'll say that for her. My daughter-in-law put a few foolish notions in her head that I quickly put to rout, you may be sure. 'Tis a good thing that Isobel took off on a honeymoon, or heaven knows what she might have done regarding Chloe's future."

Chloe wanted to cry out that her dearest mama would not have compelled her into a marriage with someone like the odious Lord Twisdale just to punish Chloe for refusing another man. But the short stay with Grandmama Dancy had forced Chloe to realize that her grandmama firmly believed in harsh punishment for anything she deemed impertinent. She was strict, stern, and never showed a speck of affection or compassion. Chloe felt as trapped as any fox at bay.

At this point Theo Purcell, the son of their hostess, properly presented himself to claim the next dance. Chloe gratefully left the stultifying presence of her grandmama and Lord Twisdale for the lighthearted romp of a Scottish reel.

"Dashed pleased to see you here this evening," Theo offered while they danced madly down the center of the line.

Before taking her place opposite him, Chloe flashed a grin at him and nodded. "I couldn't have missed it for anything."

Theo frowned at her choice of words, causing Chloe to berate herself for perhaps revealing too much. She'd have been forced here even if she'd had a fever.

They concluded the dance and Theo suggested they pause for a glass of lemonade.

Chloe gave him a grateful look. Even if he was reputed to be somewhat of a sad rattle of a fellow, he was deemed amusing, if a bit outrageous. She sipped the pleasantly tart beverage he offered her with pleasure.

"I sense you are less than happy, Lady Chloe," Theo ventured.

"Oh, nothing that will not mend, as they say. Do you long for the end of the Season so you may retreat to the peace of the country? Or are you one of the gentlemen who remain in the city to enjoy the delights found here?"

Surprised at the passable conversation from a girl he had deemed dull and dreary, Theo said, "St. Aubyn and I plan to remain for a time before repairing to his country estate. He has a few loose ends to conclude." Julian had informed Theo that the friendship with Mrs. Hadlow had run its course and he intended to end it as soon as possible.

"You are good friends with the gentleman?" Lady Chloe held her glass of lemonade before her as though it might bite.

"I am," Theo replied with agreeable modesty. "I daresay you are not acquainted with him, for I doubt your dra—, that is, your grandmama would permit such an introduction. Although, in St. Aubyn's defense may I say he is the best of fellows." Theo was surprised that Lady Chloe would dare show an interest in a man who was, to put it kindly, a bit of a scoundrel—one beyond naive girls.

"I suspect that grandmamas have a somewhat different point of view from a gentleman's friends," Lady Chloe said, fortunately overlooking his near blunder of referring to Lady Dancy as a dragon, which she definitely was.

"True. St. Aubyn is a prince of a fellow, but the ladies will persist in pursuing the chap. Lucky dog," Theo added under his breath.

Chloe studied her companion from beneath partially lowered lashes. Theo Purcell was a spindly fellow with blond hair that fell into what she supposed was romantic locks. His brown eyes had held a kindly look in them, however. Why was he considered so audacious?

"I understand you are quite musically gifted, Mr. Purcell. You perform on the pianoforte?"

"For my sins, I do. My father wants me to hunt and I want to be musical. Fathers never seem to be satisfied with their sons. Look at St. Aubyn. His father demands he wed and set up his nursery, else face a drastic cut in funds. Seems to think that since the viscountcy traces back to the Conquest that Julian ought to do him proud. Demands a bride of wealth and background—as though they were thick on the ground. Mind you, both of us wish to please our fathers. It isn't always easy."

Then Theo, who admitted a reputation for being a bit of a rattle, even if he was musically talented, looked most surprised at the serious conversation he was holding with young Lady Chloe. "Are you a mesmerist, Lady Chloe? I vow I do not usually spout so to a charming young lady."

"You underrate yourself, for you are an entertaining gentleman," Chloe protested. She had learned what it was that blue-deviled poor St. Aubyn, thanks to the chattiness of his good friend. "I hope I shall have the pleasure of hearing you play one day. I should like that. I have no such talent and I envy those who do."

"Miss Walsham said you are clever with drawing. Do you take a pad and pencil with you when you go about?"

Chloe blushed at the reminder of the sketch in her generous reticule. She unconsciously clutched the cords of her reticule more tightly in her hands.

"I suspect you do," Theo said gently. "Will you permit me to see them?"

"I doubt you would find them of interest."

Theo smiled, figuring he would see an amateurish drawing and steeled himself not to shudder. He boldly plucked the reticule from her hands—ignoring her gasp of protest—then opened it to peer inside. He removed the little pad, returning the reticule to Lady Chloe. As usual, he was breaking every rule in the book, but his curiosity had blossomed out of control. Then he opened the book to see the first of the little caricatures.

"Good heavens, it is Twisdale to the life. That is, it expresses him to a tee," Theo hastily added. The nastiness he had suspected was concealed behind Twisdale's bland veneer was bared to the viewer in all its ugliness when Lady Chloe had depicted Twisdale as a pompous serpent with sideburns. With an accurate portrayal of Twisdale's head above a starched cravat and gaping coat, the scaly body of a serpent coiled below.

"You ought not be looking at that. I never intended anyone to see it. I merely do them for my own amusement." She stretched out her hand, giving Theo an accusing look that ought to have put him to shame.

Theo acted as though he did not hear her softly spoken words. There was no way he could return the pad, although he knew he should, until he had seen the lot.

"By Jove, there is St. Aubyn. Incredible! You have caught that hint of pain he tries to hide, even though you show him as a lion. Handsome devil," Theo concluded without a trace of envy in his voice. A lifelike Julian's face topped a noble lion, poised to do battle. "Devilishly good sketches, Lady Chloe. Pity you cannot show them around, for they cut to the heart of a person, though I quite understand that you prefer to keep them to yourself. Oh, this one of Mrs. Hadlow is choice. She *is* like a mongoose, just as you have depicted her." The sly look in her aunt's eyes accurately caught her nature, as did the predatory paws. If he thought it a pity that the mongooseish Mrs. Hadlow couldn't consume the snakelike Lord Twisdale, he said nothing of the sort.

Chloe snatched the pad from Theo's hold and stuffed it into her reticule. "I implore you to say nothing of these sketches to anyone. I do them for my diversion, certainly nothing more. You are truly as naughty a gentleman as I have been told," she scolded, albeit with a strained smile. She curtsied, then whirled away, retreating to her grandmother's side.

Theo felt like a cad, breaking the rules of etiquette. But then, he frequently did so with impunity. He had no justification for his behavior, other than overwhelming curiosity. But he intended to tell St. Aubyn about that frightfully good drawing of him. Trust St. Aubyn to be depicted as a lion rampant. Then he paused to wonder how the clever Lady Chloe would draw him.

Chloe could not recall when she had been so angry. Really, that Theo Purcell went beyond what was acceptable.

"You appear flushed," her grandmother scolded. "A lady never appears flushed in her face. I suggest you retire at once until you have calmed yourself."

It did not occur to her grandmother to inquire as to what had turned Chloe's cheeks pink with annoyance. Rather than explain, Chloe gratefully walked from the ballroom in the direction of the Ladies' Withdrawing Room.

The hall was quiet when she made her way along the hall. At the entrance to the little anteroom where she had known the delightful, if brief, lesson in flirting from Mr. St. Aubyn she resolutely kept her face averted, her eyes downcast. She had no desire to know if her lovely aunt still lingered there with the reputed scoundrel.

Although, if he had been ordered to marry and set up his nursery, perhaps he intended to make her aunt his bride? Chloe hoped that was not the case, for even if she was related to the lovely Mrs. Hadlow, she did not like her in the least.

"There you are," said a familiar voice, quite low and from the shadows of an architectural niche.

"Mr. St. Aubyn," Chloe whispered back as though the walls had ears and might report to her grandmother.

"I intend to leave, but I had hoped to see you first. I do not wish you to think I have forgotten your predicament. Your aunt has not harassed you regarding what she thinks she saw, has she? Or said anything to your grandmother?"

Surprise rang clear in Chloe's voice when she replied, "Not yet. But she is not related to Grandmama, you see, being the daughter of my grandfather's brother. There is no reason for her to tell on me, for there is little love lost between the two families. She is a Maitland, not a Dancy," Chloe concluded, as though that explained everything.

"Yet she has similar hair," the gentleman mused, reaching out from the shadows to lightly touch one of Chloe's curls.

"That is on both sides of the family," Chloe reported back, thinking this a very odd conversation to hold with a gentleman reputed to be a dashing rogue. Never had she revealed so much about herself, or her family to anyone—and then to such a man! He had a kind of magic, she supposed, the sort that drew all the secrets from you.

"I wished to speak with you," he began, then paused. "I must see you again. We have not finished your lessons, nor have I found a solution for you. It is unthinkable for you to wed Twisdale. On that we are agreed. The problem is to find an acceptable alternative."

Chloe drew in an amazed breath. He did hold a concern for her. He had not forgotten his offer. Somehow she could not accept the opinion of the ton. This man was more than a scoundrel, if indeed he was that. Could a scoundrel care about a young girl being forced to marry a man with a shadowy past, a man she feared? Girls were compelled to marry that sort of gentleman quite often. Society accepted it, for necessity frequently required a melding of fortunes and families.

"I am to take a drive in the park with his lordship tomorrow at four of the clock," Chloe revealed.

"Could you manage to escape from the house for a ride in the park early morning? You do ride?" he thought to add.

"Indeed. My brother saw to it that I was well taught by the head groom. I shall meet you in the park at nine of the clock tomorrow morning—if that is not too early." She gave him an anxious look, aware that gentlemen often did not seek their beds until dawn.

"I intend to head for my house shortly, following a brief meeting with a friend. I will be there, near the Stanhope gate." He melted back into the shadows and Chloe fled to the Withdrawing Room.

Was she quite mad? Could she really have arranged a meeting with St. Aubyn? Suddenly life seemed a trifle less dismal and her future appeared to have expectations.

"Ready?" Julian inquired of his friend Purcell.

"Think my dear mama will not take it amiss if I decamp now. Goodness knows I've done the pretty with all those chits who don't take—the demure little things whose mamas have such hopeless hopes for," he concluded righteously.

"See any with potential?" Julian asked while waiting for the carriage to be brought around. He had ordered it before speaking with Lady Chloe, so it ought to be here shortly.

"No. Well," Theo amended, "did chat with an unusual dab of a girl, not the ordinary kind at all. Lady Chloe Maitland. Clever with a pencil. Did you to a tee." He chuckled at the memory of St. Aubyn as a lion. "With all her money, you'd think she would have her pick of the crop, as it were. Grandmama's compelling her to marry old Twisdale. Dashed stupid thing of her to do, if you ask me. Chit thinks of the man as a snake, as least she drew him as one."

"You have heard the rumors as well, then?" Julian entered his carriage as soon as it drew to a halt, first instructing his coachman as to their destination.

Theo climbed in behind Julian and settled on the cushioned seat before attempting a reply.

"About Twisdale? Not widely spread about, but yes, I caught one. Suppose the old dragon don't know anything about it, if it is true." Theo drummed his fingers on the seat beside him, then said, "Off to the usual spot?"

"Indeed, although I won't stay late tonight. I have an early morning appointment I have no desire to miss."

No amount of hinting could wrest this intriguing bit of information from Julian. Theo did his best, then good-naturedly gave up. He'd only inquire so far.

The carriage drew to a halt before the elegant and re-strained entrance to White's, that most esteemed gentle-men's club.

"Dashed pity you have to leave early," Theo jibed two hours later when Julian rose from the card table.

"Indeed." He had been winning steadily and hated to go. But the hour was late and he wanted to be alert come morn-ing. "Tell you what, my friend. You take my place. Perhaps my luck will rub off on you. And ... if I need to involve you in the business I discuss come morning, you shall know directly what it is all about."

Leaving a mystified Theo shifting over to his chair, Ju-lian ran lightly down the stairs to where his carriage awaited. Fortunately his coachman had an excellent mem-ory and when Julian had instructed him to return in two hours, the fellow was prompt. Among other things Julian demanded of his employees was promptness.

Come morning Julian intended to slip from the house with no one the wiser. Just why he was being so protective of the troubled Lady Chloe, he was not certain. But every gentlemanly instinct had been aroused at the mere thought of that pretty little innocent being forced to wed Twisdale.

Chloe hugged her secret to her all the way home from the Purcell ball.

"You were passable this evening, my girl," the dowager declared just before her elaborate Town carriage arrived at her residence. "However, I expect you to be a trifle more gracious to his lordship when he comes this afternoon to take you for a drive in the park. Do you understand what I mean? Encourage the man. Even a chit like you ought to know how to flutter your lashes, how to please a gentle-man."

"Yes, Grandmama," Chloe said in reply, wishing she dared to object.

"See that you do."

The Dowager Lady Dancy left her carriage, totally ig-noring Chloe. She bustled into the house and left her grand-daughter to wander up the stairs to her room all by herself.

"It would be lovely to have one of my cousins to confide in," Chloe said to a painting on the wall. "Dear, impetuous

Hyacinthe, practical Julia, adventuresome Elizabeth, even the daring Victoria would be most welcome. How I envy them. They avoided the clutches of Grandmama and found their own husbands. Why, oh, why did my dearest mama have to marry just now?"

Chloe slipped quietly into her neat little room feeling a bit lost and rejected. New clothes—although she truly did not admire her grandmother's taste—did not compensate for loving attention.

Following a good sleep, Chloe felt a trifle more optimistic. Surely if Mr. St. Aubyn felt there was a possible way out of this quagmire in which she was stuck, she ought not give way to a fit of the green melancholy.

Since her grandmother did not leave her room before noon, Chloe was able to exit the house with no one the wiser save the scullery maid.

Chloe cast a concerned glance at the thin little girl. Her grandmother did not believe in providing decent rooms or food for her lower servants. Chloe suspected that the child slept on the stone floor beneath the kitchen table so as to catch a bit of warmth from the stove. If she owned so much as a change of clothing it would surprise Chloe.

"I will see to it that she has a decent blanket and pillow," Chloe whispered to her horse once she was mounted and on her way to the park. Although she risked a scolding for interfering with the running of the house were she to help the girl. Grandmama did not approve of coddling servants, particularly a scullery maid. Yet Chloe's tender heart found it difficult to snuggle in her bed—although it was firm, for her grandmother did not believe in softness for anyone save herself—when she thought of the poor child several floors below.

Her groom, a quiet, tolerant fellow, trailed behind her. He had not objected when she softly informed him that she wished to ride ahead of him, for she had someone to meet.

When Chloe reached the Stanhope gate she looked all around her. There appeared no one in sight and her heart sank, although she supposed she ought to have known that it was too good to be true.

"Good morning," came a voice out of nowhere, it seemed.

Chloe whirled about in her saddle to see Mr. St. Aubyn coming forth from the shade of a large tree.

"You are prompt. I appreciate that." To Chloe's groom, he added, "I will take the greatest care of Lady Chloe. If you like, you may trail along behind us to see that I have none but the best of intentions."

The groom nodded and waited until the couple had ridden off before following them.

"What nonsense this all is," Chloe declared. "I should not have to scheme to avoid marriage with such an odious creature. You would think my grandmama would wish the best for me. It seems all she can think about is punishment."

"I have given your problem a great deal of thought since I spoke with you last evening."

Chloe gave him a surprised look. She had not expected to hear such a thing.

"And did you reach a solution?"

"My father insists I marry soon. He has no patience in the least. Why, I have years before I must wed," Mr. St. Aubyn added softly.

"And?" she prodded when it appeared he had sunk into a reflection.

"You must not marry Twisdale. So . . . my thought is that we join forces. My father will be pleased, as you are the very sort of proper young woman he wants me to wed. And I believe my fortune and prospects are better than Twisdale's. My family is older and quite respected. Even if your grandmother may have heard a tale or two about me, she cannot deny I am of the highest ton," he said with careless modesty.

"Join forces?" Chloe said, her breath nearly taken away by this audacious offer—or whatever it was. "Precisely what do you mean?"

"Well, not actually marry, just pretend to have a deep interest in each other, an understanding, if you like. What do you say to that?"

"Pretend to show particular attention?" Chloe stared at him in utter astonishment.

Chapter 3

"*I*t is utterly outrageous," Lady Chloe declared. She paused, looking ahead through the bower of trees and off into the distance. "Do you think we might actually dare try such a thing?" she added, hope clear in her voice.

"Well, as long as you and I knew that it is all a hum, I suppose we might," Julian said, looking over at the slip of a girl clad in the most dreadful riding attire he could recall seeing in some time. It not only fit badly, it was quite the wrong hue for a woman of her coloring. Rather than drab dark blue, she ought to have leaf green, he decided, with smart black braid trim and a jaunty little hat perched on those pretty auburn curls.

"You could not possibly think that I would care to hold you to such an agreement. I would never wish to compromise any gentleman and thus force him into a distasteful marriage," she snapped back at him.

Julian liked her indignant response. It bode well for the success of their pact—should they actually proceed with it.

"If you want, we could wait to see if Twisdale really does ask you to be his wife. You would refuse him, I gather?" Julian chanced a look about them, observing that no one was close enough to detect their identities.

"Need you ask?" she said in a quiet voice. She permitted her horse, a reluctantly allowed treat dispensed by her grandmother, to pick its way through some long grass. When Julian looked at her she wore a troubled expression.

"You will see him this afternoon," Julian reminded her. "Should he dare to offer marriage, try to contact me. If I see you, for I believe I will also take a drive in the park, signal me as to what has happened."

They decided on the sort of signal, then Julian said, "I

had best be off before we are observed by someone. Although if we are to proceed with the pact, I suppose we really ought to permit others to see us together."

But he realized that if they were seen together, Elinor would not be pleased. He hoped she would have the good sense to lavish her attentions on another more receptive gentleman. He felt sure there were any number of men who would welcome the intimacy Elinor offered with such careful generosity. He wished to be done with her and hoped this escapade with Lady Chloe might do the thing. When the girl at his side chuckled at his remark, he recalled himself.

"No one would believe it otherwise," Chloe joked. "A dashing man like you with an inexperienced girl like me." She felt the oddest liking for Mr. St. Aubyn. Surely he could not be the scoundrel as so many claimed. A scoundrel would not care what happened to her. Even her own grandmother seemed indifferent to her future.

"That is no lie," he said with a chuckle of his own, then gallantly added, "although I misdoubt you are as green as you claim."

"La, sir, you flatter shamelessly," Chloe said with amusement. "Although I see you do not disclaim the designation of dashing!" She gave him a distinctly arch look and actually fluttered her dark lashes at him. The sparkle in her eyes caught his interest, for it hinted at other, more interesting talents.

"You learn your lessons too quickly, I think. Now, pay attention," he said in a more serious vein. "We will wait to see how affairs go this afternoon and then proceed accordingly. Is that agreed?"

With a good deal of trepidation Chloe sobered, then nodded. "Agreed."

Chloe, heart fluttering madly with dismay, watched him dash off across the park leaving her to sedately trot along in his wake.

Was she utterly mad to trust the man, a near stranger? She knew so little about him, other than brief comments. But . . . she admitted, she had never heard anything truly evil, such as the nasty rumor regarding Lord Twisdale and his late wife. No, remarks about the roguish Mr. St. Aubyn

were inclined to be wistful—when made by ladies—and
admiring—from gentlemen.

Then Chloe burst into wry giggles of the infectious sort
that even made her dour groom soften his expression.
Fancy her becoming entangled in such a predicament. This
was more like something her cousins might do. At this
thought she sat a trifle straighter in her saddle, tilted her
chin up a bit, and contemplated the coming afternoon and
what it might bring.

Upon her arrival at her grandmother's house, she went to
her room to change from her detested riding habit—chosen
by her grandmother for its modesty—and turned to her
drawing pad and pencil.

She intended to make a sketch of Mr. Purcell today.
With an excellent memory at her command, it was no time
at all before she had the face of Theo Purcell atop the drawing of an inquisitive and very naughty-looking magpie.

Once satisfied she had captured the look of unholy glee
that crossed his face when he had seen the drawing of Lord
Twisdale, she ranged all the drawings along her little desk.
It was a bit like looking at the cast of characters for a play.
She had seen such a sketch once, depicting all the roles for
a comedy on the stage. Only, this was her life and it did not
the least seem like a comedy to her.

That afternoon Chloe was not surprised when Lord
Twisdale was announced shortly before four of the clock.
She had expected him to be early.

The gentleman bowed faintly when she entered the
room, giving Chloe the impression that Lord Twisdale felt
he was doing her a vast honor. And so he was, she supposed. What a pity she did not appreciate it in the least.

"I feel sure that you are aware why I am here," he began
with a pompous air. "Your grandmother would scarcely
permit me to be private with you otherwise."

Since Chloe had most carefully left the door wide open
and even brought her maid along to remain just inside the
entrance to the sitting room, she merely bowed her head.

"Indeed," she replied with a docile air. She crossed the
room to seat herself on a straight-backed chair that was as
uncomfortable as it looked. However, it had the advantage

of being some distance from Lord Twisdale and that annoying scent he wore. Folding her hands neatly in her lap she waited for what was to come with a meek pose.

"Lady Chloe, I have the distinct satisfaction of soliciting your hand in marriage," he announced abruptly with total disregard for any romantic notions Chloe might harbor. "The dowager agrees with me that our marriage would suit us both admirably."

Chloe knew the wildest desire to ask if Lord Twisdale intended to wed her grandmother, for it certainly sounded that way. She doubted if he would appreciate her lamentable sense of humor and remained properly silent for a moment before attempting a reply while searching for a means of playing for time.

"This is very precipitous, is it not? I scarcely know you, sir." Chloe wondered if she ought to attempt to stall or if she should just reject the man immediately and incur the wrath of everyone on her head at once.

"You know all you need to know, my girl," he said in a sharp tone and with a look of annoyance. "I sought approval from your grandmother and she has granted it after a proper investigation."

"I am dreadfully young, sir, and perhaps a trifle absurd. Pray allow me to consider your offer for a time, for I would not wish to err in my judgment. Marriage is such a permanent arrangement." Unless, she added to herself, one is nudged into the grave. Chloe studiously kept her gaze on her lap where her hands fidgeted with a scrap of linen. It was the only sign that her nerves were tried.

"I am confident you will see the wisdom of an alliance with me," he said with a hint of impatience.

Curious at his change in tone, Chloe glanced up to catch a smug expression settle on his face. He must feel greatly confident, she thought. What a pity. He appeared even more the serpent to her with that unctuous look in his eyes. She would be glad once she could deny him and be free of this threat to her peace.

Repressing her aversion with care, Chloe rose from her chair and crossed to the door. Her maid stepped forth with a pelisse and bonnet in her hand.

"Excuse me and I shall prepare for our drive. That is, we

are still to take a turn in the park, are we not?" She paused by the door, taking her bonnet in hand before facing him.

His smile was rather thin when he replied, "But of course, Lady Chloe."

Chloe was very prudent in her actions. She did not wish to arouse any suspicions. Rather, she attempted to act like the innocent she was, but one who truly could not make up her mind and appeared excessively shy. If she aroused his concerns he might say something to her grandmama, who knew that while Chloe might appear shy, she knew her mind well enough, more's the pity. She might sneeze. Since he appeared to suspect weakness of any kind in a future bride, it could possibly help. Her sneeze was a glorious one, rattling the very windows.

Her ploy seemed to be most effective. The aggravated, yet resigned look from Lord Twisdale proved her strategy was working. Now if they could just encounter Mr. St. Aubyn in the park. Chloe depended upon her gallant rescuer to come to her aid. Precisely what he intended to do she was not certain. But anyone as dashing and debonair as Mr. St. Aubyn must have dozens of ideas in his brain.

Julian had endured a devil of a day in but a few hours. Try as he could, there was no way he might fob off Elinor Hadlow from the drive she demanded. She insisted upon traversing the park at the height of the afternoon promenade by the stylish of the ton. He had fully intended to ride today, just in case Lady Chloe signaled him a message. How the devil was he to cope with Elinor languishing at his side?

He guided his team through the gathering throng that led into the park. It proved tedious and awkward going, particularly when one inexperienced driver of a high perch phaeton became entangled with a tandem rig.

Elinor remained silent at first, somehow sensing that he was less than thrilled to be summoned to her side. She wondered if her twit of a niece could possibly have had any bearing on his attitude, then decided that had to be the silliest piece of nonsense ever to enter her head.

She bowed to a passing dowager with the sort of regal air she intended to cultivate once she became Mrs. St.

Aubyn and wife of the heir to the substantial St. Aubyn fortune, the superb estates, not to mention the famous St. Aubyn jewels. She had glimpsed a few of them when Julian's mother was still alive and they were magnificent. Elinor fully intended to be the next to adorn herself with those diamonds, rubies, emeralds, and other gems she had heard of but not seen.

Her eyes narrowed at first when her niece came into view. The chit seemed even more dowdy than usual. How fortunate, Elinor thought, the girl looked as though she couldn't say boo to a goose.

Then Elinor noticed Lord Twisdale and her smile widened. Lovely. Not only would her niece soon be out of the way—Lord Twisdale had kept his first wife safely in the country and far from Society's eyes—but if the rumor was true, she wouldn't be around much longer, either. Pity all that wonderful money was legally tied to Chloe. Elinor would so love to get her hands on it.

Julian flinched when he saw the look in Lady Chloe's eyes. Her hand raised to the brim of her bonnet to adjust the feather just so and he shook his head. It had been as he had predicted. Twisdale had not waited long—not that *that* was unusual these days. When a peer of the realm needed a wife following the death of a first, Society proved most forgiving of his ignoring the time of mourning. Even though he did not actually marry Chloe, he could attach himself to her in such a manner that she would be as good as wed to him.

Julian signaled to her that he understood her dilemma with a lift of his hat, an unexceptional gesture.

"You met my little niece the other evening while at the Purcell ball, I believe," Elinor said when it appeared Julian had nothing to say.

"Indeed. Theo said she is a talented little artist. I have not seen her work. Have you?" Julian skillfully wove his carriage through the press of carriages in the direction of the serpentine.

"I had no idea that she possessed any talent whatsoever. I fear I have been far too occupied with my search for a new residence to look in on my little niece. Usually, girls making their come-outs are so tediously naive." Elinor gave a sigh, as though to remind Julian that she was wondrously beyond that stage.

"Odd, she struck me as showing distinct promise. Theo appeared much taken with her." Julian decided it best to deflect attention from Lady Chloe. He well knew it would not do for him to evince too much interest in the girl.

"Theo Purcell? That rattlepate has an interest in my niece? I doubt it will do him any good. The dowager will most likely select a much different gentleman for little Chloe. Mr. Purcell has little to recommend him other than his family and an ill-advised interest in music."

Julian made no reply, for he knew precisely the financial standing of his good friend and it was far better than Elinor suspected.

He tired of her waspish comments on those in passing carriages long before they left the park. It was with distinct relief that he drew up his team of matched chestnuts before the Hadlow establishment.

"Do say you will come in for a moment. Your groom can easily look after your horses. I would show you the list of properties that my man of business presented to me. You know I value your advice." She gave him a melting smile and Julian decided that perhaps he had best have a look at that list. There was a definite hint of triumph in her eyes that he could not trust.

Leaving his cattle in the capable hands of his groom, Julian escorted Elinor into the house with a wary step. The curvacious Mrs. Hadlow was not to be trusted. Julian was thankful that Hadlow House stood in a quiet corner of London and that Elinor had a companion of unimpeachable propriety.

Elinor led him along the hall to her study, once her late husband's. In a dull and dreary room heavy with dark oak and deep blue draperies the splash of white paper on the desk caught his eye immediately.

"Which one do you think I shall choose to buy?" She whisked the paper from the desk to place in Julian's hand. In the background, Miss Wingrove, the elderly woman who offered a note of decorum to the dashing widow, rustled to a halt by the door.

He barely refrained from an exclamation. The house at

the top of the list was one across the square from his own. He had not known it was for sale, not that it mattered.

"How convenient for you," he murmured, which he supposed was near enough to the truth of the matter.

"Yes, is it not," she murmured back at him in a seductive voice. "You will be able to visit whenever you please." She sidled forward to lean suggestively against him.

"I am able to do that with anyone," he reminded her. He barely refrained from taking a step back from her as he wished he might. What a pity she was such a tantalizing piece of baggage.

A flash of annoyance was quickly wiped away from her lovely face. "I expect you to do the right thing, Julian. You do know what I mean? Your father would not like to hear of your activities these past months." Her eyes narrowed with intent; their meaning was not lost on Julian.

"Truly, dear lady? He rarely concerns himself with my doings, but if you say so . . . " Julian cleverly extricated himself from her clasp, feigning a reluctance while he said, "I am devastated that a prior appointment takes me from your side, dear Elinor. Until later?"

She did not appear happy to see him go, but there was nothing she might do to hold him here . . . at least for now. She must cling to his promise—for it was that, surely—to come to her later on. Elinor needed to bind St. Aubyn to her in a more permanent way and time was not standing still.

Chloe entered her grandmother's house at the chime of the clock. Five of the afternoon. Had it been but an hour that she was gone? She must try to meet with Mr. St. Aubyn. As to how, she was not sure, but she would find a way. Knowing she must report to her grandmama, she went to the drawing room and paused at the doorway.

"My dear girl," her grandmother began from her place on the sofa, "am I to wish you happy?"

"Not as yet, Grandmama. Lord Twisdale did indeed ask for my hand, but I begged for more time."

"More time?" her thunderstruck relative cried. "And what does a chit like you need with more time, pray tell?"

"Marriage is such a permanent affair," Chloe said in defense of her behavior. "I would know that this alliance is right for me."

"Foolish child. Trust one who knows what is best for you to make that decision for you."

"There are times when I wish I were at home in Wiltshire again," Chloe blurted out in dismay.

"It is no longer your home," the dowager reminded her. "Your brother John—if he still lives—claims title to it. You shall be buried in the country if you do not marry soon. Your mother and stepfather may elect to spend their time there."

Privately Chloe thought that no bad thing.

"I insist that you make up your mind soon. Accept Lord Twisdale. It is highly unlikely that you will have a better offer." The dowager rose to cross the room. She stared down at Chloe with a chilly look. "I shall give you time as you request, but it shall be brief, for the conclusion is settled in my mind." The dignified lady tapped her fan against her palm as though deliberating what to say next. "Mark these words: should you choose to go against my wishes you shall remain in your room with naught but bread and water until you see matters in my light."

The dowager walked across the room to stand by the window, then turned to confront Chloe with a haughty stare. "That you would dare to question my judgment is insufferable. Go."

Aware that she could soon be captive in this house and not a soul in the country would lift a hand to help her, Chloe curtsied to her grandmother, then backed from the room as though leaving royalty.

Actually, Chloe had wished to remain with her relative, hoping she might persuade her to relent. But now Chloe knew her fate was sealed. There was nothing for her to do but marry the odious and deadly Lord Twisdale. Chloe might be a trifle defiant, but she was not so stupid as to risk starvation. She suspected her grandmama would never relent and would instruct the servants to be strict in their administration of her orders.

On her way up the stairs to her room, Chloe desperately hunted for a way to convey her dilemma to Mr. St. Aubyn. What he might do to help her was beyond her imagination at this point. *If* Chloe were permitted to attend a party this evening there was no guarantee that St. Aubyn would be there as well. But, if she were more like her cousins she could just run away.

Once in the seclusion of her room, she picked up her pad and pencil and began to sketch her grandmother. By the end of the hour a very lifelike and vicious dragon with the unmistakable face of the Dowager Lady Dancy graced the thick white paper of the drawing pad. Chloe tore the sheet from the pad and placed it with the other drawings she had done of the members of the ton she had closely observed.

"I fear I am undone," she said softly before finally giving way to tears.

Hope rose when an hour later the dowager sent a message to Chloe that she was to attend the theater in the company of Lord Twisdale that evening. Naturally the dowager would accompany them and they would sit in the Dancy box. With her grandson and heir to the title off in the country, the box sat empty, but for her use.

Chloe debated on what to wear with an optimistic view. She hoped Mr. St. Aubyn might be there this evening. Certainly if her prayers were answered he would be. However, if he was not, perhaps Theo Purcell might? And maybe, just maybe, she could contrive to send a message through that nice gentleman.

Since the contents of her wardrobe were limited to either the dresses she had brought from the country—out-of-date and a trifle tight—or the unflattering garments purchased for her by Grandmama, she did not truly care what she selected

"Oh, miss," her maid, the usually inarticulate Ellen said. "Do you think to wear that gray?"

It was a dull gray sarcenet trimmed with navy ribbon, high-necked and long-sleeved. The gown made Chloe feel as though she were in half-mourning. Perhaps that was why it seemed to appeal—she felt quite in that mood.

"I think it perfect, Ellen." Once dressed—Ellen having retreated into her usual silence again—Chloe studied her reflection in her cheval looking glass. While not a vain girl, she wished she could look fashionable and pretty for a change. She thought she had appeared prettier when her mother had the dressing of her, with colors such as soft peach and bright peacock blue.

Turning her thoughts from such a useless topic, Chloe decided she had best write two notes—one for Mr. St. Aubyn, the other for Mr. Theo Purcell. Using a stiff sheet of white paper, Chloe bluntly informed St. Aubyn of her fate. On the second sheet—a lighter weight piece of cream paper, she asked that Mr. Purcell tell his friend that Chloe was in trouble.

With the two notes safely tucked into the depths of her reticule, along with her ever-present drawing pad and pencil, she joined her grandmother for dinner.

"Enjoy the meal, my dear. Bread and water can be so tedious—not to mention slimming." Her grandmother eyed Chloe's slender figure with a raised brow. Her comment had the effect of putting Chloe quite off her food, in spite of the warning.

Chloe determined that she would find a way out of this predicament with or without Mr. St. Aubyn. However, she concluded with a touch of wistfulness, it would be far nicer to have his support and sympathy.

In the meantime, she put her mind to work figuring out a great number of ways and means of stalling Lord Twisdale. She could try sneezing again, for he seemed to always wear that dreadful scent and he abhored any sign of frailty.

Lord Twisdale had looked askance at a woman who sneezed a great deal during the Purcell ball. Perhaps, Chloe thought with optimism, he held a dread of colds or maybe his wife's death instilled this apprehension.

The theater was comfortably crowded this evening, Chloe decided with pleasure. It offered her a wealth of faces to draw if she might snatch a moment or two away from her grandmother and his lordship.

Across from the Dancy box Chloe espied her beautiful aunt. Elinor looked so lovely this evening. How could any gentleman resist such a creature of delight as she? Of course he would not know of her temper tantrums—famous within the family circle.

Next to her sat the docile elderly relative who was so obscure that Chloe could not even recall a name for her. She was one of those unfortunate unmarried ladies who drifted from household to household in the hope they could be useful and thus keep a roof over their head.

With a surreptitious slip of her hand into her reticule, Chloe withdrew her pad and pencil. The lights had dimmed and most of the audience seemed to pay some attention to the stage. The rest gossiped and chattered in quite loud tones.

She began to draw her impoverished relative. Within a short time—for she was some distance away so it was difficult to capture details—Chloe had her likeness on the paper atop a rather wilted-looking dove.

Before she knew it, the first intermission was upon them. She concealed her tablet and pencil, smiled dutifully at every comment her grandmother and Lord Twisdale made, and waited.

"I wish to speak with Selina Wingrove," the dowager said. "I wonder how she can tolerate living with that Hadlow woman." The Dowager Lady Dancy turned to his lordship and ordered, "You will be so good as to assist me. These corridors can be exceedingly hazardous. Chloe, wait here."

Chloe nodded, then sneezed as Lord Twisdale's scent assailed her nose. "Perhaps I may have a drink of water?"

Lord Twisdale seemed about to offer his assistance, although he appeared somewhat reluctant, when the dowager shook her head. "Nonsense. Stick your head out of the door and send someone to fetch you something."

Chloe sneezed again and the dowager, with Twisdale in tow, left with more than usual haste.

Watching to see where her grandmother and his lordship might appear, Chloe saw them enter the opposite box. When they began to chat with the wilted dove in Chloe's drawing, she saw her chance.

Retreating to the rear of the box and well into the shadows, Chloe searched the theater again. She had seen St. Aubyn earlier. If only she could think of a way to fetch *him* to bring her the water she had claimed to need.

"Looking for someone?" came a voice from directly behind her. "Do not turn around, rather stay as you are."

Chloe relaxed as though into a safe haven. "St. Aubyn, I am very glad to see you—even if I cannot, if you know what I mean." She turned her head so she might catch a glimpse of him. He had looked smashing from a distance and she would wager he was quite devastating up close.

"Heliotrope again," he murmured. "I would find you anywhere." He inhaled with appreciation. "What news do you have for me?"

The smooth wool of his coat brushed against her arm, sending tremors through her. Even her sheer sleeve could not prevent her awareness of his touch. "Grandmama continues to insist I must accept Lord Twisdale. I pleaded for time and she has most reluctantly granted a little respite. I fear it is not much. I confess I am afraid of him. It will be bread and water if I refuse him, however."

Her drawing tablet slid to the floor and St. Aubyn hastened to pick it up for her. "Miss Wingrove? A wilting dove? How fitting. Yet it is not malicious. Tell me, do you often sketch people in this manner?"

Forgetting her problems for a moment, Chloe smiled. "Indeed. Mr. Purcell is a naughty magpie."

"Let me guess. . . . Lord Twisdale is a serpent?"

"True," she said with downcast eyes. Then she turned her head, accidently brushing her cheek against his lips to say breathlessly, "And Grandmama is a dragon."

Chapter 4

"*H*urry, I fear they are leaving the box opposite us. Try to meet me tomorrow—say at the panorama in Leicester Square, just inside the door at two of the clock," he urged.

Still very much aware of the slight touch of his lips against her cheek, Chloe marshaled her nerves and nodded. "I will do my best. Perhaps Grandmama will allow me to visit there, with my maid, Ellen, along. I could say it is an educational venture."

"I will be there," he promised. "I know how difficult it is for you, so I will wait an hour before leaving."

Chloe felt a faint rush of air from the hall and knew, even without turning to see, that he had gone. She moved forward to the front of the box and watched, wondering if he might appear elsewhere. Within a brief time, she saw him enter the box opposite her, bending forward to speak with her aunt.

She had no right at all to feel this pang of dismay, yet she did. Quite obviously there was something between them. What it might be she refused to speculate.

Behind her a rustle of skirts informed her that the Dowager Lady Dancy had returned with Lord Twisdale behind her.

"Ah, you remained in the box. I told you she is an obedient girl, Twisdale." Grandmama sounded odiously triumphant.

"True, Grandmama, I did not leave the box. Alas, I could not find anyone who would bring me a glass of lemonade, but I will wait until we take our leave." Chloe wondered if her cousins would have been as meek and mild as she was now—given the same circumstances. Somehow she could not see her Cousin Hyacinthe behaving so passively. Yet, Chloe dare not anger her grandmother. Not if she hoped to achieve the appointment with Mr. St. Aubyn tomorrow. She felt deliciously wicked, planning a tryst with a gentleman—even if it was nothing more than to scheme how to escape a distasteful marriage to another man.

Distasteful? She studied Lord Twisdale while pretending to look beyond him at the stage. The sharp scent from Lord Twisdale wafted past her and she held her handkerchief to her nose. One did not wish to overdo the sneezing. Every bone and nerve in her body felt him a dangerous man. Surely she was being fanciful? Yet Mr. St. Aubyn had known of the rumor.

Her dear friend Laura had just told her that *she* had heard that Lady Twisdale had taken a powder of arsenic from her medicine chest by mistake. Chloe thought it peculiar that a woman would not know what she had in each container of her very own chest. And why would she want arsenic there in the first place?

The farce concluded before Chloe realized it was being performed. She was sorry not to have paid attention, for usually the farce was the best part of the entertainment, she not being given to tragedies, particularly of the family sort. She assisted her grandmother with arranging her shawls, finding a fallen fan, and making certain nothing was left behind them. Her silence was not marked by either her relative or the guest. They were busy tearing the farce into shreds.

"And what do you think, child?" Lord Twisdale inquired as they settled into the Dancy carriage her grandmother had kept for her use. The lights and bustle of the theater faded from view and the clatter of the horses' hooves on the cobbles of London streets made conversation difficult.

"The scenery was extremely pretty and I thought the music quite nice," Chloe responded, believing those comments safe enough.

"Chloe admires the lighter offerings," the Dowager Lady Dancy explained somewhat unnecessarily.

This appeared to be sufficient to satisfy Lord Twisdale, for he chatted with Lady Dancy the remainder of the drive.

For once in her life Chloe did not mind in the least being treated like a witless child.

Once they were safely in the house again, she waited until she thought it prudent to speak. She approached her grandmother in the gold-and-white drawing room.

"I have a great favor to ask, Grandmama. A lady told me how very educational she found the display at the Rotunda at Leicester Square. Mr. Barker has an admirable painting on view and I should like to see it. Might I take Ellen with me tomorrow afternoon—unless you have something for me to do, that is?"

Since Chloe knew her grandmama always took tea with Lady Sefton on Tuesday afternoons to discuss Society events, she thought she had a chance to be free.

"What? Educational, you say? So I have heard tell. No little friend to go with you as well?" The dowager gave Chloe an inquiring and too-searching look.

"I could invite Miss Laura Spayne along, I suppose." Chloe hoped her good friend would be otherwise occupied.

"Do that," the dowager commanded. "Remember, I have given you but a short time before you must accept Lord Twisdale. He is being most understanding about your miss-ishness, my girl. It is imperative he acquire an heir and he needs a dutiful wife to accomplish that. He is convinced you will be most dutiful," the lady concluded with a nod of her feather-bedecked head.

Chloe bowed, reminding herself that she must guard her tongue more than ever before. It would *not* do to anger Grandmama at this moment. She stood by the fireplace, regal and elegant, resembling a queen far more than the present one.

Taking her grandmother at her word, Chloe backed from the room, then hurried up the stairs before any change of heart could occur.

Come morning her grandmother would be busily employed scanning the newspapers to glean every shred of news and gossip to share with Lady Sefton. As long as Chloe remained out of sight, she doubted if her grandmother would think about the matter again.

It was difficult to sleep, for Chloe kept thinking about that accidental touching in the theater box. She stroked her cheek where his lips had so lightly grazed. It was nothing more than skin, she reminded herself. Skin touching skin. Yet it had such a profound effect on her. She could not allow such a fancy.

Mr. St. Aubyn was not the least like the boys at home. He had such polish, smelled deliciously of spice and cost-mary—not the stables—and was so considerate. He simply could not be the scoundrel his reputation proclaimed. Scoundrels did not help green girls.

With that thought in mind, she drifted off to sleep.

In the morning Ellen touched her on her shoulder with her silent greeting of the day.

Chloe recalled what was to occur this afternoon and bounded from her bed with new enthusiasm for life. St. Aubyn would think of something. He had to.

But first she must write a missive to Laura. Could she trust her to remain silent about the assignation once she learned of it? With a studied look at Ellen, who was quietly going about her business of making up the bed, then plac-ing the gown to be worn on the coverlet, Chloe decided she might as well ask. Penning the missive with care, she folded and sealed it.

"Ellen," Chloe said some minutes later, "I have a letter for Miss Spayne. Could you be the dearest of maids and de-liver it for me?" Chloe offered a shilling with the letter, knowing that Ellen would speechlessly accept both.

With a nod of her head, the maid took the letter, tucking both shilling and note in the pocket of her apron. Then she insisted upon helping Chloe into her gown of pale gray sprigged muslin.

Oddly enough the dress, intended to be nunlike in ap-pearance proved quite different when worn. The double frill at the neck framed her face nicely and the demure puffed long sleeves flattered her slender arms. It was Chloe's favorite gown. Ellen had found a pink silk rose to sew onto Chloe's chip straw bonnet so that she thought she might be fair to being presentable when she went out this afternoon.

Somewhat to Chloe's dismay, Laura wrote back that she would adore going to Leicester Square this afternoon and would present herself at Lady Dancy's house at half past one of the clock.

Ellen did not question the outing, not that Chloe expected she would. Laura was another matter entirely. When she was ushered into Chloe's neat room, she burst into question. With her pert, sweet face she strongly reminded Chloe of the drawing she had done of her friend—that of a sweet and cuddly kitten.

"What a mysterious invitation you sent me. I simply had to come. Fortunately, Mama approves of you as being a young lady of unimpeachable manners and integrity." Laura's brown eyes danced with mirth and she tilted her head to one side before she inquired, "Is it dreadfully tedious?"

"It is." Chloe ignored the erroneous assessment of her character and wondered how best to explain their mission.

At last she said, "You know that Grandmama insists that I must marry Lord Twisdale."

"I know," Laura said, her voice devoid of expression but her eyes watchful.

"Oh, Laura, I am not perfectly mannered and obedient as your dear mama believes. I simply cannot marry that utterly odious man." Chloe waited for her friend to react to such an outrageous pronouncement.

"Well, I wondered how you could endure such a thing. He is a complete toad." Laura settled on Chloe's favorite chair near the window and surveyed her good friend. "I fail to see how you may manage to avoid the fate, however."

"That is what you must promise to keep as a secret. Will you? Cross your heart?"

Laura solemnly promised, then, eyes agleam, leaned forward in anticipation. "Tell me, oh, do," she implored.

"I cannot go into the details, for it is too long, but Mr. St. Aubyn has taken pity on me and offered to help."

"The Scoundrel?" Laura jumped up and began to pace back and forth on the rug, her dark eyes flashing with her surprise and consternation.

"Indeed, and I do not see him as a scoundrel. He believes me, Laura. He agrees that it would be a disaster were I to wed that dreadful man." Chloe rose from where she had perched on the tufted bench to confront her friend.

Laura paused in her steps, turning to study Chloe. In a whisper, she said, "You mean he also thinks there is something odd about Lady Twisdale's death?"

Chloe nodded. Then, with a glance at the mantel clock, she said, "We had best leave before something happens to prevent our excursion. Grandmama is off to Lady Sefton's house, but I shan't be at ease until we enter the Rotunda."

With Ellen and Laura's maid beside them, the girls entered a hackney summoned by the butler. The trip across London was accompanied by soft murmurs of, "What do you think he will say?" and "I cannot believe you are so daring as to risk this."

They left the hackney, advancing upon the building with hesitant steps. They passed the little shop selling coffee and tea, tobacco and cigars, then walked to the entrance that was set back some distance from the street.

Inside, after paying four shillings for herself and the others, Chloe searched the area. She hadn't realized how tense she was until she relaxed upon seeing Mr. St. Aubyn advance from the shadows.

"Good afternoon, Lady Chloe. Miss Spayne, what a pleasant surprise." He half turned to speak to another person who had remained in the shadows. "Theo, my good fellow, why not join us? Surely you do not need to go to Jackson's just now?"

Theo grinned and walked the distance with flattering haste. "Lady Chloe and Miss Spayne! The lure of Jackson's cannot compare with this treat. Shall we?" He offered his arm to Laura, who accepted with apparent delight. Her glance back at Chloe was one of pleased conspiracy.

"That was fortuitous," Julian said quietly as he ushered Lady Chloe up the stairs to where the panorama would be seen. It claimed to offer a comprehensive and most lifelike view of the Swiss Alps in full and glorious color.

"Indeed, but Grandmama insisted I have someone besides Ellen along with me," she replied sedately. Then forgetting to be composed, she turned to him and said anxiously, "Have you thought of something? Anything?"

"I have considered your situation at great length." Julian failed to add that he was approaching desperation himself. Elinor had been pressing him again, and he suspected she was quite willing to create a scene to suit her purpose if needs be. What that might consist of, he did not even wish to contemplate. However, he surmised that nothing would be beyond her capabilities as he had come to know them.

"And?" Lady Chloe prompted.

"I believe it would be a good idea if we proceed to appear as though we have reached an understanding." Ignoring the gasp from Lady Chloe, he revealed, "You are not the only one who wishes to escape an unwanted marriage. While I have no desire to name anyone, there is a lady who is pressing her intent. I have no wish to marry her and my father would not be pleased at that union."

"He would not be dismayed to see *our* names linked?"

Julian allowed a wry chuckle to escape. "On the contrary, he would think all his prayers have been answered. My father is convinced that an amenable wife would be the making of me."

"I fail to see how we may accomplish this scheme in a short time, for you know that Lord Twisdale is urgently pursuing my marriage to him and Grandmama has endorsed his suit," she argued, prudently ignoring his comment on a wife.

It was plain that she was highly dubious and Julian could not say he blamed her. He simply could not think of anything better. He had no wish to leave London merely to escape Elinor Hadlow. And he also knew a desire to help this young woman elude marriage to a man he strongly disliked—even distrusted.

"Theo has agreed to help us. He will tell everyone he was with us this afternoon, imply that we were quite taken with each other, that sort of thing. He's rather good at implying things, actually."

Lady Chloe turned a grave face to him. They had reached the top of the stairs and were about to join the others inside the Rotunda to view the spectacle. "It is agreeable to me. I would do anything to avoid marriage to Lord Twisdale."

"Even appear attracted to me? How you do flatter a chap," Julian said in his most mocking manner.

"Oh, Mr. St. Aubyn, it is not that at all, and I believe you know it," she said with a hint of a smile. "Why, a plain girl such as myself could never interest a dashing gentleman like you in the normal course of events. It will cause a deal of talk, you know," she concluded with a sage nod.

"I can weather the storm. Can you?" Julian looked at the fragile, heart-shaped face so trustingly turned to him with a faint pang in his heart. Was he doing the right thing to involve her in his affairs? Yet she desperately needed his assistance as much as he desired hers.

"I can." Her face lit up with a smile when they entered the room with a light step.

Julian wondered why she referred to herself as plain. She had a piquant air about her and with that pink rose nestled inside the brim of her chip bonnet next to her equally pink cheek, she looked rather adorable.

He placed a protective arm behind her, guiding her to the first viewing place with solicitous concern.

"Oh," she breathed, quite forgetting her dire circumstances for the moment, "it is more spectacular than I had believed."

They slowly circled the viewing platform, studying the magnificent scene before them. "How do you suppose he achieves that lighting effect?" Chloe asked when they had completed the circle. "I vow the mountains appeared so real I could almost feel a chilly wind from them."

"I've never heard. But then," he said, turning to a topic he wanted to pursue, "you are also talented. I should like to see more of your clever little sketches. Were you serious when you said you had done your grandmother as a dragon?" He guided her along behind Theo and the lively Miss Spayne.

"Yes, for all my sins, I did. It was rather wicked of me, but she had just told me that if I did not accept Lord Twisdale soon she would put me in my room on bread and water until I changed my mind."

Julian's grip on Lady Chloe's arm tightened as he contemplated a grandmother who would treat her own kith and kin in such a manner. His conclusion was that if he could, he would take Lady Chloe away as far as he might from the old dragon. Chloe was far too sweet to be forced into a frightful marriage.

They left the Rotunda, then took a hackney to Gunter's

for ices. For as Theo put it, "If you are to begin this thing, 'tis best to begin at once."

Laura smiled at Chloe while the gentlemen presented their order to the waiter. "Please do not worry. Theo told me about the plan and I believe it just might do the thing. Knowing your grandmother, she will feel compelled to alter her intentions once she catches wind of your gentleman admirer. However did you manage it?" she concluded in a wondering voice.

"Later," Chloe cautioned. "How she will react is more than I can guess."

Soon pineapple ices were placed before them and the four consumed the treat with relish, even the gentlemen, who could have pretended to be jaded and beyond such things. They parted shortly after that, but not before having been observed by two of the greatest gossips in Town.

"Remember, Theo has promised to do his best and I suspect Miss Spayne will assist him in the task," Julian reminded her. "All that we need to do at this point is wait to see what develops. Believe me, I am as anxious as you are. I have no wish for a forced marriage, either."

"We face a similar battle, it seems. And how would I draw your opponent?" she dared to ask.

"I see her as a falcon or other predatory bird," Julian replied in a musing tone. "Allow me to see what you have done today."

Lady Chloe hesitantly withdrew her little pad and offered it to Julian with that twinkle in her eyes. "You may not approve, sir."

He studied the drawing and chuckled. "It is her to the life." A drawing of the lovely Lady Jersey, portrayed as an elegant butterfly, charmingly illustrated the lady's true nature. He turned the page and chuckled again. "Mrs. Drummond-Burrell as I live and breathe and as a hawk!" The haughty stare from the noble bird was Clemintaria Drummond-Burrell to a tee. The next page was blank and he looked at Chloe with questioning eyes.

"I cannot quite decide on the next one to do."

"Do Emily Cowper next," he suggested.

"As a lamb?" Lady Chloe said in a teasing voice.

Julian laughed heartily at this sally and then bowed to

Lady Chloe. "You have a delightful wit, my girl. It would be a shame to have it wasted on Twisdale." Julian could have bitten his tongue when he saw the laughter fade from her lovely eyes.

"We shall prevail, never fear," he said to encourage her.

"I trust we will." She was again the shy and worried young miss he had first seen.

Julian took her hand in his and smiled down at her. "Until later, my dear Lady Chloe." He was reluctant to let her hand go. He was truly concerned for her. She seemed such a little thing to stand up to that wicked old woman.

"Until later, my dear conspirator," she dared to reply with a mischievous look in her eyes that surprised Julian even as it delighted him.

When back at the house, Chloe awaited the return of her esteemed grandmother with an anxious heart. For once, the knowledge that little happened in London that did not reach her grandmother's ears was comfort for Chloe. She wondered which of the gossips would reach Lady Sefton's drawing room first, for most of the female half of the ton knew where the dowager spent Tuesday afternoons. Few had any love for her, and nearly all would be eager to lower her arrogance if possible.

Feeling a bit hungry and not knowing if she'd be sent off to bed without any supper, Chloe silently slipped along the hall and edged her way into the kitchen. Only the scullery maid took note of her.

"Rose," Chloe whispered when the girl peeked around the corner from the scullery and into the kitchen. When she ventured close to her, Chloe asked, "Could you find me some food? I fear I may not eat later."

Understanding how it was to be deprived of food when hungry, the girl darted off. She returned shortly with a plate holding a slice of ham, a roll, a savory, and a piece of plum cake.

Chloe accepted the largesse, but not before observing how the child's large eyes followed the food.

"Are you hungry, Rose? Do you even get enough to eat?"

"Bless you, miss, us below the salt dassent ask for more of anythin' to eat," Rose replied with an anxious glance at the cook, who had just returned to the kitchen from her rooms.

"Rose," she commanded in a firm tone, "back to work. Do not be bothering Lady Chloe." The girl skittered from the kitchen and soon was heard banging pots and pans.

"Mrs. Beeman," Chloe said in her soft voice, "I would that Rose be given more to eat. She looks too thin by half."

Casting an astounded look at Chloe, who rarely ever raised her voice regarding anything in the house, the cook nodded. "Don't see any harm in it, though what your grandmother might say with coddling of a scullery maid, I don't know."

"Well, if she is not hungry, she might well work better." After hurriedly eating the food on her plate, Chloe placed it on a sideboard in the butler's pantry, then spirited herself off to the front parlor. When Grandmama returned, it was well to be forewarned.

She stood close to the window holding aside the golden draperies with one slender hand, apprehensive and nervous.

At long last the dowager's Town carriage drew up before the house. The groom in his dark blue-and-gold livery hurried to let down the steps, then assist the dowager from the vehicle. She sailed up to the front door, which was whisked open for her so she need not so much as pause in her stride.

Chloe turned to face the doorway, wondering if she would be able to withstand what she feared was coming. She licked her dry lips and quickly folded her hands before her lest Grandmama see her trepidations.

Apparently the dowager had been informed as to Chloe's whereabouts, for within seconds the imposing figure appeared framed in the doorway. With narrowed eyes, she advanced upon Chloe.

"I heard the most outrageous story this afternoon. Mrs. Robynhod claimed she observed you exiting Gunter's with not only Miss Spayne, but Mr. Purcell and Mr. St. Aubyn as well. I said nothing, not wishing to risk a falsehood. It cannot be true, or can it?" She glared down at Chloe, who stiffened her spine lest she wilt.

The ordeal was ever worse than Chloe had feared. Her

grandmother was twisting the scene to sound sordid and dreadful instead of an innocent dish of pineapple ice.

"We encountered Mr. St. Aubyn and Mr. Purcell at the Rotunda. They were most kind to assist us and offered to treat us to an ice. Even Ellen enjoyed a treat." Chloe sought to remind her relative that she had been properly chaperoned, although it was but a maid. Ellen was of sober and decent reputation, not one of those maids who flirted and got into trouble.

"I do not wish you to speak to these gentlemen again," the dowager said in the most repressing of voices. She drew herself up and prepared to go to her room for a rest.

"Is it true they are not only wealthy in their own right, but due to inherit a vast fortune as Laura said?" Chloe inserted before her grandmother left the room. "Laura said her mama told her the St. Aubyn jewels are worth a queen's ransom."

The Dowager Lady Dancy pirouetted to face Chloe, a most peculiar expression crossing her face as she did. "I had heard something of the sort, true. However, St. Aubyn has a dreadful reputation," she concluded with a wave of her hand.

"He was all that was proper and kind to me," Chloe said in reply.

"Indeed." With an exceedingly thoughtful expression on her face, the dowager left the room.

Once alone, Chloe sank on the nearest chair, her legs finally refusing to support her any longer.

"I did it," she crowed in a whisper. "I managed to stand up to her in my own way and survive. I must tell Laura." With that she dashed up to find her bonnet and gloves.

In the drawing room of her new abode, having been forced to remove there even more quickly than she had believed necessary, Elinor paced back and forth. Mrs. Robynhod had told her little tale with such glee. To think that Elinor's own twit of a niece should humiliate her in this way.

Oh, that girl! To be seen laughing and flirting with Julian St. Aubyn in public, just outside of Gunter's. He had expressed great glee over something Chloe had shown him. Drawings, perhaps?

Elinor stopped her pacing to contemplate this thought. After a time, she rang for her maid, ordering her pelisse and bonnet, and the carriage to be brought around. Something must be done to halt an attraction before it could bloom. Although what St. Aubyn might see in that dab of a girl was more than Elinor could imagine.

Her mind working furiously for the next half hour while she awaited her carriage, Elinor had a vague plan when she finally left her new house across the square from Julian's elegant home.

She darted a malevolent glance at it when she drove past, wishing she might make things most unpleasant for him. How dare he insult her so!

When she arrived at the Dowager Lady Dancy's home, Elinor sought an interview with her. Upon finding the lady unavailable, Elinor turned a speculative gaze on the butler. In her experience most of them were corruptible given the right sum of money.

She withdrew a gold coin from her reticule, holding it so it might be seen by an observant eye. When he straightened and blinked, she knew she was closer to success. "Is my dear niece Lady Chloe also absent?"

"Indeed, madam. I believe she has gone to the bookshop with her maid."

"I loaned her a trifle which she has failed to return. Might I just whisk myself up to her room to fetch it? Then I would not have to embarrass the child. One must be considerate of these young people, for they have such delicate nerves." With a discreet and most graceful wave of her hand she transferred the gold coin to the butler's.

Within minutes Elinor found herself in Chloe's little room. She looked around her with distaste.

"I vow, 'tis as plain as she is. Where could she hide that pad of paper Mrs. Robynhod mentioned seeing? Surely she'd not take it to the bookshop."

Then Elinor espied a stack of what appeared to be drawings on the dressing table. Darting to quickly peruse them she suddenly let out a horrified gasp. When she viewed herself as a sleek mongoose who looked ready to consume the

nearest snake in the grass Elinor's eyes grew huge with outrage.

"She will pay for this," Elinor vowed. "I shall make her
wish she had never been born."

Chapter 5

*C*hloe peered about the bookshop to see if Laura was there.

"Around the corner," Ellen counseled.

Hatchards was crowded with book lovers and most likely a few others who were there like Chloe, to meet a friend. The area in the front of the shop was full of gentlemen engaging in pleasant debate. Chloe hurried around the stack of books to find her confidant.

"You survived," Laura exclaimed softly when she saw Chloe's face peering over a stack of books.

"I do believe I gave Grandmama something to think about, for I repeated what you told me regarding you-know-who's fortune, not to mention the family jewels. She had the most peculiar look on her face before she went up for her afternoon rest." Chloe shared a pleased look with her friend over her tiny victory.

Laura beamed a smile of satisfaction at Chloe, then said, "Allow me to pay for this book of verse, then perhaps we might go for a stroll along the edge of Green Park?"

"Afraid of the cows?" Chloe said with a gurgle of laughter, knowing her friend would never venture close to the animals that roamed in the park.

"I have never liked animals larger than I am," Laura said with a twinkle in her pretty dark eyes. "And, yes, that includes horses."

Once outside, the two girls, with their maids close behind them, strolled along the border of the park, admiring the scenery and animals from a safe distance.

"How does your drawing proceed?" Laura asked after a time.

"I have completed all the patronesses at Almack's and

quite a few others. Oh, Laura, it is such fun. I study a person to see what part of his or her character stands out in my mind, or perhaps how they appear to me. Then, I simply draw a likeness of that animal, bird, or whatever and bestow the facial likeness on it. For instance, Lady Jersey is a beautiful butterfly."

"Delightful. And what about me?" Laura said with some hesitation.

"You are the dearest of kittens, the sort one loves to pet and cuddle."

"How lovely," Laura cooed with delight. "I'd give a shilling to know how you portray Mr. St. Aubyn."

"A lion rampant, but you need not look at me like that. He feels sorry for me and desires to help, nothing more," Chloe said with a prim nod in a voice that warned Laura not to tease.

"Oh, do not look now, but there is Sir Augustus Dabney approaching. I cannot believe he is walking! Gracious, he must have sold his carriages and horses to pay his gaming debts," Laura confided in a soft undertone.

"Perhaps he wished to merely take the air?" Chloe offered, not wishing to impugn Sir Augustus, for he had been very kind to her.

"Do you never think ill of another?" Laura said with a hint of impatience.

"Indeed—my grandmama often, and my aunt Elinor every now and again, and Lord Twisdale constantly. But they are an exception, you know. I tend to think good of someone until shown otherwise."

Laura shifted her parasol to her other side so she might have a better look at the gentleman who approached. Chloe closed hers up and then swung it to and fro by the handle on her left side.

"Ah," exclaimed Sir Augustus, as he met them on the walk. He raised an ornate quizzing glass to one eye to survey Chloe. "May I wish you happy, Lady Chloe? If I must, I shall be utterly devastated."

Chloe bestowed a confused look on him. "No, indeed, sir. Wherever did you acquire such a notion?"

"Your parasol, ma'am. Swinging your parasol at your

left side signifies to me that you are engaged." He gave her an arch look with a knowing expression.

"Truly? How amusing. I had no idea a parasol could hold such meaning! I believe I must take lessons in this art, else I shall be sending all manner of messages I know nothing about," she declared with a smile.

"Some of those French chaps offer lessons in that sort of thing—fans, parasols, handkerchiefs, and gloves. Amazing what can be learned from them." He permitted his quizzing glass to swing idly from his superbly gloved fingers while studying Chloe with an intent gaze that soon made her uncomfortable.

"La, sir, and what does it mean when you dangle your quizzing glass from your fingers?" she ventured at last.

"Not a thing." He instantly ceased and allowed the glass to fall against his waistcoat, where the dull gold chain gleamed softly against the ivory mull.

They exchanged a few pleasantries, then the girls went on their way while Sir Augustus headed in the direction of White's, off Piccadilly on St. James's Street and not far from the esteemed Hatchards and the environs of Green Park.

"And what animal or bird is Sir Augustus?" Laura inquired with a tilt of her head, looking at Chloe with a mischievous gleam in her eyes.

"A peacock?" Chloe said with a grin hastily smothered by her gloved hand.

Laura chuckled with appreciation at her friend's wit.

"One thing, we had best use care how we behave with our handkerchief, the fan, our parasols, and above all our gloves," Chloe admonished. "Heavens, we could be sending messages all over the place and not know a thing about it."

The two girls exchanged amused looks, then at last went on their respective ways after promising to see each other that evening at the Robynhod party.

Hailing a hackney, for her grandmother deemed it an extravagance for Chloe to use the Town carriage, Chloe contemplated the day's events.

She wished she might send word to St. Aubyn regarding her success with Grandmama. Of course she might then also have to explain that she had dropped that hint about the St. Aubyn fortune and the family jewels. These were not terribly important to Chloe, but she knew her grandmother set great store by such things.

Perhaps she could suggest she needed another lesson in flirting. Sir Augustus was amusing, but he did remind her of a point. . . . Chloe was woefully ignorant on that subject. She dare not ask to have a French teacher of such skills. When Laura had told her how she had lined up with several girls to receive instruction on flirting with the fan, Chloe's first reaction was to smile. Then she considered the matter and decided it would be no bad thing to know.

Once inside the house, and after sending Ellen up with her pelisse and bonnet, parasol and gloves, Chloe entered the drawing room.

Over by the window stood a gentleman with his back to her. He was garbed much as all the society gentlemen were—except this man wore an impeccably tailored gray coat over darker gray pantaloons, and leaned just a trifle on a fine malacca cane.

"Mr. St. Aubyn!" she declared with a rush of pleasure that surprised her. She almost felt as though she had conjured him up after thinking about him all the way home from Green Park.

He turned to face her, a smile lighting his face to make him even more handsome. Chloe experienced a sense of frustration, for she was such an unsophisticated girl compared to the women this gentleman usually sought for company. Could she converse with him without sounding utterly gauche?

"Lady Chloe," he said with a faint bow, "I trust you had an enjoyable outing."

"Miss Spayne and I took the air along Green Park after meeting at Hatchards." With a slight glance at the open doorway, she added, "We had a very educational conversation."

"Indeed?" He also looked at the door, apparently surmising that Chloe suspected that either her grandmother would shortly join them, or that one of the staff would eavesdrop on their chat.

Ellen slipped into the room, perching on a straight-backed chair near the door.

"I came to see how you fared after the visit to the Rotunda earlier. I heard a rumor, you see."

"So did my grandmama. I explained and she is not terribly displeased. She also said nothing more about my impending engagement to Lord Twisdale."

"Good. You go out this evening?" He caressed the elaborately carved handle of his cane with an absent stroke of one gloved hand. He looked as though he wished to sit down, but Chloe was not certain it would be wise to encourage him to linger.

"The Robynhod party," Chloe replied with a shrug of her shoulders. "I fear I shall need another lesson or two, however," she added with great daring. "We met Sir Augustus Dabney while strolling along the edge of the park. When I swung my parasol along at my left side, he asked if he might wish me happy. I suppose everyone expects an announcement of an engagement to Lord Twisdale," she inserted on a reflective note. "At any rate, I did not know anything about flirting with a parasol."

"No, one might say you are not well versed in the art of flirting. However, that is not so reprehensible. It is refreshing to see a young girl who is not madly fluttering her lashes, dropping her handkerchief, twisting her gloves in her fingers, or sending signals with a parasol."

"You do not object to placing the fan against the lips?" she said softly with a dash of daring.

"Never that, but you had best be careful with such an invitation. The wrong man might take advantage of you." His look seemed paternally tolerant of her girlish remark.

Chloe was quite certain there were few gentlemen so inclined, but remained silent on that score. She merely shook her head and stood, hands held politely before her, while she waited for him to take his leave.

He advanced toward her, an odd light in his eyes. What a provocative tilt to his mouth and such an intriguing look in his eyes. Perhaps he was a scoundrel after all?

"I must go, for the time is slipping past and I would not have your grandmama think me improper." He looked for all the world as though he silently laughed at her or someone.

Chloe wished with all her heart that she might dare to lift the handle of her fan to her mouth. What would it be like to know the touch of his lips on hers, rather than the faint brush of them against her cheek. Then, quite scandalized that she would harbor such outrageous thoughts, she sought a decorous reply.

"That would never do," she said. Then the words "Dragons must be given proper respect" popped out before she could consider how *im*proper she was being to speak of her grandmother in such a manner.

"I shall consider what your next lesson should be," he added in a soft aside before leaving the room.

Chloe stood utterly still, contemplating his words. Her next lesson? What it might be? A shiver of delight fluttered through her.

Suddenly her dread of the Robynhod party dramatically lessened and she began to look forward to it, even if her gown was a gray thing she had worn a number of times before.

When she hurried to her room, Ellen cautioned her that time passed far too quickly and her grandmother would expect her down for an early dinner tonight.

Chloe had intended to sort out her drawings and study the one of St. Aubyn again. She wondered if she had captured that sparkle in his eyes just right. Well, she concluded, the drawings must have been tidily placed in a drawer and out of sight, for they were not where Chloe had left them. Ellen's work, most likely.

Her inspection must wait until later. So she hastily changed from her day dress into the gray silk—such as it was—for this evening.

Ellen had found another pretty pink silk rose that she tucked into Chloe's curls and pinned into place with care. When queried about her source, the maid replied, "I was sent to the attics for something else and I chanced to see a hatbox full of silk flowers. I doubt any would be missed, there were so many." For Ellen it was a loquacious reply.

"Well, it does improve my looks. This gray silk needs a touch of pink," Chloe mused in a considering way.

Ellen produced another pink rose to pin to the bodice of

Chloe's gown. "There now, you look as well as possible without a new gown."

"And we both know that even if it is my money that is spent, Grandmama will not deign to purchase that!" Chloe declared with affront.

When she joined her grandmother for dinner, that good lady said nothing about the touch of pink silk roses. Rather, she had something else on her mind.

"Scroggins said you had a visitor."

"Mr. St. Aubyn stopped by for a few minutes to see how I managed after the excursion to the Rotunda this afternoon. Ellen joined us."

"Hmpf," Lady Dancy said with a calculating expression crossing her face. "Most considerate of him. Behaved himself, you say?"

"Yes, Grandmama. He was all that was polite."

"Maybe he is thinking about choosing a wife. Even a scoundrel must consider what is due his family name." Lady Dancy dismissed the butler and stared at her young relative with a most penetrating gaze.

"Perhaps. I should not refine too much on his attentions to me, however," Chloe dared to explain. She did not wish her grandmother to acquire any outrageous notions.

"How is that? You said he was polite."

"He was and is. He just did not seem as though he is interested in me in that way."

"But then, what do you know about such matters," the dowager concluded with a wave of her hand. She rang for her tea and hurried Chloe through her sweet, nattering on about the Robynhod rout.

Once they arrived at the Robynhod home, it was easy to see that the ton had turned out in grand numbers to grace the event. True, while some parties bordered on the insipid, word had seeped out that Mrs. Robynhod offered something out of the ordinary.

Chloe heard whispers of it while ascending the stairs and wondered what it might be. She adored surprises.

While mingling with the throng of guests, she caught sight of Laura with her parents, her Aunt Elinor—who looked exceptionally beautiful, in fact, rather dashing— Theo Purcell with Sir Augustus, and off to one side Mr. St.

Aubyn. Although he had his back to her, she would recognize that back anywhere, even without sight of his cane.

Her grandmother set off for the card room at once, leaving Chloe to find Laura and asylum.

Miss Wingrove sidled up to them and gave Chloe a significant look. "How are you, my dear?" she whispered, or as near to a whisper as one could get in the midst of a mass of people.

"Well, thank you." Chloe shot her a puzzled look. Miss Wingrove usually never spoke to Chloe.

"I hope you will continue to enjoy good spirits," she said with an apologetic expression. "One never knows what is around the corner."

Chloe murmured an agreement, then watched, still puzzled, while the lady edged her way back to Elinor's side. There she remained in the shadows, ready to fetch a shawl, a glass of lemonade, or simply disappear if her benefactress so wished.

"How odd, but then she never is what you might call commonplace," Chloe said in an aside to Laura.

"Come, let us wander about the rooms. Perhaps we shall find other friends and make up a game of something."

With a murmur of assent, Chloe asked, "Did you hear something about a surprise the Robynhods have for the guests this evening? Someone mentioned it while we were on the stairs."

"I doubt if it will be out of the ordinary. But Mama said she always serves a delicious supper. Mama said Mrs. Robynhod gossips so frightfully about others, she daren't serve but the best of foods." Laura searched about as though hunting for the dining room.

"How fitting that her gossiping should benefit us," Chloe said with a smile.

They turned a corner and nearly bumped into Theo Purcell and Mr. St. Aubyn. Laura exclaimed with delight and said, "Do let us get up a game of something. Cards? Charades? Cranbo?"

"Well, we could have Lady Chloe portray her favorite characters," Mr. St. Aubyn said in a drawl.

In the background Aunt Elinor spoke with Lady Jersey, but it seemed to Chloe that she was quite conscious of all that was said in her hearing. She stared at Chloe as though she'd become a nasty worm. What in the world did she think might be said by St. Aubyn to a slip of a girl like Chloe?

Not liking his casual drawl, she glared at him and moved away. "Come, Laura, I see Sir Augustus across the room. Perhaps he may be able to give us more information of those teachers he mentioned earlier."

Not understanding her motives in the least, Laura gave Chloe a confused look, then followed along.

"I thought it would be fun to have a game of something," she hissed at Chloe when they were at a safe distance.

"Really," Chloe hissed back, "can you see the elegant Mr. St. Aubyn playing at charades?"

Laura turned to look back at the gentleman, who now stood by Lady Jersey and flirted with her in a very sophisticated manner.

"I would say that your Mr. St. Aubyn could most likely play at charades with the best of them." Then she looked about them and said, "Have you seen Lord Twisdale here? He usually manages to show himself at every event you attend."

"I have seen very little of my tormentor in the past day or two and hope to see still less. Maybe Grandmama forgot to tell him."

"Look the other way," Laura suddenly urged. "He just paused by the entrance. We do not wish him to spoil things for us."

Glad to have someone who appeared to care for her interests, Chloe obediently turned her back to the entry and wondered if she might be successful at eluding the man by this method.

"I say, Lady Chloe, are you planning to get up a game of *attitudes*?" Sir Augustus said from where he had popped up at her side.

"No," she replied, even as Laura said, "Yes, we are."

Nothing would do but that the diversion was organized, and Chloe shortly found herself the object of all eyes in the room while she sought to reveal her subject. Posing in an *attitude* tired one quickly and she objected to being the cynosure of all eyes.

"You represent the goddess of wisdom," Laura cried with delight.

Actually, Chloe had attempted to portray an instructress, but was so happy to be out of the limelight, that she gave way with more than a little eagerness. She retired to the shadows to watch Laura perform.

"Were you truly wise, you would depart immediately," advised a voice from behind her.

Chloe pretended not to hear St. Aubyn, but wafted her handkerchief across her brow to indicate she guessed they were watched. "Lord Twisdale?" she whispered.

"Have you not noticed the malicious looks darted at you by your aunt? I fear she is up to something. When I arrived she was in close conversation with our hostess. Both wore an expression of unholy glee. I cannot be at ease when I think about it. What have you done to displease her?" His softly spoken words disheartened her.

"Nothing at all." Chloe turned slightly so she might speak without seeming to be talking to the man behind her. She noted he held his hand to his mouth as though pondering the performer.

In the softest of voices, and from behind the security of a spread fan, Chloe continued, "Perhaps you were not the only one to hear a bit of gossip this afternoon, sir. If she is very good friends with Mrs. Robynhod it may well be that she was informed of the visit to Gunter's and the conversation between us that followed."

"By Jove," he said in a faint undertone of disgust.

"I understand that some ladies resent attention paid elsewhere, even if it is of the most innocent kind." Chloe turned again to face the person performing and behaved as though she had no idea who had been standing behind her for a brief time.

He eased himself away, not trusting himself to answer that last remark. Blast Elinor anyway. What made her think that she could snoop and pry into his doings as though she had a right to know all he did. That Chloe should know anything of the liaison that had existed between himself and the beautiful Elinor bothered him. A young girl like her ought not be exposed to such knowledge.

Julian sought and found the elegantly beautiful Mrs.

Hadlow arm in arm with Lady Jersey. Elinor still wore that smug expression of elation she had worn earlier. What could she be up to, he wondered.

"Julian," she purred, "you became bored with the game? Perhaps they ought to play something more interesting?"

"Like Hunt the Slipper? Or Blind Man's Buff? What sort of game would you play at, Mrs. Hadlow?" Julian fixed her with a stare that she could not seem to break. At her side Lady Jersey stirred, then drifted away to find something less intense.

"I do not play at games, Julian. Can you say the same?" She tore her gaze from his to search the room. From the way her eyes narrowed with displeasure, Julian guessed her gaze had come to rest on Lady Chloe.

"You must be proud of your talented niece," Julian offered suddenly, not liking the expression that had flitted across Elinor's face. "She seemed to play the game rather well."

"Did she?" Elinor turned her face back to him and smiled. It was a strange smile—smug and a trifle triumphant. It made Julian distinctly uneasy. "Well, as to that, we shall soon see." She drifted away from him to chat with Lord Twisdale.

And that was odd, for Julian would have sworn that Elinor detested Twisdale. His attention was captured by a round of laughter from the assembled group clustered about the attitude posers. Theo posed as Neptune and had a dickens of a time keeping a straight face.

Julian decided to take him from his misery and identified him. Whereupon he discovered that when he had named the character, he must take the following turn.

Theo thanked him for saving him from disgrace, then muttered, "You had best be a lion rampant, someone is bound to guess."

Not understanding in the least, Julian agreed to pose with good grace and was astounded when Lady Chloe immediately called out his portrayal.

"Well done," Julian said with relief. "Did Theo tell you?" he added when the group had dispersed because Lady Chloe declined a second attitude.

"Not exactly." She turned her attention to the doorway

where Mrs. Robynhod was inviting people to partake of her little supper. "Perhaps I had best find Grandmama and enjoy the delights to be found at the table our hostess provides."

"I meant what I said earlier; beware of your aunt. I do not trust her in the least."

Chloe tossed him a worried glance before wending her way to the dining room with Laura.

The usual buzz of conversation met her ears when she entered the pleasantly sized room. After selecting a plate of rather delectable foods, she sought her grandmother and Mrs. Spayne, who were seated on a sofa in the next room. Laura followed, but not without several backward glances at Theo Purcell.

Settling herself on a chair while balancing her plate and glass of lemonade most carefully, Chloe listened to the flow of conversation about her.

"I say it is nothing more than one of her little whims. I doubt if Effie has anything extraordinary planned. After all, who does she know that the rest of us do not also know?" Mrs. Spayne pointed out when the topic of the supposed surprise came up.

It was not long before they discovered what it was that Mrs. Robynhod intended as her treat.

When the people were about finished with their supper, the hostess climbed on a step that had been placed at one end of the drawing room. Rapping for attention on a wooden stand that somewhat resembled an easel, she spoke when all was quiet.

"My dear friends, it is not often that we are given the pleasure of enjoying true talent found among one of our own. This evening I have that pleasure. Through the assistance of a dear friend I am able to display the extremely clever drawings of our dear Lady Chloe Maitland. They are arranged on this stand for all to see and enjoy. Lady Jersey, perhaps you would care to be the first viewer. Or Lord Twisdale?"

Chloe knew she must have paled considerably. She felt chilled and her hands had turned to ice. Turning slightly, she met Laura's horrified gaze with one that must have been equally shocked.

"Good grief," Laura cried softly in an understatement of the very highest. "This could destroy you."

"It depends on how they view themselves and how others react, I fancy," Chloe whispered.

Since she adored the unusual, Lady Jersey had managed to stay close to her hostess and now was among the first to study the clever little sketches. When she saw herself depicted as an elegant butterfly, she merely laughed with apparent delight. When she viewed Mrs. Drummond-Burrell as a hawk, she smiled a trifle wickedly. She turned to the gentleman not far away. "Come, St. Aubyn, see yourself."

The press of people around the drawings was impossible and Chloe alternately turned pale and blushed when the patronesses present looked at the sketches.

Lord Twisdale, who had not the slightest sense of humor, was utterly furious, although he concealed it fairly well.

"These are delightful spoofs," St. Aubyn declared in a loud voice that carried throughout the room. "What a charmingly witty talent Lady Chloe has, to be sure."

Those in the room appeared to relax after that pronouncement from one depicted and the buzz of conversation rose to a more intense degree while this was discussed.

Chloe wished she might sink through the floor. When Mrs. Robynhod sidled up to her, wagging a finger beneath her nose, Chloe stifled her wild urge to bite it.

"What a naughty girl you are, to hide such ability from us all. May I beg you to sketch me? I cannot wait to see what wicked little thing you draw. It will be the thing, you know, to have a fiendishly clever sketch of one to display."

Chloe murmured something that must have sounded like an assent, for the hostess went off trumpeting that *she* was to be the next victim of the drawing pencil belonging to the talented Lady Chloe.

"You have survived, just barely. But I fear you have not heard the last of this, my girl," predicted a voice over her shoulder.

Chloe feared that Mr. St. Aubyn had the right of it and she wished with all her heart that she was back in Wiltshire. But one good thing—what misfortune could befall her after this?

Chapter 6

"*I* am most displeased," the Dowager Lady Dancy declared after whisking Chloe along with her to a small library down the hall from the drawing room.

While dreading the confrontation, she appreciated her relative's desire to keep this meeting private. The warmth of a small fire drew Chloe to it, for she felt dreadfully chilled. She glanced about the wood-paneled room glowing with rows of leather-bound books in many hues, all touched with gold lettering and trim. She found a small comfort in the quiet, appealing setting. Then she turned to face her grandparent.

"Believe me, Grandmama, I had not the least intention of ever showing those drawings to anyone," Chloe said with a catch in her voice. "They were done for my own amusement. However, I have a notion that my dear aunt had something to do with their appearance here this evening."

"And how could that dreadful woman have had access to your personal things?" the dowager inquired in an ominous voice.

When her grandmother glared down at Chloe with those icy green eyes, she wished to be somewhere far, far away. They made her feel so frightfully small, somehow.

With a gulp, Chloe made a stab at what must have occurred. "While you had your afternoon rest and I went to Hatchards, she must have wormed her way to my room. When I returned to the house, I noticed the drawings were not where I had left them, but I believed Ellen had neatly stowed them away." Then Chloe's fears burst forth. "What am I to do now?"

"Lord Twisdale is furious, as well he might be. How

dare you portray your intended in such a light!" Fury and disgust were equally clear in the dowager's voice.

"I do not wish to marry him," Chloe countered, wishing she were not quite so timid. "Perhaps he will choose to end his interest?" She devoutly hoped so.

"It would serve you well if he did." The dowager glanced away before continuing in a different tone altogether. "He informed me that he feels you merely exhibited poor judgment and he is willing to overlook this little faux pas. He said something about schooling you to learn discretion in your actions. Your mother has done poorly in training you, my girl."

"My dearest mama is a wonderful mother; none could be better," Chloe whispered, daring to challenge that assessment.

"In spite of those odd starts she has from time to time?" The dowager gave Chloe a knowing look as though to remind her of the little superstitions and beliefs Lady Maitland, now Lady Crompton, had harbored.

"Well, they came true. Lord Leighton was the first man Cousin Elizabeth saw on Valentine's Day and she ended up marrying him." Chloe realized she had a "so-there" note in her voice, but it irritated her when anyone, even her mother's mother, criticized her beloved parent.

"My son's girls are a harum-scarum lot and I washed my hands of them years ago. Best not offer any of them as an example." The dowager sniffed her disdain for the celebrated Dancy girls.

"But they all married extremely well into the peerage." From the dull rose that flooded her grandmother's face, Chloe suspected that it rather galled the lady that her granddaughters had made excellent marriages without her assistance. Not that it had been sought. Chloe thought the girls were clever to have kept their distance from the old dragon. Goodness knows, Chloe wished she might.

"It remains to be seen how things go," Chloe said, after recalling the disheartening words regarding the lessons from Lord Twisdale. Had his first wife needed such lessons? And what, pray tell, were they?

Opening the door to the hall, the dowager motioned Chloe before her and walked at her side to where people still clustered about the clever renditions of the cream of Society.

"Disgraceful," the dowager murmured. "A true lady never does anything to call attention to herself."

"It is *not* my fault," Chloe whispered back.

Lady Sefton approached and Chloe wanted to crawl beneath the carpet. Then a smile from the lady brought a ray of hope.

"Depicting me as an adorable spaniel with soulful eyes is most intriguing. Am I really like that?" the lady demanded with a twinkle in her pretty eyes.

"I am very fond of spaniels; they are so dear." Chloe gave her ladyship an affectionate look.

Then Lady Castlereagh followed her, waving her fan energetically before her as she shook her head at Chloe. "A fancy bird, all plumes and dotted feathers. I do not know about that, a trifle exotic for a plain barnyard hen, my dear. But Emily portrayed as a lamb is delicious."

Lady Sefton nodded, then added, "Brummell may not forgive you for depicting him as a preening raven with a black hat and cane."

Chloe closed her eyes and prayed that she might be able to leave before long. While reaction had not been too bad so far, it was bound to change sooner or later. Lord Twisdale had yet to approach her, nor had Aunt Elinor.

"I thought you might wish to take these home with you," Mr. St. Aubyn said from over her shoulder.

Lady Chloe whirled about to accept the pile of drawings from him, her gratitude shining from luminous eyes. "Thank you," she said in a soft little voice.

The chit looked near to tears, Julian decided, glad he had thought to gather all those outrageous sketches up before someone decided to sneak one or more away.

"If you will have the goodness to assist Chloe, I should be pleased," the dowager unbent to say. She was quite aware that Mr. St. Aubyn was of the highest ton and well liked by all the patronesses.

"I shall escort Lady Chloe with the greatest of pleasure," the elegant gentleman said with a correct bow to the dragon.

Chloe gave him an amused look, then willingly walked at his side to where the maid waited with her hooded cloak.

The dowager rustled along behind them, intent on a dignified escape.

"Excellent anticipation," Julian murmured while he slipped the velvet garment over her shoulders. In the soft candlelight her curls shone like polished mahogany above the dove gray nap of the fine velvet. Heliotrope wafted up to tease his nose. His hands lingered for a moment longer on her slender shoulders, feeling the delicate bones, the surprising strength she must have to endure the old dragon.

"Laura sent for it, just as soon as everything exploded. The dear girl knew I would wish to leave as soon as I might." Lady Chloe moved and broke the spell that had transfixed Julian for those odd moments.

"And you leave with me, not Lord Twisdale," Julian reminded, feeling more like his usual self.

"And Grandmama," Chloe added in an afterthought.

"Never mind the dragon," he said softly, close to her ear. "What sort of scold did she read you while closeted down the hall?"

"She informed me that contrary to my expectations Lord Twisdale did not cry off, rather, he said I was in need of a few lessons in discretion, which he would be happy to administer." She turned to give Julian a worried look. "What do you suppose he intends to do?"

Julian thought it sounded ominous, but merely said, "Most likely, nothing." Nonetheless, he intended to do a bit of investigation regarding Twisdale's first wife.

When the dowager joined them, the trio bade farewell to their triumphant hostess. Mrs. Robynhod was aware that her party would be talked about for weeks and she gave Chloe the warmest of smiles for her unwitting contribution.

They left the house to enter the carriage. Julian elected to go along. He thought the little Chloe could use someone to deflect the dowager's anger. He had another reason to leave; the party had become too dangerous for him to remain.

Julian had approached Elinor regarding the drawings after the initial flurry of revelation. She was the only one he could think of who might have access to them—other than

Chloe, and he knew she wouldn't release them to anyone. Elinor's response had nearly undone him.

"Julian," she had purred after tacitly admitting she had taken the drawings, "if you think dear Chloe is in trouble now, I can do far worse. Ignore the chit. I have a much better proposal for your time." Her look had been inviting and insinuating. Her words had chilled him to the bone.

Upon arrival at the Dancy house, he walked into the entry with the ladies. Then he turned to the dowager and said, "I wonder if I might beg a glass of something. The evening has been not without trials. Mrs. Robynhod is not the hostess you are, ma'am."

Gratified to be praised—even by a scoundrel, for he was the darling of the patronesses—she responded with an invitation to join them in the drawing room.

While she conferred with Scroggins, Julian drew Chloe up the stairs with him, indulging in harmless chit-chat on the way. Once inside the drawing room, he put his hastily formed strategy into action.

"We agreed you are to pretend to have an interest in me, Lady Chloe," he reminded her. "If you wish to survive this affair unscathed it would be better for you to be thought to be my intended instead of Twisdale's. I am far better ton," he said in a matter-of-fact way, acknowledging what Society accepted.

"I thought I *had* been showing an interest in you," she retorted quietly.

"You will have to do much better than that, my girl. Can you not gaze after me with a sigh? Or look at me with stars in those lovely eyes? Or place your hand on my arm in the most confiding of manners?" He tilted his head, considering her, then added, "We had best have another lesson in flirting, I believe. I shall pick you up for a drive in the park tomorrow afternoon at five of the clock."

Chloe swallowed the astounded reply that had longed to leap from her lips. Just like that? He dared to assume she would jump at the chance to drive in that superb carriage with him, parade with a handsome gentleman before all of Society? Of course she would, but he was so odiously sure of himself.

"I shall ask Grandmama if it is acceptable." That she felt dubious about permission rang clear in her voice.

"Allow me, infant. She will bow to my wishes more quickly than yours," he said with that supreme confidence that Chloe was beginning to find annoying.

She almost kicked the wretched man in his shins. He was so frightfully self-confident, and the worst of it all was that he had earned that right by his polish, looks, and wealth, not to mention his surfeit of exquisite manners.

When the dowager entered the room she gave Julian an assessing look, then turned her gaze to where Lady Chloe stood far from his side. Chloe appeared ready to erupt.

"Your port will be here directly. Tea for you, my dear?" she asked Chloe, who looked surprised to be consulted.

"Indeed." She sent Julian a challenging stare, daring him to approach her grandmother with any sort of a request.

"I have been considering the work of this evening, ma'am," he said politely to the dragon. "Do you not believe it might be well to have Lady Chloe appear in public as soon as possible? I should like to offer my services to that end. I thought perhaps a drive in the park tomorrow at five in the afternoon might have a dampening effect on any gossip flying about." He assumed a casual pose near the fireplace.

The dowager considered his words and kind offer while Scroggins served the tea, port, and a light supper.

"I suspect you are right," she admitted at last, over a plate of smoked salmon, macaroni salad, and a cream cake.

"Good," he said, feeling like his plan just might work. "I shall be here." He chatted a bit longer while consuming the excellent port, then bid the ladies good night.

Jauntily running down the stairs and out to the street, he hailed a hackney and headed for White's. He wanted to know what was being said, and where better to begin?

"Well, well," came a hearty voice the moment he stepped into the gaming establishment and most desired gentlemen's club. "Hear you were one of the select this evening. Dashed clever drawings, so I heard tell. Wish she would get them published so the rest of us could see them. Doing Sally Jersey as a butterfly," the portly Austin-Featherstone declared, "was rich, but I'd give a pony to see the

Princess Esterhazy as a poodle." He gave a genial laugh at the very image it evoked.

"Did she actually portray the Lieven as a snipe?" asked another who leaned against the stair rail while Julian walked up the steps.

"Better than a widgeon, perhaps," Julian replied with a lift on one brow and a knowing grin.

"True, she is always whispering into someone's ear," the other man replied, then drifted off to share his new information with those in the other room.

It proved to be not nearly as bad as Julian had feared. Brummell declared that from what he had heard the raven was most elegantly portrayed and that he thought the girl dashed clever. He as well wished he might see the collection of drawings. "I should like to see you as a lion rampant. However do you suppose she arrived at *that* image of you?" he added with a disparaging twist of his mouth.

"Imagination, I fancy," Julian replied with his temper well under control.

"It is a nine days' wonder," Brummell concluded to Julian in an undertone while others had turned the conversation to the next race at Newmarket.

"They haven't heard all of it," Julian offered, knowing the Beau would like to be first with a tidbit of gossip.

"And what might that be?" came the bland, but intent, question.

"That I find Lady Chloe to be utterly charming. Taking her for a drive tomorrow afternoon and I suspect you will see me near her more often in the coming days," Julian replied with a most offhand air.

"What about Twisdale?"

"Well, the chap's bad ton, is he not? It would never do to see talent such as Lady Chloe reveals to be stifled beneath a load of criticism. Understand he intended to do a bit of training," Julian concluded with an exchange of looks.

Brummell gave a nod of understanding. "Quite so, old boy."

Julian drifted off, then later watched to see others crowd around Brummell. Soon after, Julian left for his home, certain that he had deflected the plan that Elinor was trying to place into effect. Courting Lady Chloe was a small price to pay for escaping Elinor's clutches.

He could always manage to slip out of any entanglement later. He always had in the past.

Chloe hurried up to her room after her grandmother had excused her for the night. First she placed the drawings in a large folder, then into the back of a drawer in her highboy chest. Then she slumped down onto the small chair near the fitfully burning fire.

Ellen quietly entered, stirred up the blaze, then began to arrange Chloe's night things for her. "Good evening?"

Surprised at the question from her usually taciturn maid, Chloe shook her head. "Someone—my aunt, I think—came up here and made off with all my drawings."

The maid stopped her preparations to stare at Chloe. "And?"

"Everyone at the party inspected my work. I never intended that *anyone* should see those drawings. Grandmama is right—they are very wicked."

"I will ask around to see if Mrs. Hadlow has been here," Ellen offered.

"Mr. St. Aubyn is coming around tomorrow to take me for a drive. I wonder how *that* will go?" She gave up trying to stay awake and mull over her dilemma. With eyelids that declined to remain open, she had best sleep now.

Yet once in bed, sleep refused to come and it was some time before she succumbed to her fatigue.

Chloe decided that her feelings were somewhere between delighted and dismayed. She faced St. Aubyn arrayed in her best gray pelisse and bonnet, which, while trimmed in gray, had a clutch of jaunty green feathers tucked behind the satin ribbon. She suspected that Ellen had raided the box in the attic again. And Chloe wondered if the feathers fluttered as much as her heart did.

The drive to the Stanhope Gate was unexceptional—unless you consider the instructions given her on how to flirt while in a carriage. It was when they entered the park that her ordeal began with stares from all sides and amused looks from several. Others bestowed glares of outrage and Chloe felt her heart sink.

"Courage," Mr. St. Aubyn murmured as they viewed Elinor Hadlow approaching in the carriage driven by Lord Twisdale.

"What a peculiar pair they make," Chloe whispered, placing that confiding hand on his arm just as he had ordered. She received a most puzzling reaction to this gesture. She felt oddly comforted and yet stirred by her proximity to him. That firm, well-muscled arm felt more than just reassuring to her. It gave her other, stranger sensations.

"Now give me that melting look you practiced while on the way over here," he muttered at her. The other carriage was drawing close enough to see a facial expression and he wanted Elinor to realize that he had no intention of bowing to her wishes.

Lady Chloe obediently turned to bestow a warm look of regard on him. Her look of adoration and trust had a most profound effect on his senses. Innocence, he decided. It was most likely as dangerous to a bachelor as consoling a new widow. Although he admitted that his reaction to her confiding touch surprised him. He'd been pawed by a number of ladies and normally shrugged it off. Chloe's gentle touch was different—not to mention the delicate scent of heliotrope that always surrounded her.

"Mr. St. Aubyn—Julian," Elinor purred a trifle stridently—which made it sound more like a snarl. "Is it not a lovely day? Although I am surprised you are out, Chloe, I must say," she added in a less than gracious manner.

"Indeed," Lord Twisdale began with pompous intonation. "Thought you would have the good sense to remain secluded after the debacle of last evening. Poor judgment, my girl."

He frowned at her and Julian could see why she drew him as a serpent. Bloody snake-in-the-grass! How could the dowager even think of letting that blasted fellow lay a hand on the fragile Lady Chloe.

Julian narrowed his eyes at Twisdale and said in a dangerously bland manner, "I was not under the impression that you had a jot to say about what Lady Chloe does, Twisdale."

The older man blustered, "Her grandmother decides what is best for the chit."

"Quite so," Julian said smoothly. He hoped the self-assured tone of his reply rattled Twisdale's complacency. And he also counted on Elinor seeing which way the wind was blowing and looking elsewhere for a husband.

"We are holding up the parade," Lady Chloe murmured with another look of seeming adoration at Julian.

"So we are," Julian agreed, gazing down at her with what he hoped to be fond regard. With a flick of the reins, his superb grays were off through the traffic and lost to the fulminations of Twisdale and Elinor.

"There is something between you and my aunt," Lady Chloe observed. "Do you find her appealing?"

Shocked that Chloe would ask such a thing, he snapped, "No, and you ought not ask."

"Why not? Oh, I know it is impertinent, but I suspect we have gone far beyond that point. She is very beautiful," she concluded a trifle wistfully.

"First of all," Julian said, bending his head so she could hear, but none other, "she knows she is beautiful and uses her beauty in a cunning, displeasing manner. And you, my dear Chloe, have an inner beauty that Elinor Hadlow does not know exists."

"That was a very pretty speech," Chloe replied, looking up at him with a skeptical expression on her sweet face. "Is that a part of flirting? Making a girl feel special?"

"Blast it, I meant what I said."

She did not look one whit convinced. Julian sat in silence for a time, fuming at relatives who depressed a girl's natural beauty and dressed her in dowdy clothing.

"Perhaps you are a scoundrel after all," she said in very soft tones that he barely heard.

A strained silence existed in the carriage all the way back to the Dancy house, where the dowager reigned supreme for the nonce.

When they paused inside the door—Julian having left his superb grays in the care of his expert groom—he stared down into that artless expression she wore with such success. "I may have earned the sobriquet of scoundrel but that does not mean that I am not sincere."

"I must learn to discern that particular moment, is that it?" she said, her incipient dimple flashing into reality when she gazed gently up at him, her smile as fleeting as it was pretty.

"Did anyone ever tell you that you have a lamentable sense of humor?" He shook his head at her, liking her candid, open gaze.

"Quite often, I fear. It is what drew me into trouble, if you recall," she said, grinning when he made a face at her dreadful pun.

Julian groaned, then considered her somewhat elfin charms. That dainty heart-shaped face revealed little of what went on in her active mind. What a clever chit she was proving to be.

His somewhat reluctant admiration grew when she patted his arm and said, "It ought not be so terrible, you know. We can pretend to rub along tolerably well for a time, then just drift apart once Aunt Elinor has turned her attentions elsewhere and Lord Twisdale has found another to be his bride—or my dearest mama returns." She prudently withdrew to a discreet distance. Even if Ellen lingered in the shadows and servants crisscrossed the rear of the hall from time to time, she appeared to be concerned about appearances.

"Of course." He studied her, wondering why he had thought her plain. She had magnificent eyes when she dared to raise them. And her hair made him wish to thread his fingers through the curls to see if the color gave it a vibrant warmth of its own. She definitely had possibilities. Pity there was not someone truly knowledgeable to guide her into a better choice of clothes and bonnets, a more self-assured manner. She could be quite bewitching.

He cleared an odd obstruction from his throat and sketched a slight bow. "I had best depart. Intend to stop by White's for dinner and then on to the Kitteridge party. Nothing like London in the height of the Season."

Chloe murmured an appropriate farewell, then watched him leave the house. Scroggins appeared seemingly from nowhere to open and close the front door with great ceremony. He bestowed a cold look on Chloe which prompted her to pause before going up to her room.

"What time did my Aunt Hadlow come yesterday? I was sorry to have missed her." Chloe slipped her bonnet off and fiddled absently with the gray satin ribbons, watching Scroggins with an uncertain gaze.

"She arrived whilst you were at the bookshop, milady," the butler intoned with sublime dignity.

"What a pity I was not here to see her. Grandmama, as well, since no one saw fit to announce her."

"The Dowager Lady Dancy," he said in a voice loaded with starch, "does not receive Mrs. Hadlow, ever."

"Nor do I anymore. Mark my words, Scroggins, Mrs. Hadlow is not to be permitted in this house again. She greatly displeased my grandmama by her actions yesterday. Were I to inform the dowager of your part in the fiasco, I have no doubt you would be fired." Chloe made to turn, then paused again to add, "I trust that is perfectly clear?"

The normally hatchet-faced butler actually looked a trifle shaken at Chloe's words. "She indicated she wished to return or retrieve something, I do not recollect which," he began in his defense, an indication of how badly he was rattled.

"Just see that you *recollect* that she is denied entry into this house under any and all circumstances. *I* shall try to remember not to inform on you."

With that thrust Chloe trudged up the stairs, wondering if she would remove a spear from her back when she reached her room. At least it felt as though the stare given her would result in something projecting from that part of her anatomy.

When she reached the sanctuary of her room she found an agitated Ellen.

"What has stirred you to such a dither," she asked, surprised to see her normally uncommunicative maid so highly upset.

"I ought not say, milady," Ellen said, burying her nose into the depths of a scrap of cambric.

"If I ask politely will you tell me?" Chloe said with a twinkle in her eyes.

"While I was in the kitchen fetching you a pot of tea and

a plate of biscuits, I found that poor little Rose in a heap, crying her eyes out. It that affected me." Ellen blew her nose again, then sniffed a couple of times.

The plight of a scullery maid was far from her thoughts at the moment, yet Chloe halted by her bed, recalling the pitiful sight of the too-thin child who had no doubt slept under the kitchen table.

"Now what?"

"One of the footmen has been bothering her."

"How dreadful! But . . . she is merely a child," Chloe cried in horror, understanding the implications even if she was a supposed innocent. Country girls heard and saw things if their eyes and ears were not closed.

"She is twelve, milady. Old enough in spite of her size."

"I must do something. Why, it could kill her to become in the family way. Grandmama would surely put her out on the streets. What would become of her then?" Chloe looked at Ellen with concern for another girl, not so terribly much younger than herself.

"Precisely, milady," Ellen said, returning to her reticent manner.

"Oh, mercy. What could I do with her? I need help, but who?"

And then Chloe thought of Mr. St. Aubyn. Since they were helping each other to escape unwanted marriages— for Chloe knew her aunt well enough to guess what it was that she desired—perhaps he might assist here as well?

If she chanced to see him at the Kitteridge affair she would seek his counsel. He might be termed a scoundrel, but she just knew that buried beneath that fashionable facade was a heart of sorts. All she had to do was to find a way to reach it.

Surely she might manage that?

Chapter 7

The Kitteridge affair would be pronounced a glittering event of the first water. Not only did Brummell stop in to view the assembled merrymakers, but the intriguing Lady Chloe Maitland attended. By the evening of the party word of her positively wicked little sketches had filtered through the ton, the news spreading like a grass fire.

When Chloe entered the vast ballroom, she immediately became aware of heads turning in her direction, ladies' faces half-disappearing behind suddenly raised fans, and the elevated quizzing glasses of nearby gentlemen.

"Pay them no heed, my dear Lady Chloe," Mr. Brummell said close to her ear with his usual attitude of ennui. "Any new thing excites their curiosity. No doubt you will be besieged by ugly matrons and fat, pompous men to have their sketches done. Shall I show you how to depress their encroaching ways? I fancy you need a lesson or two, not accustomed to being a Lion of Society."

She turned to meet his amused gaze with a look that was quite dubious. "Lion? Scarcely that, sir. I suspect curiosity is closer to the truth. Perhaps novelty or oddity might express their impression as well. However, since I do not own one of those odious quizzing glasses, I shan't be able to mimic you."

"God forbid! Never ape another's clever little tricks. Invent one of your own." He tucked his glass away in a pocket, the dull gold chain looped down as a soft accent to his austere attire of dark blue coat, black pantaloons, and white waistcoat topped by a restrained cravat.

"My own! Well, and I should like to know what there is left?" she said in an amused undertone, for the Marquis of Hammersleigh approached. He was disgustingly obese, as pompous as could stare, and dangled his ornate gold quizzing glass from the pudgy fingers of his badly gloved right hand. His beak of a nose protruded over a petulant mouth, and beady eyes stared avidly at Chloe as though she were a tender morsel to consume.

"He reminds me of a Christmas goose," she confided to Brummell before remembering she ought not say such outrageous things.

"Ah, Hammersleigh," Brummell said with unctuous smoothness. "Lady Chloe was just telling me she intends to do you as a Christmas goose."

"By Jove, that is a clever snippet to relate." His corset creaked violently as he bowed over her hand and he actually beamed a smile at her. "Purbrook insisted that you would snub me. Wait until I tell him. Do you require your victim to sit for you, Lady Chloe?" he inquired in seeming seriousness.

Chloe found her voice and said in an indignant huff, "I had not planned . . ." She halted in midspate when nudged by Brummell. Darting a glance at him, she caught the faintest shake of his head. "But then, you so marvelously fit the image." Where had those shocking words come from? Oh, she was turning into the veriest wretch.

"Oh, by Jove, how delicious. I see you possess great wit as well as beauty, Lady Chloe." In an aside to Brummell, with a voice that may have been intended to be confidential but reached Chloe's ears quite clearly, he added, "Shame to let all that talent be sent into rustication by Twisdale. Her fortune, you know," he concluded with a solemn nod.

Chloe listened in furious silence until the obnoxious man left, whereupon she glared up at the premier gentleman of London. "I was under the impression you were about to teach me how to get rid of that sort. I do not consider that a lesson!"

"A thousand pardons, my lady. It was just too delicious to let pass by. I promise I will do better. On the other hand, you may have to either continue your wicked little drawings or go into seclusion. I trust you overheard our pompous friend's remark?"

"I do not intend to marry Lord Twisdale."

"Good. I liked your firmness of manner when you said

that. I suggest you continue with the drawings, in that event. Twisdale has absolutely no sense of humor." He looked beyond Chloe as another man approached.

"Are you corrupting the ears of a delicate female, Brummell?" Mr. St. Aubyn said when he confronted the pair, leaning slightly on his ebony cane with the clouded amber handle that was all the rage these days.

"Not in the least. I *was* going to give her lessons in how to depress an encroaching mushroom."

"Instead he trapped me into doing a sketch of Lord Hammersleigh as a Christmas goose." She gave St. Aubyn a repressive look, trying not to smile at him. Could a man possibly appear more appealing than Mr. St. Aubyn, with his charming manner and the devilish gleam in his eyes?

St. Aubyn looked after the man and struggled not to laugh. "He does fit the image, I must say."

"Oh, you are as wicked as I am," she fumed in soft accents, for another star of Society approached where Chloe appeared to be holding court—Brummell to one side and St. Aubyn on the other. No girl could have been in more stellar company.

"Lady Cowper," Chloe said, suddenly subdued. She liked this lady and felt a trifle sorry for her, for she had overheard tales regarding that dear woman's life.

"So you see me as a meek little lamb, do you? Well, perhaps I am," Lady Cowper said with a smile. "Are not a great number of women? For after all, what else can we be?" She gave Chloe a searching look.

There was not a single thing Chloe could think of to say in reply. She had based the drawing mostly on the name connection—Emily having been a Lamb prior to marrying the fifth Lord Cowper. But there was also the thought that she meekly tended her much older husband. A friend had revealed that Lady Cowper rejoiced when the earl came home drunk, as he talked more to her then than at any other time.

They chatted briefly before Lord Palmerston claimed the lovely Emily for a Scotch reel.

"And now for that much-needed lesson," St. Aubyn declared.

"Actually, I suggested that Lady Chloe continue her

drawing," Mr. Brummell said with a perceptive look at his friend St. Aubyn.

Chloe could feel Mr. St. Aubyn tense at these words and she wondered why it mattered to him what she did.

"And why should she?"

"Twisdale has not the slightest sense of humor, you know," Mr. Brummell said blandly as he raised his quizzing glass when a matron went by wearing the silliest evening cap Chloe had ever viewed.

"Oh my," Chloe whispered behind her fan.

"Spangles, gauze, feathers, and satin all in one creation?" cried Brummell softly. "By Jove, I think I need a restorative. How would you depict her? A peacock?" He dangled his quizzing glass from his sublimely gloved hands while watching Chloe.

"No, I fear I have assigned that bird to Sir Augustus Dabney," Chloe said, following her confession with an engaging little giggle.

"Yes, he is, I agree," St. Aubyn chimed in as though wishing to supplant Brummell in the conversation.

"I am off to sample the delights of the buffet," the Beau declared. "Then it is White's for me. Shall I see you there later, St. Aubyn?" Brummell paused before his departure.

"Perhaps. I have a bit of business to take care of first." St. Aubyn stood, feet planted firmly at Lady Chloe's side and looked to take root there. He handled that cane with the air of one who would not hesitate to beat off an approaching intruder with it. There was something most assuredly protective in his attitude.

"Indeed." Brummell bowed slightly to Chloe with a sagacious look on his face, then wandered off toward the dining room.

"I need to discuss something with you," Chloe said, recalling the problem of her grandmother's scullery maid. Tender-hearted Chloe could not bear to think of that poor little scrap of a girl being hunted by an upperservant. It would be difficult for the girl to refuse a superior. He could easily report her for some infraction of the house rules and Rose would be fired. But there was a limit to what Chloe might attempt, and that was why she needed Mr. St. Aubyn's help.

"I am at your service. Twisdale giving you trouble?"

"Not at the moment. No, our scullery maid needs a refuge for the nonce. Do you know how I could spirit her away from the house into a safe place where she will not be troubled by an importuning footman?" Chloe dared to touch St. Aubyn's arm with a gentle hand, her eyes pleading with him to understand.

"Your scullery maid?" Julian said in amazement. Most women he knew did not know the existence of such a creature in their home much less their difficulties.

"I would hide her upstairs but the footman would tell tales, I feel sure—if he did not trap her there to have his way with her. There is nothing like a thwarted male for vengeance, so I have observed," she concluded with a glance in the direction of Lord Twisdale, who had entered the room a short time before.

"I heard—not to change the subject from your worthy scullery maid—that Lady Twisdale attempted to run away from their country home not long before she died. The man I talked with said the girl seemed dreadfully unhappy." St. Aubyn absently caressed the handle of his cane while studying the ominous gentleman across the room.

"But no one did a thing about her?"

"She was married to Twisdale. It is not proper nor legal to interfere in a marriage," St. Aubyn reminded Chloe.

"Married for life," she said sadly, "which was not long in her case. I should not wish to follow in her steps."

"God forbid," Julian said, echoing her sentiment. "Although there are cases when a marriage may be dissolved for one reason or another."

"I remember reading about the Pouget case some time ago," Chloe said thoughtfully, referring to the marriage dissolved by the father of the groom because he claimed there was false and imperfect publication of the banns.

"I recall that one. The female involved was older and had most likely tricked the lad into marriage to place her hands on his money."

"A good many marriages take place so one of the parties may have access to the money of the other," Chloe said with a glance at her grandmother. The old dragon was making her way around the ballroom with an intent expression on her face. Chloe suspected that she was about to bestow a scold on her granddaughter for spending time with Brummell and St. Aubyn. "I do not give a fig what she says," Chloe murmured in anticipation of her defense. "I have had the best of company in the entire room."

Julian smiled, delighted that she viewed him in such a charitable light—even if he was lumped with Brummell. All the women adored that fellow, who seemed pleased to flirt with them yet never offer anything beyond that.

"Your maid. You said you wished help? I shall consider the matter and contact you tomorrow. A drive in the park?" Julian spoke in a rush, for the dowager neared them at a goodly pace.

"Are you trying to bring me into fashion, sir?" Chloe said, fluttering her dark lashes while lightly touching the handle of her fan to her lips, then suddenly dropping it in a rush of confusion.

"And are you sending me messages, you silly girl? Never mind, one day I shall collect all that is due me."

"Are you to stand there nattering all evening, St. Aubyn, or do you take my granddaughter for a whirl on the floor?" the dowager demanded of him when she reached their sides.

Chloe felt her cheeks flame, for she had believed that it would be difficult for Mr. St. Aubyn to dance, given his continual use of a cane. He surprised her.

"I would like nothing better, Ma'am." Propping his cane against the wall, he escorted Chloe to the center of the dance floor, whereupon he demonstrated his skill in the quadrille.

It was a new dance Chloe had studied with intensity before trying it. With a partner like Mr. St. Aubyn it proved to be a delight. Small wonder that Lady Jersey had brought this variation from France. Chloe leaped and pirouetted with what she hoped was grace. She observed that St. Aubyn acquitted himself well, even if he did not do the entrechats as perhaps they should be performed. He rose lightly on his toes and looked quite superb to her eyes.

When they returned to the dowager, she sniffed with what seemed approval. "Well done."

"I suspect that Lady Chloe is thirsty, as I am. Might I escort her to the refreshment table, ma'am?" St. Aubyn asked with utmost respect after reclaiming his cane.

"Indeed," the dowager said, looking bored with the entire matter. She turned away to greet a friend and Julian guided Lady Chloe in the same direction that Brummell had gone earlier.

"I trust you survived all that in good state," she said with a look of concern.

"My disability is but slight and I only resort to the dependance on a cane when I must." Julian did not volunteer the source of his affliction. Childhood accidents were of little interest, or so he had discovered over time.

"Lady Chloe," Sir Augustus demanded, stepping between them and their objective, his quizzing glass in hand, "I am most devastated that you portrayed me as a peacock. A more aggravating, detestable bird I cannot imagine."

"None of us see ourselves as others do, Dabney," Julian said blandly, annoyed that the peacock had intruded on what he had hoped would be a few quiet words with Lady Chloe.

"I was not aware that you had assumed the duty of answering for her," Sir Augustus replied with a raised chin and stiffened spine.

"I am her lion rampant," Julian said with a bored drawl, as though that settled the matter.

Sir Augustus considered this statement for a moment, then bowed, murmuring something about toddling off to Boodle's, that favorite club for country gentlemen.

"Really, sir, you are truly outrageous. I fear you have planted a silly notion in that empty head of his. He has, I am told, a habit of emptying his brain-box at the slightest provocation." Lady Chloe gave Julian a vexed look, then she accepted the glass of lemonade handed to her by the footman stationed at the beverage table.

"Forget about him. I want to settle this business about our drive tomorrow afternoon."

"I was under the impression that it *was* settled. At least, you made your invitation sound like a command." She wished she might complain, but she desired this meeting far too much to do so.

Julian darted a look of amusement at her. "You are coming along quite nicely, I think. You are learning to speak your mind in a telling manner. It will give you a certain cachet to be seen with me, you know," he reminded her.

"I did ask if you were trying to bring me into fashion," she reminded him.

Julian liked the flash of her eyes and the hint of that dimple that lurked at the side of her mouth. Such a tender little rosebud, her mouth. Then he tore himself from a contemplation that was most likely fruitless and escorted her back to her grandmother's side.

Across the room Elinor seethed with well-concealed fury at what had been going on when she was able to snatch a view—the throng of people permitting. That Brummell should champion her niece was bad enough, but when Julian joined those two, it had inflamed her sensibilities to a high degree.

How could he possibly prefer that insipid little nobody—Elinor ignored Chloe's relationship to the Dancy family and the fortune she inherited—to herself! She had hoped to bring Chloe to disgrace, even ruin, with those nasty little sketches. Instead, Chloe had been lionized from the moment she entered the ballroom.

Did the little twit know what consequence she derived from standing between Brummell and St. Aubyn? Did she even care? Elinor placed a hand over her heart to calm her thwarted nerves. Well, she would not permit dear little Chloe to triumph where she, the beautiful Elinor Hadlow, failed. This time she would succeed. She must. Chloe would yet be sorry she had been born.

Chloe looked across the ballroom to meet her Aunt Elinor's gaze and shivered. The malevolence in her eyes was most clear, even at this distance with naught but candlelight for illumination—although the Kitteridge family had not spared use of fine wax candles.

When Chloe observed her aunt sidle around the room until she reached the spot where Lord Twisdale stood in disapproving silence, Chloe began to worry anew. There was something odd in those two talking together again. Particularly when they both glanced up to stare at her. She pretended to scrutinize the room as though admiring the decorations, and tried not to look back at them. This was not the first time they had conferred and Chloe wished she knew the topic of their conversation. She very much feared it was herself.

Another search of the room revealed that St. Aubyn was nowhere to be seen. She would have liked to ask his advice, but then she scolded herself for thinking she might turn to him whenever she was troubled. Yet . . . he had promised to help her about Rose. It was certain that Chloe had not the least idea where it would be safe to hide a scullery maid.

Tomorrow when they went for the promised drive in the park Chloe would seek his advice about Aunt Elinor and Lord Twisdale as well as the scullery maid.

The following morning Chloe awakened to Ellen's gentle touch and the aroma of hot chocolate and scones.

"Did you find out as to how Rose can escape, my lady?" the faithful maid inquired.

"I sought help from a gentleman I trust," Chloe said, then considered how strange it was that she should think the scoundrel to be so depended upon.

"Mr. St. Aubyn." Ellen apparently had no doubt as to the identity of the one consulted. "When do you see him again? That James is impatient." The maid continued her unaccustomed speech by adding, "I took the child in with me last night. Poor mite. I fear for her."

While Chloe had only a small idea what those fears might be, she knew her maid well enough to believe they were very real and a fate to be dreaded.

"Flowers came," Ellen continued in her more customary abrupt talk. "Want them?"

"Indeed," Chloe said with a smile. Who thought to court her with blooms after all that had happened? She drank the last of her chocolate, popped the final bite of her scone into her mouth, then slid from her bed. Donning a soft, faded green robe, she curled up in the chair near her window, waiting.

Three bouquets had been delivered. One of rich burgundy roses held a card from St. Aubyn. She glanced at Ellen to see the maid standing, arms folded, an expression of interest on her kindly face.

"Unconscious beauty, that tells you," Ellen offered.

Chloe shrugged, refusing to accept that bit of nonsense. "They are merely in season and very lovely."

"Hmpf," the maid commented.

A cluster of bright red carnations had a card from Sir Augustus. Chloe looked to her maid with raised brows. "What have you to say to such an unremarkable arrangement?"

"Alas for my poor heart. The gentleman feels thwarted?"

Chloe did not comment on Sir Augustus but rather looked at the remaining bouquet, a selection of various June flowers: single roses, striped carnations, and others just as pretty. "Well, Ellen, I cannot see any message in these."

"He means to confuse you, miss. But that sort of rose implies love is dangerous and the striped carnation sends a message of refusal."

Chloe stiffened in her chair, looking at the inoffensive blooms with distrust. When she unfolded the stiff paper that had been tucked inside the cluster of flowers, she almost dropped the blooms. "Lord Twisdale!"

"Take care with that gentleman," Ellen counseled.

"I intend to, you may be certain," Chloe replied softly. She placed all the flowers in the containers Ellen had set out, then with Ellen's help changed into a day dress.

"I had best tell little Rose that we will find her help. She may not believe you," Chloe told Ellen before leaving her bedroom. Knowing enough of the lower orders to be aware of their awe for a lady, she suspected Rose rightly would be skeptical of forthcoming help.

When she reached the kitchen she complimented the cook on the scones, although they might have been made by the housekeeper, who often created delicate pastries. Lucky for Chloe the cook beamed her pleasure. Chloe pursued her mission, finding Rose at the stone sink just inside the scullery door, arms deep in greasy water.

The girl looked up in fright, then subsided into watchful suspicion. She bobbed a wobbly curtsy, not removing her arms from the water where she scrubbed at a kettle.

"I shall see that you are safe," Chloe said in an undertone sure not to carry far. "Once I find out where you may be housed, I will send for you." She knew there was nothing for the child to pack, for she likely owned no more than what was on her back. "When I send Ellen for you, be sure to come at once, you hear?"

"Yes, mum," the girl murmured, turning back to her task.

Since Chloe suspected the maid would be scolded if she did not complete her task soon, she was not offended at this lack of respect. She slipped from the room, taking a lemon biscuit with her as a reason for invading the hallowed halls of the kitchen. Back in her room, she told Ellen what she had said, and the maid nodded her agreement.

The hours dragged by slowly until time came for her drive. Although both Sir Augustus and Lord Twisdale had sent flowers, neither had come to pay a call on her . . . or grandmother. For that she was profoundly thankful.

After donning her best gray pelisse and the bonnet with the green feathers, she awaited St. Aubyn's arrival in the drawing room with her grandmother.

"Another drive in the park? Do not acquire any notions, my gel," the dowager said in a disparaging manner. "I doubt St. Aubyn has naught but his own reason for escorting you about," she offered, far closer to the truth than she suspected.

"I shan't," Chloe said, clutching her hands before her so as not to betray her nervousness.

When Scroggins ushered St. Aubyn into the drawing room, Chloe felt the urge to nudge him out of the door, fleeing to a far place with him, away from the dangers of London.

"Ma'am, Lady Chloe," St. Aubyn said with a bow to each. "Lovely day for a drive in the park. It feels as though summer has arrived."

"Enjoy it while you can. Never lasts long, you know," the dowager replied with gloomy pessimism. She waved them from the room with a bored look.

Once at his side and driving through the Stanhope Gate, Chloe searched for words to explain why she felt compelled to champion poor little Rose.

"Your scullery maid needs rescuing, I believe you said," St. Aubyn prompted.

"Indeed, she does. I saw that odious James lurking about

on the ground floor, just looking as though he would like to slip off to the scullery room. Although why he desires to bother that slip of a girl is more than I can see," she added in a puzzled voice.

"The unattainable is always exciting, even in a plain, scared girl, it seems."

"Dreadful, that's what it is," Chloe grumbled.

"I have given it some thought and believe I can send her to my country estate. My steward came to Town the other day and is due to return tomorrow." What his steward might think of sharing a coach with a scullery maid was beyond consideration. But he was not paid to complain of the company he was required to keep while on salary.

"That would be most acceptable," Chloe said with joy lighting her heart. She placed her hand on his arm and turned her head to gaze up into his face. "You are a sham, sir. I believe you are the very best of gentlemen. There is no scoundrel lurking in your heart."

"Take care, Lady Chloe. I would not have anyone else hear those scandalous words," he said in mock horror.

"Oh, pooh," she said. She compressed the lips that longed to break forth in a huge grin.

"Your aunt approaches," he cautioned.

Chloe swiftly turned to observe her aunt being skillfully driven through the park by none other than Sir Augustus Dabney.

"How curious," Chloe murmured. "Whatever is a diamond like my aunt doing with a fellow like Sir Augustus? Not that he is not acceptable ton, mind you."

"Naturally. I cannot fathom what possibly could bring those two together, however I doubt it is anything for the good of man or womankind." Julian met the hostile gaze from the woman with whom he had been so closely associated and felt a frisson of alarm. He had no knowledge of any liaison between Elinor and another, much less the worthy Sir Augustus, and that also worried him. When Elinor was not kept occupied, she could well fall into mischief. Precisely what form that mischief might take concerned him.

Chapter 8

"*H*e really does resemble a stuffed goose," Chloe observed over her shoulder to Ellen, who was fussing around with Chloe's humdrum-hued gowns.

The maid crossed the room to peer over Chloe's shoulder and smiled. "That he does. 'Tis a wonder he is able to walk."

"Ah," Chloe said, "he waddles, not walks." They both chuckled before Chloe placed the drawing of the Marquis of Hammersleigh with the neat stack of her other caricatures. She had drawn a perky ribbon around the plump neck of the goose, with a bunch of mistletoe berries tucked in at one side. There was no mistaking who it was, nor her intent to portray him as a *Christmas* goose—for they were the ones often forcefed to produce an exceedingly plump bird.

"You will put them away, I gather," the maid suggested in a quiet voice.

Chloe picked up the stack, placing them carefully into the cloth-covered folder. The one of her grandmother stuck out at an angle. Chloe pulled it from the stack so she might study the sketch.

"Not kind," Ellen commented from nearby, where she now attempted to do something with one of the dresses.

"The drawing or my grandmama?" Chloe answered with a sad sigh. Not waiting for a reply—which was not likely to come anyway—Chloe took that picture and tucked it under the things in her bottom bureau drawer. She ought not express her feelings for her grandmother in such an infamous manner, even if the old woman was as mean as could stare.

She found herself in a peculiar dilemma. She truly desired to obey her grandmother—as was most proper, for the old lady was in authority over Chloe. She had been reared to respect authority, and particularly older relatives.

On the other hand, Chloe experienced a growing spirit of resistance. How could a relative—even one who found her more of a nuisance than a joy—consider marriage for Chloe to a man like Lord Twisdale? So very much older and with a questionable history, he hardly seemed like the sort of chap to wish on a girl, a granddaughter you ought to love.

She was considerably torn in her regard for what was due Grandmama.

Aware she was expected to join that lady in the drawing room, for it was her day to receive callers, Chloe rose from her little desk, brushed down her simple gray-sprigged muslin, and marched down the stairs after wishing Ellen good luck with her project. That poor gown had been adapted twice now. Chloe knew an intense desire to buy a new one.

"About time you came down from your room. Drawing again?" Lady Dancy said with a shrewd expression.

Chloe knew she must look guilty. "Yes, Grandmama."

"Who?"

"Lord Hammersleigh," Chloe replied meekly.

"I should like to examine those drawings of yours. Get them immediately," the dowager ordered.

"Yes, Grandmama." Chloe backed from the room, running lightly up the stairs to fetch the neat cloth-bound bundle. She paused, looking at the bottom drawer and wondering if she ought to bring the other sketch—the one of her grandmother—along. Perhaps she was cowardly, perhaps she was merely being kind—she left it behind.

She deposited the cloth-covered folder on the table at her grandmother's side, then sat down awaiting a verdict, if there was to be one. Anxious eyes followed the dowager's thin, elegant hands as they picked up the folder, placed it on her lap, then opened it.

"Hmm," Lady Dancy intoned when she viewed the drawing of Lady Jersey as an exquisite butterfly, then Emily Cowper as a sad-eyed lamb. "You took a terrible chance, you know."

"I did say I never intended anyone else to see them," Chloe quietly insisted.

"Ah, yes, that wretched aunt of yours. Why Hadlow had to marry a second time—and then to one so much younger than he—is beyond me. The old goat." The dowager surveyed the sketch of the Christmas goose, a faint smile touching her mouth for a few seconds before she returned to her usual expression of severe blandness.

"Pity I did not know him well enough to draw him as one," Chloe said, her eyes beginning to twinkle with mischief.

A glare from the dowager dimmed the twinkle to a mere flicker. "I truly mean no harm," Chloe began, then was cut off with a wave of the dowager's plump arm.

"Where is the one you did of me, pray tell?" she asked in a most ominous, albeit quiet, voice. "Sally Jersey said it was an excellent likeness."

While Chloe furiously tried to think of an answer that would not be a lie and yet might allow her to escape the revelation of her opinion regarding her grandmother, Scroggins announced a caller.

"Sir Augustus Dabney to pay his respects, my lady," he said with a stiff bow, ignoring Chloe completely.

Since she did not care in the least whether she talked to Sir Augustus or not, Chloe made no move to welcome the gentleman when he entered the room. She sat, stiff and silent, on the straight wooden chair where she usually retreated when in this room. Yet she supposed she ought to be grateful to the peacock, for he saved her, at least for the moment, from revealing the sketch of her grandmother.

"Madam," Sir Augustus said, making an elegant leg. As an afterthought—or so it seemed to Chloe—he turned to her and sketched the faintest of bows to her as well. "How lovely to see you both in the best of health."

"Did you expect otherwise?" Lady Dancy said with a narrowing of her eyes. She closed the folder and placed it on the little table again so that none might see the contents.

"No, indeed. Merely thought it delightful to see such esteemed ladies in prime twig, y'know," he said with more haste than charm.

He then proceeded to pour the butter boat over the dowager's head with such extravagant encomiums that Chloe near ached to laugh aloud. What his purpose might be in courting her grandmother she couldn't guess, until a sudden, rather bizarre, thought struck her all of a heap.

"Miss Spayne and Lady Spayne," Scroggins announced with a dignified bow.

James the footman entered behind them with a tea tray loaded with every one of the little dainties her grandmother adored plus the necessary for a fine tea.

Shooting him a narrow look, Chloe set aside the problem of little Rose and crossed to greet her dearest friend. "I am so happy to see you," she said with a darted glance at the dowager, who was holding forth with Lady Spayne on the evils of London Society.

"Miss Spayne," Sir Augustus said after greeting Lady Spayne. The wife of a prosperous baron and country gentleman was not to be ignored, nor was her pretty daughter. "You look most charmingly."

"And you, sir, look quite elegant, as usual," Laura said in reply.

Chloe studied the Petersham trousers worn by Sir Augustus, noting how they flowed to spread widely around the ankles and over the foot. How did he manage to walk? Over this startling creation he wore a coat that was nipped in at the waist and had huge brass buttons. His amazing cravat looked to swallow him.

"Indeed," Chloe murmured, "garbed in the very latest mode as usual."

"Quite true," he said modestly. "One always wishes to be dressed *à la modalité*." He cast a patronizing glance at Chloe's frequently worn gown, but most fortunately said nothing about her lack of modishness.

"Who does not wish to appear to be dressed in the latest fashion?" Laura said lightly, then changed the topic— which she knew to be a touchy one with Chloe—to the next party to be attended.

Scroggins paused in the doorway to survey the room, then said in stentorian tones, "Mr. Purcell and Mr. St. Aubyn, madam."

The two gentlemen followed on his heels, not waiting for him to usher them up.

Chloe smiled in welcome to these gentlemen. They were closely followed by two ladies. Mrs. Robynhod and Miss Springthorpe cast coy glances at the young men, then clustered about the tea table for a bit of gossip.

Suddenly Mrs. Robynhod spoke up, turning to Chloe with a simper. "My dear, I am awaiting my sketch. I will be devastated if you fail to draw me."

"Oh, I have not had time as yet," Chloe began.

"I forbid her to create any more of those scandalous sketches," the dowager declared in a loud voice.

"What?" St. Aubyn said with a shocked look at Lady Dancy. "Why, she is a sensation. Everyone in London is clamoring to be sketched by your granddaughter."

"*I* am a peacock, that most beautiful of birds," Sir Augustus said with obvious pride, waving his handkerchief about in the air and quite forgetting his annoyance of the evening before. "Poor St. Aubyn has to content himself with being a lion rampant, and Purcell is naught but a horrid magpie—sorry, Lady Chloe," he added when he realized he was criticizing the artist.

Laura and Chloe exchanged looks. Chloe glanced to where the batch of sketches were safely tucked in the folder, thankful that they were hidden from view.

Sir Augustus unfortunately followed her gaze and smiled with triumph. "Aha! Do I detect the presence of the celebrated drawings?" He darted across the room—no small feat given the nature of those beastly Petersham trousers—and grabbed the folder up from the table with a cry of achievement.

Mrs. Springthorpe, not having seen the drawings before, hastily moved to peer over his arm when he removed them from the folder.

"How terribly clever," she cried with surprise. "I have always thought Lord Hammersleigh resembled a plump goose," she said with appreciation.

"I'd not viewed this one before. Dashed clever," Sir Augustus said promptly and with evident approval.

Julian watched for his chance, then drew Lady Chloe to one side after an appealing look at Miss Spayne.

"I saw your aunt with Twisdale again this morning while

I was out riding. They were driving alone in his carriage and deep in conversation."

"Heavens!" Lady Chloe whispered. "What are they up to now? I fear I do not trust them in the least. That makes several conversations they have had—that we know about. What do they find of such great interest, I wonder?"

"We had best be prepared."

"Are we to have our drive this afternoon?" she said hesitantly.

"Bring your scullery maid," Julian instructed with a patient look at the unfortunate girl at his side. She resembled a ghost in her soft grays, as though she might waft through a wall, or something. Had he the dressing of her she would be a vibrant chrysanthemum or a ripe peach.

"Rose will be most grateful. And I will, as well. I think it is quite beastly that she has no protection, no one to turn to, and must bow to the importunings of a servant of higher rank . . . or lose everything."

James the footman entered the room bearing a tray with fresh tea and additional biscuits and cakes.

Casting a pensive look in his direction, Chloe said, "I find it reprehensible that a man is permitted to have his way with a maid and not be punished."

"I gather that he is the one involved," Julian observed, taking note of the footman's sleek, possibly pleasing looks.

"I say, you two, not fair to leave us out of your discussion," Theo said in his jovial and totally improper manner. "Do you still drive out this afternoon? If so, Miss Spayne and I will join you, if you have no major objection. After all, we are in on nearly everything going on so far."

Julian did not allow his annoyance to show, but gave Theo a gracious nod. "But of course, we would be delighted with company."

"Probably wish me to perdition," Theo mumbled, "but dash it all, I cannot hope to match your grays."

Julian laughed, forgiving his friend for his interference.

Following a promise to complete a drawing of Mrs. Robynhod as soon as might be, Chloe walked with the younger people to the landing. She made her farewells, which were brief as they planned to meet in a short time, then watched while they strolled down the stairs to the front door. Here they all paused, while Laura adjusted her bonnet and readied her parasol and Lady Spayne checked her reticule.

Scroggins opened the door in response to a pull of the bell and before Chloe could move, ushered in Lord Twisdale.

At once Julian looked up to where she still stood. He wanted to call out to her to have a care, the enemy approached. However, he figured that she would guard her words while the older peer was around. If her grandmother would only reconsider. But then, Julian realized that his problem would most likely not go away at once and he required Lady Chloe's support and assistance.

There was a flurry of comments and polite exchanges before Julian left the house with Theo and the others. First seeing Lady Spayne and her charming daughter safely to their carriage, he urged Theo along with him.

"Saw an uncommon sight this morning," Julian began. "Old Twisdale and Elinor Hadlow out for a drive. They were alone—no groom for propriety who might repeat anything that was said. Twisdale tooled along the road north from the park, quite as though he wished to chat with the charming Elinor and not be overly bothered with traffic."

"And what do you suppose was the topic of conversation between that unlikely pair?" an intrigued Theo inquired.

"I'd give a pony to know," Julian said with a wry twist of his mouth. "She is a schemer—we both know that. Lord Twisdale I'd not trust as far as I could throw him. And since he is no lightweight, that is not very far."

The two gentlemen exchanged looks, then hailed a hackney to take them to Jackson's for a round of sparring.

Chloe watched Lord Twisdale huff his way up the stairs, then politely walked at his side into the drawing room. She said nothing beyond her cool words of greeting. When the fragrance of the eau de cologne he had poured over his head reached her nose, she could not restrain her sneeze. It exploded into the quiet of the room.

At once his lordship left her side to make his bow to the dowager. "Lady Dancy, so charmed to see you again."

Chloe searched her reticule for her dainty handkerchief, then she sneezed—rather violently—again.

"I say, Lady Chloe," Sir Augustus cried in dismay, "I do hope you have not contracted something dreadful."

"No," Chloe replied with a faint sigh. "I often sneeze when encountering certain scents. I cannot say why it happens. It is a frightful nuisance, you may be sure."

"Wonder if it is catching?" he mused, looking at Chloe as though he debated something of significance.

"That I cannot say," she replied, thinking she might have discovered a highly useful tactic.

"Dabney," Lord Twisdale said in an overly hearty voice. "Delighted to see you. Been on the lookout for you, my boy."

"Really, sir?" Sir Augustus looked rather alarmed at this remark from a man who usually ignored his existence. As he did not owe the fellow money, it was clear that something else was on his mind.

Chloe could not imagine what in the world Lord Twisdale might have to do with a twiddlepoop like Sir Augustus. And she suspected that Sir Augustus was not best pleased to be threatened with an encounter from his lordship.

A glance at her grandmother revealed a look of puzzlement on her face as well. So, this was not a part of the plot to marry Chloe to the odious and slippery Lord Twisdale. Chloe thought of a serpent, how one could slide in and out at will wherever it wished.

The hour for paying afternoon calls had drawn to a close. Sir Augustus had far overstayed his time and Chloe could not help but wonder at his motive. Goodness, she was becoming more suspicious by the day. But, truth to tell, his behavior was decidedly odd. So was Lord Twisdale's, for that matter.

She watched the two gentlemen pay homage to her grandmother and barely sketch a bow in her own direction before departing together. Lord Twisdale determinedly clutched the elegant coat that covered Sir Augustus's arms. With a darted glance at her grandmother, who was leaning back on her chair as though in fatigue, Chloe backed from the drawing room and then slipped along the upper landing.

From here she could watch the entry below. Although

she could not hear the words, she perceived that Lord Twisdale commanded Sir Augustus join him for something.

The look of fright on that young man's face might have
been amusing had not Chloe wondered at the cause.

When she peeked into the drawing room again, her
grandmother had gone out the far door. Empty teacups lit-
tered the tables and little remained of the elaborate tea
Grandmother usually ordered.

Chloe ran over to gather up the remaining biscuits to
take to her room for later this evening. Catching sight of the
fabric-covered folder with her sketches, she snatched it up,
then returned to her room with her bounty.

She really had to make a drawing of Mrs. Robynhod.
That woman would give her no peace until she saw herself
depicted as a wicked something or other. Now what might
she be? Chloe settled onto her favorite chair, curling one
foot beneath her while contemplating a solution.

Ah, she decided at last, she would draw Mrs. Robynhod
as a cat—not a kitten like dear Laura, but a mature, inquisitive, sly cat. Sleek and shrewd, Mrs. Robynhod would
make an admirable cat.

Once decided, Chloe set to work, quickly delineating the
gossip. Before long the sketch was complete to her satisfaction and there on the pad was the cat in a pose of watchful-
ness with the gaze of a predator. Perfect, even if Chloe
knew it was as wicked as could be.

"That is the woman who came to visit your grandmother
earlier," Ellen observed quietly. "Is she as disgraceful as all
that?"

"I suspect she might be, or perhaps she is naught but an
innocent gossip—if such a thing exists."

"And you draw her as a cat?" The maid studied the little
sketch again, then shivered. "Improper," she concluded.

"On the contrary, she will be thrilled," Chloe predicted
with a grimace. "It strikes me as distinctly odd how one can
do the most outrageous things and get by with them. They
think it wickedly clever that I sketch what I see within their
hearts. I must admit, I wish I had not begun this pastime."

"Shame to let talent go to waste," Ellen said quietly
while gazing at the contents of Chloe's wardrobe.

She wore such a gloomy face that Chloe had to smile and shake her head.

"Is it so very bad? Perhaps I might think of a way to convince Grandmama that I need a new gown and hope that she will be too busy to accompany me. I hope I may have need of your presence." She exchanged a significant look with Ellen, then began her search for her grandmother.

The dowager was discovered in the library, of all places. She was examining a book on wild animals of the world, a collection of drawings Chloe had looked at time and again for inspiration.

"Dull," the dowager pronounced.

"But frightfully accurate, I have no doubt," Chloe countered.

"I imagine your clever renditions are more likely to provoke interest," the older lady said with a shrewd nod.

"Perhaps," Chloe admitted reluctantly. She would rather avoid that topic if possible.

"Laura said she was going to the mantuamaker's for a new gown to wear to Lord and Lady Sefton's party. All my gowns are becoming dreadfully shabby. I should like to order a new one—or possibly two. I am certain my man of business will not cavil at such an expenditure."

Where she found the daring to speak so boldly Chloe did not know. She had thought of the man who believed and supported her and found the image of St. Aubyn inspired her to defy her grandmother as never in the past.

"You think to go off with Laura Spayne and her mother?" the dowager said in a dreadful manner.

Refusing to back down, Chloe gave her grandmother a stubborn look with a tilt of her heart-shaped chin. "I do."

"Well, then, go. I am tired and must rest before we go out this evening. You have a drive in the park late this afternoon. Do not forget your obligations, my girl."

With those astounding words, the dowager rose from her chair and marched from the room, looking every bit as tired as she claimed.

Chloe stood still, pondering the results of her daring. Her grandmother appeared to actually feel the effects of the rushing about in Society. For this Chloe felt sorry.

But . . . she had succeeded wildly beyond her dreams. She ran from the library and up the stairs to her room.

"Quick, fetch Rose. We shall take her along with us in the event I am late for the drive in the park. I have permission to buy two gowns. I need you along to assist me in my selection, for I have never had the choosing of a dress for myself before and I may make a mistake. I cannot depend that Laura will be able to help me."

Ellen said nothing in reply, but helped Chloe into a pelisse, then whisked herself down to the scullery. Since the cook was in the stillroom at this hour, she had no difficulty in sneaking the child up the back stairs and into Lady Chloe's room.

Rose looked utterly terrified.

Dismayed by the girl's appearance, Chloe dug around in a bottom drawer to find an old but presentable dress she had once liked and hated to toss away. When held up to Rose it proved to be large, but still acceptable.

The trio who tiptoed down the stairs and out the front door escaped from the house with no one being the wiser. Scroggins was no doubt harassing the housekeeper and the rest of the servants were about their duties, which did not involve a presence in the entry hall.

At Laura's house they discovered she was out.

"Do you know this means we shall be on our own!" Chloe declared with glee.

"Indeed," Ellen agreed with a snap of her head.

The hackney had just deposited them in front of the mantuamaker's when Chloe caught sight of St. Aubyn. He was studying the window of a shop that catered to gentlemen who used canes and umbrellas.

Heartened merely by the sight of him, she took a deep breath and entered the elegant little establishment. She had not been there before, but her cousin Elizabeth had mentioned the woman to her.

"Madame Clotilde," Chloe began, "my cousins referred me to you . . . the Dancy girls?"

At the mention of that name the woman beamed a smile and drew Chloe to a chiar. "You have need of a gown or two, perhaps?"

"I have permission for two gowns." Chloe unwittingly

revealed her longing when she gazed at a bolt of peach blossom sarcenet.

The door opened behind them and the mantuamaker gazed with affection at the person who entered.

"What? Lady Chloe here and alone? Where is the dragon?" He ignored the presence of Ellen and her little shadow, who perched in a corner in awed silence.

"Mr. St. Aubyn!" Chloe cried with pleasure.

A shrewd look from the glowing young woman to the premier scoundrel of London and the mantuamaker sat a trifle straighter. Quite obviously all was not as she had suspected, her expression said had Chloe chanced to look at her. That beloved scoundrel gazed with more than fondness at this girl, if he but knew it.

"Madame," St. Aubyn said with suave persuasion, "I wish you to spin forth a gown of incredible daring. It must be somewhat discreet—Lady Chloe is unwed—but it must reveal luscious promise, intriguing possibilities. Dare I hope you can invent such a thing?"

"Not only can I, I have," the mantuamaker declared with a certain triumph. To Chloe she added, "Every once in a while I permit myself free reign of my talent. I dream of a special design, then create it with my own hands. I thought of such a one not long ago. Come with me, for it just may be near enough of a fit for you to wear."

Within short order Chloe blushingly exited the fitting room. With the pins fitting the dress to her figure artfully concealed, she hesitantly walked to the room where she suspected that St. Aubyn waited to see what had been conceived.

Julian stared with amazement at the delicious apparition that hovered in the doorway. He could not have envisioned a more apt gown for his little protégé. Delicate peach aerophane crepe swirled about her figure, revealing, concealing in a tantalizing manner. Beneath that almost transparent fabric, a shimmer of pale gold gossamer satin hinted at a lovely, youthful figure. A scandalous gown for one so young, for she resembled nothing more than a naked peach blossom.

"Oh, miss," Ellen ventured to say. She was quelled to silence by a look from St. Aubyn.

"She will take it," he ordered without consulting a stunned Chloe, who had just caught sight of herself in a looking glass and most likely wouldn't have been able to say a word anyway.

"Oh, but . . ." Chloe managed to sputter.

"What else for you this afternoon? You have not forgotten we are to have our drive?" he said with a lift of his brows.

Chloe darted a glance to where Rose huddled behind Ellen and nodded. The change of topic took her mind from the incredible garment she wore for a moment.

Not St. Aubyn. "You can have this altered for her in time for the Sefton ball?"

With a decisive nod, the mantuamaker agreed, then suggested, "Perhaps Lady Chloe will like to consider a new carriage gown?"

"Carriage gown, evening gown, day gown, especially a riding habit, she needs everything!" St. Aubyn declared with an apologetic and understanding look at Chloe.

Her resistance faded at his apparent comprehension of her problems with Grandmama and gowns. "She said I might have two," Chloe admitted. "But, sir . . ." she began, only to be interrupted by St. Aubyn.

"You need more, however. Forgive me for asking, but does she pay the bill? If so, I will see to it."

Blushing furiously, Chloe shook her head. "My inheritance covers all my expenses." Then, determined to be heard, she said, "It is scandalous for you to help me select one gown, much less several. What would Society say if we are found out?"

"It will support my claim to your interest," he said with such great authority that she decided not to argue.

"Very well," she said with spirit, "I will proceed."

"Well, then." St. Aubyn tilted his chair back against the wall and smiled a trifle wickedly, "Forget the drive in the park. I believe we shall be entirely too busy to go. You, my dear Chloe, are to have an entirely new wardrobe. Your man of business may expire from the shock."

With a delightful sparkle in her eyes, Chloe grinned at him and then whirled about to face the fascinated Madame Clotilde. "First we shall choose the designs, then the fabrics, and then you may take my measurements, for St. Aubyn has the right of it. I am turning over a new leaf."

And thus began the emergence of a new Lady Chloe, darling of the ton.

Chapter 9

*E*linor Hadlow paused before a milliner's shop, a look of fury crossing her face before she carefully smoothed her expression. She was not mistaken in what she had seen. An assignation!

She never could confuse St. Aubyn's distinctive figure in gray with his signature cane in hand for another. And she had most assuredly seen that twit of a niece enter the expensive mantuamaker's establishment—one Elinor could afford to patronize only once or twice a season.

When she casually strolled past the shop window she caught a glimpse of Julian with Lady Chloe, discussing something with Madame. Julian had *never* assisted Elinor in selecting her gowns, laughingly complaining about the tediousness of the matter. Yet here he was with Lady Chloe Maitland—the little baggage—instead of Elinor Hadlow, her far more experienced and beautiful aunt.

That Julian St. Aubyn might have a genuine interest in the girl never crossed Elinor's mind. She could not conceive of such a circumstance, at least with a scoundrel like St. Aubyn. No, Lady Chloe must be conspiring to lure Julian away from her aunt, in spite, perhaps—jealous of the other's beauty and poise. That, Elinor could comprehend, for it was something she would have done in an instant, the situation being reversed.

Forgetting her intention of selecting a charming new bonnet to enhance her carriage gown, she summoned her waiting carriage and fumed all the way to her new home.

Once there she paused on the top step to gaze across the square to St. Aubyn House. Oh, that man would regret spurning her. And as for Lady Chloe, well, something was bound to answer if she just thought hard enough. All Elinor needed to do was put her devious little mind to work.

She had discussed the problem with Twisdale only that morning and he had said something that might offer promise. Now she had greater provocation and motive for revenge. Oh, it would be so sweet, she would do both of them in at the same time.

It was close to six of the clock when Chloe took a delighted parting from Madame Clotilde. The vast number of garments ordered had put Chloe into a dizzy whirl. And she adored every minute of the momentous occasion.

It was a major step in her life, a declaration of independence, if you like. Although she would remain as dutiful as she might, she would not permit her grandmama to again place her under an unwanted thumb. A way would be found; St. Aubyn would help her find one.

Even her knowledge that she was most improper in allowing St. Aubyn to assist her in selecting her gowns had not brought it to a halt. She suspected that only ladies of questionable virtue allowed such familiarity. And yet she had not sent him away, even though she knew she might experience a punishment of sorts for her outré behavior. His charm and indisputable good taste had tempted her and she had succumbed. The look in his eyes had made the hazards well worthwhile.

They paused on the walkway. Chloe was about to send Ellen for a hackney when St. Aubyn put out a staying hand.

"And now to the scullery maid," he said, surprising Chloe with his astonishing memory. Although she supposed she ought to have expected him to remember his offer of help, it pleased her that he did.

"Rose came with us, sir," Chloe said with some hesitation. Even with a decent dress on, the child looked what she was, a maid of no background or education.

"So you are little Rose," the awesome figure in smooth gray Bath coating said to the young girl who peeped from behind Ellen.

"If y'please, sir," she whispered back, looking astonished that she had managed to utter a word.

Bored with the chit, and wanting to savor the memory of

Lady Chloe in the peach aerophane crepe over pale gold gossamer satin that appeared to be a second skin, he motioned to his carriage that had drawn alongside the walkway at the sight of him. "Inside."

Rose scrambled inside the carriage, huddling to the far side of the rear-facing seat. Huge eyes studied the adults who remained on the walkway as though she wondered if her fate would be any better off with them.

"Take her to the house and feed the chit. Keep her below until Rogers goes to the country in the morning. She is to go along with him." He dismissed his coachman with a gesture, then turned to Lady Chloe.

Chloe stared after the carraige and the little face that dared to peep from the window. Waving an encouraging good-bye, Chloe turned to the maid's benefactor.

"Just like that you can alter her life," Lady Chloe marveled. "And I suspect you did the same for mine. What my grandmama will say to my surfeit of new clothes I shudder to contemplate."

"You will not back down?" he queried, gently leading her along the walkway and away from the mantuamaker's. If seen together in front of that place, a few might draw intelligent conclusions.

Ellen gave a sniff of disdain. "Not likely, she won't."

Surprised that the silent maid would so much as dare to utter a word, St. Aubyn was about to offer a reproof when he caught sight of Chloe's bemused face.

"Ellen is right. I have made my decision and will abide by it, even though I may know reproof for permitting your part in this escapade." She confessed her knowledge of her somewhat improper behavior with a prosaic spirit, and not the least hint of the coquette in her manner. "But tell me, sir, what do I do when the dresses begin to come?" She bestowed on him a look of complete faith in his ability to give her an answer that almost undid him.

"Why," he improvised, "tell her you simply were carried away and could not make up your mind, so you took them all. Surely she will understand that?"

"Mama might, but I doubt Grandmama will. Unless she has something else to worry about," Chloe replied in a considering voice.

"In that case, perhaps we should think of something!" St. Aubyn said with a dashing twinkle in his eyes that quite captivated Chloe until she absorbed what he had said.

"What?" she baldly asked. "I doubt there is little that would ensnare her attention."

"It must be of such a magnitude that all else pales into nothing beside it."

"Hullo, St. Aubyn," Sir Augustus Dabney said as he approached them. "Plan on White's for dinner?" He surveyed Chloe with curiosity, noting the quiet propriety of her dress and the maid trailing behind her.

"Gracious, the time!" Chloe exclaimed in horror. "How good of you to remind us," she said in heartfelt gratitude to the amazed Dabney, who had been hoping to needle one or both of the two, who appeared so intensely absorbed in one another that they seemed to see nothing or anyone else.

"Later," she murmured to St. Aubyn, then scrambled into the hackney that promptly appeared when St. Aubyn had raised his cane in summons.

Sir Augustus stared after the departing vehicle with a puzzled expression on his face. He tilted his head, then said, "She looks different, somehow. Agree, St. Aubyn? Wonder what happened."

He was not offended when St. Aubyn muttered some vague words of reply and then marched off in the opposite direction. Sir Augustus was quite accustomed to being ignored. Why else did he dress like a peacock if not to garner attention he would otherwise never know?

Chloe rushed up the stairs to her room followed by a cautious Ellen, who kept peering about to see if they were observed.

Scroggins came into the entry just as the two women whisked around the top step and along the hallway to the upper floor. He glanced up at the rustle of skirts, but ignored it as nothing of importance.

In her room, Lady Chloe sank on the bed for a moment to catch her breath. She exchanged a look with her maid, then said, "Did you ever know a day such as this?"

"Rose isn't likely to forget it, for sure," Ellen said. "She was terrified, but she is a game girl. I think she will do."

"I trust she will. St. Aubyn said his man Rogers would keep an eye on her until they reach the country."

"Mercy," Ellen said with a hint of amusement. "Poor man."

Chloe contemplated the scullery maid's future at the country estate belonging to Mr. St. Aubyn and wished she might be there to check on the girl. It would be terrible if she were rescued from one pitfall only to plunge into another.

Then she rudely caught herself up, for there was no way she might accomplish such a matter. She had gone quite far enough today.

As if divining her thoughts, Ellen said, "At least she has a chance to make her way now, and with good food and a bit of work, she'll likely grow up to serve for a good many years."

"Dinner, Ellen. If I am late, Grandmama will ask all manner of embarrassing questions. In her view, selecting a gown or two does not take any time at all," Chloe concluded, thinking of the little time spent at the unfashionable mantuamaker where her grandmother had taken her.

Within a brief time Chloe changed into another dress, a soft gray and white muslin that swirled about her figure in a way neither her grandmother nor the mantuamaker had anticipated. Ellen had taken needle and thread to alter the depressing gown into something halfway decent.

At the dinner table Chloe was relieved to find her grandmother totally absorbed in her own thoughts.

With nothing more to do than consume her meal, she ate well until the sweet arrived.

"I received a note just before dinner. Anonymous. But I am disturbed by the contents of it, nevertheless." Lady Dancy said with a look of speculation on her face that quite daunted Chloe.

"What did it say?" she obediently queried, as she supposed she was expected to say.

"That you and St. Aubyn had an assignation this afternoon at a mantuamaker's establishment on Bond Street. Is that true?" Sharp eyes seemed to penetrate Chloe's bones and skin to her very soul.

Her worst fears realized, Chloe searched her mind for a truthful reply that revealed enough without too much.

"Well, I did have an appointment to go for a drive with him in the park," she began.

"I thought as much," the dowager said with a narrow-eyed look at her granddaughter. "So?"

"Well," Chloe said, the very words dragged from her honest little heart, "I went to the mantuamaker alone with Ellen—Laura was unable to go along with me. And Mr. St. Aubyn chanced to see me enter the shop. He stopped in to inquire if I still intended to go for a drive with him."

"I see." There was a slight pause, then the dowager said, "And?"

"That was most of it, ma'am." Chloe pleated her napkin with nervous fingers, her mouth dry and heart a-flutter. Not being a devious girl, she suspected that did she try to lie it would be perfectly obvious.

"Would I be displeased if I discovered the remainder of that 'most'?"

"I trust not," Chloe said fervently.

"I shall say no more about it, then. It is most likely the work of a jealous woman. The handwriting looked vaguely familiar, although I could not place it. Perhaps you can?"

Thankful that her grandmother placed sufficient faith in her to give her this chance, Chloe accepted the note to peruse. "I believe it to be Aunt Elinor's," Chloe concluded. Her aunt had made no attempt to disguise her handwriting, most likely figuring that Chloe would never see the missive.

"Indeed. The troublemaker! Well, I shan't fall victim to her wiles and ruses. You look well enough after such a fatiguing day. I daresay it would be a good thing were we to attend the theater this evening. Prepare to leave within a short time."

Astounded at the turn of events, Chloe left the table to fetch her gray velvet cloak. What a blessing her grandmother had neglected to inquire if Chloe had indeed gone for that drive with St. Aubyn. She doubted if it made much difference to the dowager one way or another, and perhaps that was why she ignored the matter.

Behind her, while she awaited Scroggins, the dowager

watched her charge leave the room, noting the more confident carriage and head held high. Something had happened, and she wondered if it had anything at all to do with that dashing scoundrel, St. Aubyn.

Chloe enjoyed the theater, although the charming St. Aubyn was not present to delight the eye. While the actors droned on about some utterly silly dilemma, she dreamed about her pretty gowns and dashing new habit of leaf green that St. Aubyn had insisted she order.

The day of the Sefton ball Chloe lingered about in the vicinity of the back staircase, thinking of one excuse after another to be close by in the event of the delivery of her pretty gown. Ellen promised to keep a sharp eye and ear on the rear door, so that when the boy came, she might be the one to receive the box.

"'Tis here," came the whisper at long last. Ellen hurried up the stairs and into Chloe's room, followed closely by her mistress. The gown was reverently placed on the bed for both to admire.

"I hope . . ." Chloe began. "Oh, I hope."

Across London Julian leaned back in his leather chair at White's, watching the scene from the bow window with his friend Brummell.

"And how goes the affair à la Lady Chloe?" the beau inquired in his lazy manner. He studied the view beyond while idly swinging his quizzing glass to and fro.

"Affair? There's no affair. Merely trying to help the girl," Julian answered with matching ennui. "She is a nice child and deserves better than her grandmother is forcing upon her."

"Is that not Twisdale coming here with Dabney in tow? I keep forgetting that Twisdale is still tolerated among us." Brummell sighed and sipped his wine with a pensive air, as though debating the vagaries of the prevailing rule.

"Curious pair," Julian admitted, then lapsed into silence while considering what the unsuitable duo might be up to at the club. This so intrigued him that he signaled to Brummell that he would monitor the conversation.

"I believe they headed for the reading room, old chap," Brummell murmured.

Without a word, Julian slipped from his comfortable chair and casually strolled about the club, silent and remaining in the shadows. It was somewhat thin of company this day, considering there must be some five hundred members. At last he saw Twisdale and Dabney seated on a pair of chairs on the far side of the room. There appeared no way he might sidle up to listen to what they plotted—for plotting they must be. They had the look of schemers.

Catching the eye of one of the waiters, he motioned to him. When the man drew close, Julian made his proposition and offered a shiny gold coin, which was promptly accepted.

From the comfort of a cushioned chair, Julian watched, concealed behind the convenient pages of a newspaper, as the waiter began to check for wineglasses, wipe a table, and in general linger about the area where the two conferred. The concentration of the pair was such that they scarcely appeared to notice the man.

It was some time—with the waiter circling about as discreetly as he might—before he returned to report to Julian. With a nod of the head, Julian led him into the hallway. "Well? I trust you learned something?"

"Indeed, sir. Know you a Lady Chloe, by chance?"

"Explain, man." Julian listened attentively as the conversation was revealed to him. When done, he returned to Brummell, paused to chat a few minutes, then went on his way. He passed several friends without seeing them until Purcell came upon him.

"A brown study, Julian? What goes?"

And Julian told him what had been overheard.

"What do you think Grandmama will say when she sees this gown?" Chloe anxiously asked Ellen. "For one thing, it is not gray!"

"Indeed, miss." The usually reticent maid stood back to survey her handiwork and clasped her hands before her in admiration. " 'Tis a treat to see you, even if the dress is just short of indecent."

"Surely Mr. St. Aubyn would never have permitted me to purchase such a thing if it were," Chloe declared emphatically, but with a note of worry. She fingered the delicate edging of the bodice while glancing into the looking glass once again to see if that ethereal creature could really be her.

She did not miss the way the pale gold gossamer satin clung to her figure, nor the fascinating—to her—manner in which the aerophane crepe drifted about her like a delicate peach cloud. It was unlike any gown she had ever seen and she suspected she might garner more than a few looks this evening.

When she descended the stairs to the dining room, she paused at the doorway to give the dowager a cautious glance.

"Well? Is this the result of your shopping expedition? Come in here, girl. Let me have a look at you."

Swallowing carefully, Chloe advanced around the table until she stood before her grandmama. Then she waited for the storm to break.

"Hm." The dowager picked up a pair of spectacles she kept for reading her numerous newspapers and stared at Chloe as though examining a particularly fascinating article.

"Well?" Chloe said at last.

"You will do. Although heaven knows what Maria will say when she sees you. I hope you remember that Lady Sefton is responsible for your entrée into Almack's. If you cause her to change her mind this evening, it will be the dire consequence of your little rebellion."

Startled that her grandmother had seen so clearly what she was about, Chloe murmured something in reply, then took her place at the side of the table.

The meal was consumed in silence, and before long the two women left the house in Lady Dancy's elaborate Town coach. Chloe sat on edge, thinking pins and needles must be more comfortable than how she felt at the moment.

She thought that a great many eyes stared at her while she slowly made her way up the stairs at the Earl of Sefton's lovely home. Silly girl, she admonished herself. 'Tis your imagining, nothing more. With a fluttering heart she advanced into the ballroom where the earl and his countess stood receiving their quests. This was her first test. What would her ladyship say?

"Harriet, can this be your granddaughter?" Lady Sefton cried when she saw Chloe. "Why she has emerged from that dreadful gray cocoon you wrapped her in to become the most gorgeous of butterflies." She bestowed a fleeting kiss on Chloe's flushed cheek before appraising the gown again.

"Thank you, ma'am. You are most kind," Chloe said with proper manners.

"Madame Clotilde, I vow. 'Tis her touch, I feel sure." Lady Sefton sighed and smiled, "Oh, to be young with a figure like yours and a fortune as well. The world will be at your feet tonight."

Chloe smiled hesitantly, then passed on to greet the earl, who gave her a most appreciative look.

At her grandmother's side, she advanced into the main part of the ballroom, stopping to admire the decorations and abundant flowers that filled the great urns about the room.

When Julian caught sight of Chloe his breath seemed to vanish and he had to almost remind himself to resume that most necessary of functions. The gown was as lovely as he had recalled but she looked different. Oh, her pretty auburn hair still curled about her head as charmingly as it had before and her eyes were still that entrancing mixture of blue and green, but a mysterious something had been added and he didn't know what it was. However, she certainly did not look plain this evening.

"By Jove," breathed an awed Theo Purcell, "that *is* Lady Chloe, is it not?"

"Mind your manners, Purcell. And remember what it was that I learned today." Julian gave his friend an admonishing look, then turned to find that Lord Twisdale had entered the room.

"Right-o," Theo said, also taking in the arrival of the odious Twisdale.

"He looks utterly furious," Julian said with a great deal of satisfaction.

"Yes, he does," Theo seconded. "You actually believe he will press her to marry him this evening? Here? At the Sefton Ball? I mean," he added at the look from Julian, "it is not just any ordinary ball, y'know."

"Believe me when I say he intends to press his suit, although how he thinks to manage a moment alone with her is more than I can see."

"You forget the grandmother," Theo reminded.

"Actually, I had for the moment. That is one factor I must not overlook. Lady Chloe is properly respectful of her grandparent, although I feel the old gel scarcely deserves such devotion, considering how she plans to fob off her granddaughter on Twisdale," Julian muttered. "However, she has smiled on me once or twice as of late."

Theo followed Julian as he wound his way through the press of people until they reached the lovely Lady Chloe's side.

"Butterflies are emerging late this year," he murmured over her hand as he bestowed a proud smile on his little protégé. Oh, she had bloomed nicely. Why, any chap would be lucky to get her, not to mention all that lovely money.

She darted a glance to either side, then whispered as loudly as possible, "Grandmama did not kick up a fuss over the gown, as I feared she might. She does not know that you remained at the mantuamaker's, however. I told her that you stopped in to find out if our drive was still on for that afternoon."

"Let me sign my name to your card while we chat so none will take exception to our conversation. Twisdale approaches," Julian cautioned.

"So he does. I do not wish to dance with him," she admitted in a small voice.

"Purcell, sign here and Lady Chloe will be most grateful." At her puzzled look, Julian added, "It is the last open line on your card. Twisdale has come too late!"

"Indeed," she said with patent relief.

The first of the dances was claimed by a young sprig Chloe had met but once. He fawned over her until she longed to laugh. To hear him, one would think Chloe had just entered Society instead of having been around for a spell.

When he returned her to her grandmother's side, Chloe found Lord Twisdale waiting there for her.

"Good evening, sir," she said with a glance at the dowager. What was she planning now?

"I trust you have saved me a dance, my girl?" he said with his usual pomposity.

Chloe sneezed as a pungent scent teased her nose. Lord Twisdale looked pained but persisted in spite of the sneeze. He held out his hand for her card.

"I am sorry, sir," she said with the attitude of one speaking to an aged person requiring great respect, "it is full."

"You will give his lordship one of your dances, my girl, or I shall know the reason why," Lady Dancy said with that air of finality that could quell any spirit in most girls.

Before Chloe could answer, a cotillion was called and she sought her card to see if this was the dance that Theo Purcell had requested. He appeared at her side even as she checked one side of the little card that dangled from her wrist by a pretty blue ribbon. Opposite the first cotillion was scribbled T. Purcell.

"Mr. Purcell," her grandmother purred in a rather ominous voice, "I believe my granddaughter quite forgot that she had promised a cotillion to Lord Twisdale. Would you be so kind as to relinquish your dance with her?"

Theo bowed politely and Chloe's heart sank.

"I should like to oblige you, ma'am, but I would never survive the evening without a dance with the loveliest lady present—young lady, that is," he concluded with a charming smile and bow to her grandmother.

This lady was so bemused by the clever gallantry that she failed to admonish either Theo or Chloe and watched with a curious expression as they walked onto the dance floor.

Lord Twisdale was not best pleased.

"Later, Twisdale," the dowager said absently. She gave a languid wave of her hand, then watched the scene intently.

Theo was as proper as could stare. He led Chloe through the various patterns of the complicated dance with not one hitch. When they had completed the tenth change and were once again back in a circle, she let out a sigh of relief that she had not been required to perform this with Lord Twisdale. He seemed a trifle heavy to be flitting about the dance floor and she wondered if his hearing was so good as to hear the calls when given—for they were spoken in a voice just barely audible above the music. It certainly seemed to her that his hearing was definitely lacking—at least when it came to her refusals.

But then, perhaps he had no intention of leading her out in a dance, but planned something more sinister?

She managed to avoid catching his eye until it was time to go into supper. He began a purposeful walk toward her and she turned to search about herself in desperation. With Grandmama immediately behind her she dared not utter a word or give any sort of signal.

Laura flitted up with Theo Purcell right behind her. Mr. St. Aubyn neatly cut off Lord Twisdale and extended his hand to Chloe with gratifying grace.

"I believe you promised to have supper with me," he said with a narrow glance at Twisdale, who frowned at them as he neared.

"We shall go in together," Laura declared with a clap of her hands. The foursome drifted from the room as part of the general exodus, leisurely, calmly.

Lady Dancy found a friend who pleaded with her to join a group of older people and she went off with them, leaving Lord Twisdale fuming.

"You can stop quaking now. He is standing back there with a fulminating expression on his face," St. Aubyn said in an undertone.

Chloe flashed him a grateful look. "He requested my hand for a dance early on, but Mr. Purcell defied him and declined to yield. I was most indebted to him."

"Save a bit of that gratitude for me, if you please," St. Aubyn said with a grin.

"And why is that, sir?"

"Because of me you are able to enjoy your supper. Twisdale might have affected your appetite."

"That is not a kind remark," she said quietly. "I fear I am becoming most heartless."

"As long as you do not bestow your remorse in the wrong place," he countered with a concerned look at the placement of dainty tables in the room adjoining the dining room where the vast table was spread with all sorts of delicacies.

Chloe nodded her agreement while giving him a puzzled look. Just how far did he intend to go with his assistance?

She found herself the center of attention when she walked to the table that St. Aubyn had found for them. Gentlemen in particular went out of their way to greet her and she savored a black look from her Aunt Elinor.

"I believe my dress has met with success," she confided to Laura in an undertone when the men had gone to the buffet to fetch plates of food.

"And not merely your dress. Do you realize you have had St. Aubyn dancing attendance on you for days now? There is much speculation among the ton, or so Mama says, regarding his intentions."

"He is a friend," Chloe avowed, even as she wished it might be otherwise.

"Lady Chloe," Lord Twisdale said from behind her, causing her to start with surprise. "Your esteemed grandmother has given me permission to speak with you later this evening. I trust you do not wish to go against her wishes?"

Chloe sneezed. Violently.

Chapter 10

Lord Twisdale stiffened as though Chloe's sneeze had been a major affront to him.

"I beg your pardon," Chloe said in humble apology. "I do not know what comes over me at times." She was far too polite to mention that his scent appeared to bother her.

"Twisdale," St. Aubyn said in a freezing voice when he came up to the table and discovered the man had the effrontery to accost Lady Chloe. St. Aubyn gave him a look quite as though Twisdale had brought in an undesirable aroma. "Perhaps it is the atmosphere in here, Lady Chloe."

"Seems a trifle warm to me," Theo Purcell added in the most innocent of voices.

"Until later, my dear girl," Twisdale said to Chloe, ignoring the others as though they were not there.

"Odious man," Laura whispered as the pompous lord walked off in starched disapproval of the younger set. "He is so foolish he would choose a weathercock for a sign post."

"*I* would be foolish beyond permission to think that he is not a menace, however," Chloe said in a soft reply.

"Never underestimate the enemy, is that it?" Theo chimed in quietly, with a glance over his shoulder to make certain Lord Twisdale was some distance away.

St. Aubyn raised his hand to silence them. "Best say nothing, for you never know when ears may be around."

Laura gave him a startled look, then turned to Chloe with a troubled face. "Does your grandmother still insist upon Lord Twisdale as a husband for you?"

"She has not threatened me with such for a day or two." Then Chloe, determined to enjoy the ball—which was the high point of the Season—changed the topic. In short order they were laughing at Theo's quips and demolishing the delicious food on their plates.

If Chloe cast worried glances a time or two in the direction Lord Twisdale had taken, she said nothing more on the subject.

Restored to her grandmother following supper, Chloe gracefully accepted the hand of her next partner—young Lord John Winton—and wished the ball would never end, for then she would not have to face Lord Twisdale. Truth be told, she was enjoying her little success. The confidence from knowing she was superbly gowned had given her a glow and the daring to chat amiably during the lulls while performing the figures of the dance.

A good many of the dances required that a couple stand and wait while others went through the steps of the figures. In the past, Chloe had stood silently, wondering what on earth she might say to her intimidating partner. Tonight, she found it surprisingly easy to converse, about polite nothings mostly.

The dance concluded and Lord John promenaded her along the edge of the floor as was the custom. Chloe looked across the room and caught sight of Lord Twisdale standing at her grandmother's side. If it had not been improper, she would have begged Lord John to deposit her right here, on the opposite side of the ballroom. But, her manners being what they were, she submitted to the propriety of being returned to her relative's side.

She curtsied to Lord John, then turned to face her grandmama. "Ma'am," she said with stoic calm covering a fluttering heart.

"Lord Twisdale wishes to speak with you. Whoever was to be your next partner must yield. Is that clear?"

There was nothing for Chloe to do but nod her agreement and accept Lord Twisdale's arm. One did not create a scene in the middle of the Sefton ballroom. The young man who had signed her card for the next country dance appeared, but with a glance from Lord Twisdale, the chap melted into the throng of people.

She remained silent while they strolled from the ballroom and along a grand hallway until they reached an elegant library. Chloe paused. She did not wish to enter this room with him, for if seen, there would be no alternative but to marry him. She would be compromised.

"We are quite alone here, sir," she declared, gesturing to the almost empty hallway. Some distance along, a footman stood at attention. "What do you have to say to me that requires such privacy?" She halted in the middle of the hall, refusing to take another step.

He cast her an annoyed look, but as he could scarcely drag Chloe into the library by force—he had also observed the footman and would never disgrace himself in front of a servant—he smoothed his face into an agreeable mask.

"I seek an answer from you. When I asked for your hand in marriage you begged a few days to consider. I suggest that you have had that time." At her silence, he prodded, "Well?"

"I appreciate the honor you have done me, but I fear I must decline your gracious offer, sir." Even if it meant bread and water, Chloe would not yield to this man. Better to fade away, hoping the dowager would relent, than to know certain danger as his wife.

"What? You decline? But your grandmother said, that is, I felt certain that you would agree." For once Lord Twisdale looked shaken.

"While I should obey my grandmama, I am a silly girl, sir. I would wed for affection and I feel none toward you, nor from you." With this pronouncement she sneezed and decided that proximity to Lord Twisdale was hazardous in more ways than one.

"I shall speak with Lady Dancy regarding this. I feel certain it is her wish that we marry." Lord Twisdale drew himself up and turned on his heel and marched down the hall. Apparently he did not feel it necessary to accompany Chloe back to the ballroom, as would have been proper. Rather, he left her on her own, prey to any wandering gentleman.

She began a reluctant return to the ballroom, wondering what she must face once there. Head down, intent on her dilemma, she was unaware of another's approach.

"Of all the stupid things to do, going off with Twisdale is at the top of the list," St. Aubyn pointed out when he strode up to her side.

Chloe gave a startled jump. "I had no choice but to go

with him. Grandmama would never forgive me if I had
made a scene and she was quite determined that I listen to
him."

"What happened?" he demanded, walking protectively at
her side, one hand at her elbow to draw her closer yet.
When he took her arm he realized that she trembled—from
fear, most likely, after facing Twisdale. Julian was pleased
when she drew closer to him as though for security. It was
the first time a woman had turned to him for such a thing
and it made him feel much the—champion.

"I refused him. He went off in a huff to tell Grandmama
of my decision. I fear she will take me from the ball.
Please—dance with me, St. Aubyn," Lady Chloe suddenly
pleaded, most improperly. Especially if you remembered
that St. Aubyn was a scoundrel of the first order—which
Chloe tended to forget.

Knowing that the dowager would never haul Chloe from
the dance floor, thus creating a scene of horrendous propor-
tion, Julian clasped her gloved hand securely in his and
walked onto the dance floor with her at his side. He did not
so much as glance in the direction of the dowager, from
whom he ought to have sought permission.

It was a country dance and within minutes they were
whirling about through the first figure. When it came time
to join hands to go down the middle Chloe looked at her
partner, thinking what a pity it was he would never ask her
to marry him.

It had hit her minutes ago—when she had felt safe in
turning to him as a refuge—that she would like nothing better than to be at his side forever. She had made the stupid
mistake of plunging into love with the premier scoundrel of
London. Only for a little while would he be *her* scoundrel
and then he would be off to another. For did not scoundrels
earn their notoriety flitting from one woman to another like
a dratted butterfly?

At the conclusion of the dance, she laughed up at him,
breathless with the exertion and wondering what a girl said
to the man she just realized she loved quite madly. Of
course she could not tell him how she felt. It was not done,
or so she supposed. But as far as she was concerned her
scoundrel was exceedingly cherished and not really a

scoundrel at all—he was kind, chivalrous, and all that she could wish for in a gentleman.

St. Aubyn reclaimed his cane and they promenaded about the room. Chloe dreaded what would happen next. Her grandmother never made idle threats to Chloe's knowledge. Yet bread and water was a small price to pay for avoiding a marriage to Twisdale.

"St. Aubyn, I am afraid," she murmured as they progressed toward where her grandmother sat like a judge in chambers.

"You ought not be compelled to marry him," St. Aubyn growled softly. "We must think of something. But for the remainder of the evening, promise me that you will avoid being alone with anyone."

"I know better than to go off with a gentleman," she retorted, recalling the moments she had happily spent in his company—alone—learning about the art of flirting and in the process tumbling into love with him.

He opened his mouth to say something else but was prevented from uttering a word by Lady Dancy.

"Very naughty of you, St. Aubyn. You know better than to hare off with a young lady without first seeking permission." Her eyes were flint, her face austere. She looked as though all her clothing had been soaked in starch.

He gave her his charming lopsided smile that had the unfortunate habit of melting the heart of any susceptible woman—of which there seemed to be quite a few, Chloe thought crossly. The famous smile had no effect on Lady Dancy.

"But you most likely would not grant me a dance, my lady," he said smoothly. "Your granddaughter is delightful company. I am pleased to see that she seems to have taken so well. Not a dance unsolicited." He gestured to the little card dangling from Chloe's wrist.

The dowager looked about as Chloe's next partner came into sight. "Yes, well, the girl must learn to obey, you see," she began, then apparently realized the impropriety of such a conversation at a ball and snapped her mouth shut.

Chloe gave St. Aubyn a grateful look, but did not miss the dowager's sharp words before departing for the next dance.

"We will discuss what you did when we return home."

She felt a slight pressure on her arm before St. Aubyn relinquished her to her next partner. Glancing back she caught an understanding look in his eyes.

She might have fussed and stewed the rest of the evening over that statement, but the knowledge that for the first time in her life she had tumbled into love forestalled such a thing. She felt wondrously light on her feet and skimmed over the floor—hopping, leaping, whirling with ease through the complicated steps of the quadrille.

Julian stood along the side of the room, hands behind his back, risking the ire of his hostess by not asking some demure damsel to dance. Then he leaned on his cane and hoped that might earn his forgiveness.

He had to watch Chloe. She did not know what danger she was in now that she had refused Twisdale. The man had met with Elinor only minutes ago, pausing briefly to chat. Anyone would think it most innocent. Anyone but Julian.

Egads, but Chloe looked like a delicate peach-and-gold cherub, whirling and hopping about in the energetic dance. His leg gave a twinge when he even thought about the gyrations required. He had danced it earlier with Chloe, but he would not do it again for anyone else.

What a delight she was, so brave, facing the dragon with a lift of her chin and firm resolve. Poor little darling, he had best find her a nice husband who would treasure her, nurturing her splendid spirit. He could not think of anyone suitable at the moment, but given time surely he might come up with a name worthy of her.

Then he watched while Chloe's partner began to promenade her around the room. His gaze sharpened when he saw Elinor step into their paths, drawing Chloe from the line of people who had been dancing. He tensed, sensing that trouble was brewing in a very large scale unless he could manage to do something about it.

Without consideration for his own regard, Julian set off in the direction that Elinor and Chloe had gone—down the hall toward the library, if he did not miss his guess. He lost sight of them when a friend of his, one not seen for some time, hailed him. Julian seethed inwardly but graciously paused to speak with his old friend.

* * *

Elinor glanced at her twit of a niece and firmed her resolve. "My dear, I must have a little chat with you." When Chloe looked to refuse, she added, "Your grandmother will not object if you go with me, for I am of an age to be your chaperone." It pained Elinor to say those words, for it was admitting her age to one who looked dew-fresh and innocent. She forged ahead with her plan. "It has been an age since we last met."

"Yes, I believe that was the evening when you helped Mrs. Robynhod exhibit the drawings you took from my room. That was not a kind thing for you to do, Aunt."

This direct answer flustered Elinor. Trust dear little Chloe to issue a remark like that. Goodness, the chit was as prickly as a teasel plant. She appeared to be more than a little reluctant to go with Elinor, which served to give warning. She needed all the tact and skill at her disposal for the next few minutes.

"I thought you might be fatigued what with all the dancing this evening. Goodness, you have scarce had time to think. I believe you have taken rather well this evening." Elinor continued to draw Chloe along with her. "That is a very lovely gown, my dear. Did your grandmother buy it?"

Elinor had been seething with envy from the moment she had laid eyes on Chloe that evening. The chit glowed with health and beauty and made Elinor feel positively ancient. If that were not sufficiently horrible, the girl wore a gown that ought to have been scandalous—probably would have on another. Chloe's obvious innocence gave the beautiful dress the aura of luscious peach blossoms in a very well-tended and private garden. The chit looked good enough to eat, were one a gentleman and so inclined. Judging from the gazes Elinor had intercepted this evening, there were a great number of men who would be only too pleased to try.

"No, I selected this gown myself. Why are you taking me away from the ballroom?" Chloe demanded, slowing her steps.

Which brought Elinor to the matter at hand. "I wish to talk with you."

Chloe halted. "So you said. I believe I have been along

this passage once before this evening. I truly have no desire to view the earl's library, lovely as it might be."

Elinor stared at the stubborn tilt of Chloe's head, her firmed lips, and searched for a means of persuasion.

Chloe turned to see the genial fop Sir Augustus strolling toward her and felt distinct relief.

"Evening, Lady Chloe, Mrs. Hadlow. Splendid ball, is it not?" He preened when he glimpsed his image in one of the tall looking glasses that hung on the wall. Clearly he was proud of his reflection.

Taking a step in his direction and away from her aunt, Chloe smiled. "Indeed, it is lovely. There is nothing like pleasant company, excellent food and music, plus good friends to make an evening enjoyable."

"Right you are, dear lady," Sir Augustus said, beaming a pleased smile at Chloe when he saw she caught his meaning.

"I was trying to persuade Chloe to view the truly magnificent library belonging to the earl," Elinor said to Sir Augustus.

Chloe frowned, but said nothing.

"Is it?" Sir Augustus said, not sounding terribly interested in the idea of a library.

Chloe relaxed a trifle. Clearly there was no collusion between these two. She waited patiently, wondering what her partner had thought when she had disappeared. It was very bad manners to miss a dance without consulting your partner, she knew, and hoped he might forgive her.

Then she recalled that she was to have waltzed with St. Aubyn and could have cheerfully crowned Aunt Elinor for her interference.

How Chloe had looked forward to being held close in his arms. The reel had been nice, but it was nothing compared to a waltz. Grandmama had said she was not to partake in the scandalous dance, but she could not prevent him from signing his name across from where it was listed. Nor did Chloe wish to prevent him.

A word caught her attention and she watched Sir Augustus again when he turned to face her.

"Shall we?"

"Forgive me, I fear I was woolgathering. Shall we

what?" Chloe queried, aware of the disapproving expressions on both faces. Why did not her officious grandmother come now to haul her away? She took a step in the direction of the ballroom.

Sir Augustus gave her an amiable grin and wrapped surprisingly strong fingers around her arm. "Why, I told Mrs. Hadlow that if I might view the library in your lovely company it would no doubt appear in much better light."

Doubt entered Chloe's mind at these gracious words. While Sir Augustus had always appeared to enjoy her company, he had never truly sought her out. "I do not think we should," she began.

"What nonsense!" Elinor said briskly. "I shall come with you so what possible harm could there be?"

Appeased only slightly by the words meant to reassure her, Chloe shook her arm free from Sir Augustus, giving him a wary look. She entered the large, dimly lit room with more than usual caution.

It appeared empty, save for hundreds of leather-bound books and several comfortable-looking leather chairs. A large globe on a mahogany stand stood to one side of the room and on another wall a stand displayed a collection of prints. Paintings of previous earls and their families adorned the walls here and there. It was a cozy room, one that looked much-used.

"Quite nice," Chloe said succinctly. She turned to leave the room, feeling suddenly even more ill at ease than when she was in the hall.

"You cannot leave me now," Sir Augustus said in a coaxing way. "Why, there is much to explore here."

"No doubt," Chloe began, then gave her aunt a suspicious look when she began to stroll about the room. Aunt Elinor had never seemed the type to appreciate a well-stocked library.

"Oh dear," Elinor said suddenly with a look at her locket-watch. "I must fly, I promised this dance to a special gentleman and I dare not miss it."

Chloe wondered how Elinor knew what time the dance was to begin and said so.

"Well," Elinor cried as she ran toward the doorway, "each one lasts just so long, does it not?" With that stupid reply she was out of the door, slamming it tightly behind her.

"Sir Augustus, we must leave here immediately. I do not know what my aunt was thinking of—to leave us alone in here. 'Tis most improper," Chloe declared. She crossed the room toward the door and freedom when Sir Augustus again clasped her arm with a grip from which she could not escape.

"I think not, Lady Chloe. I have a much nicer plan in mind." His grin was amiable, but Chloe did not trust it in the least. At this point, the only person she trusted was St. Aubyn—and he was not here.

"And what is that, pray tell?" She warily faced him, wishing her grandmother would enter to drag her away. All of a sudden pleasant, foppish Sir Augustus seemed neither pleasant nor particularly desirable company.

"Why, Mrs. Hadlow has gone to inform your grandmother that you have accepted my offer of marriage. Truly, I never thought to aspire so high. But the chance to wed a lady with a fortune does not often come my way—or to most chaps in need of the ready. Here I had thought you all but wed to Lord Twisdale, but Mrs. Hadlow informed me otherwise." He advanced on her and Chloe backed toward the door.

"You have not proposed to me nor have I accepted—nor would I," Chloe fiercely declared, avoiding a library ladder that stuck out from the wall. She placed one hand on it, contemplating what she might use as a weapon against Sir Augustus. The ladder was too unwieldy, unfortunately.

"You would have no chance," he replied as smoothly as fresh-churned butter. "You would be compromised, dear Lady Chloe."

"I will never marry you," she stated with surprising firmness. She edged away from her captor, searching her mind for a way out of her peril. "Mr. St. Aubyn will never allow this to happen, he will help me," she concluded desperately.

"He will be powerless," Sir Augustus crowed with elation. "For once I shall have something he wants and cannot have." His chuckle did not bring a responsive one from Chloe. Rather, she looked at Sir Augustus as though he had gone utterly mad.

The door opened and Chloe momentarily closed her eyes, as though waiting for the executioner's ax to fall.

"What have we here, Dabney?"

"St. Aubyn!" Chloe cried with intense relief, spinning about to see her rescuer. Had she not been a proper girl, she would have thrown herself into his arms, then and there. She turned her head to look back at her foe. "See. I told you he would save me," she spat at a flummoxed Sir Augustus.

"But Mrs. Hadlow said . . ." Sir Augustus mumbled.

"Bother Aunt Elinor," Chloe said with loathing. "My aunt has nothing to say to my life or what happens with it. Fortunately."

"I thought she was merely wanting to put you out of the way of his eminence here," Sir Augustus said, gesturing with a sneer to St. Aubyn. "Must be a comedown for a diamond like Mrs. Hadlow to have competition from her own niece. How is it you turn from the aunt to the girl, St. Aubyn? Down in funds for the moment?"

"Do not permit him to rile you, St. Aubyn," she said firmly, ignoring the wrench in her heart when she heard her hero linked with her most odious aunt. Chloe put her hand out to prevent St. Aubyn from doing something drastic, like punching Sir Augustus right in his nasty little nose.

"You fear for him?" St. Aubyn inquired in a bemused voice.

"No," she admitted with a flash of her eyes. "I would not have you bruise your fists or damage your beautiful coat for the world. Nothing he can say could injure me."

"He could tell people he had been closeted with you in this library." St. Aubyn watched the pair who confronted each other with something like bemused regard.

"Oh mercy," Chloe said in disgust.

"But I do not think he will," Julian continued. "For surely we can think of something he would not wish known—like he is in dire need of funds and all had best beware of him."

"I say," Sir Augustus sputtered while edging toward the door.

"Do you know, my clever papa had my inheritance papers drawn up so that my husband cannot get his hands on my money. It must be administered by my solicitors. I am

not even certain that Grandmama knows about that clause."
Lady Chloe folded her arms, then tapped her foot on the
carpeted floor, adding, "Was there something you intended
to do, Sir Augustus? Perhaps you feel ill and find it necessary to retire to your bed? Otherwise, I imagine I could encourage St. Aubyn to punch you in that dreadful beak of a
nose if you prefer."

St. Aubyn obliged by removing his exquisitely tailored
gray Bath cloth coat. He then began to roll up his sleeves.

"Anything to accommodate a lady, Dabney," he drawled
in the superior manner of one who is accustomed to winning every altercation.

Chloe was so fascinated by the sight of the shirtsleeves
being rolled up over lightly tanned and very muscular arms
that she quite forgot to keep an eye on St. Augustus.

Before she knew it he was at the door, pausing only to
say, "I am dashed glad I don't have to marry you, if truth
be told. Had no notion you were such a termagant. St.
Aubyn is welcome to you, although what he wants with
you is more than I can see," he concluded ungraciously.

That home truth hit Chloe very hard. It wiped out all
thoughts of attractive muscles and intriguing mouths and
twinkling eyes. Indeed, she felt very much like crying. She
had just become aware of how very brave she was being
and that St. Aubyn had pushed her to change from a frightened mouse into a tiger cat—and then reality crashed
around her.

She stared after the fleeing Sir Augustus with a dazed
sensation. Giving herself a little shake, she turned to thank
St. Aubyn for coming to her rescue. "It was exceedingly
kind of you to bother with me, Mr. St. Aubyn," she began
politely. "Why my aunt felt she had to arrange an assignation—or whatever you might call it—with Sir Augustus, I
do not know, but I appreciate your rescue more than I can
possibly say." She cast her gaze on the carpet, trying to
stem the bitter tears that longed to flow.

"I believe I have made it plain that I care about what
happens to you, my girl," Julian said with a rueful look at
the precious peach package standing before him looking as
though she had lost her last pence and friend.

"Oh, St. Aubyn," she sobbed, "I feel utterly wretched! And this was to have been such a lovely ball," she wailed.

Julian stepped forward to take her into his arms, comforting her with a soothing pat on her back and thinking he was playing with fire. A lovelier bit of baggage he had not seen in ages and to have her thrust into his arms when he wanted her was testing his code of conduct to the hilt. He did not seduce innocents. Although from the way Lady Chloe fit into his arms and snuggled against his chest he wondered a trifle.

"I am a silly goose," she murmured, lifting her head to gaze ruefully into his eyes.

"Indeed," he whispered.

Then Julian did what he had desired to do for some time and could not prevent no matter how he reminded himself that he ought not. He kissed the tempting Chloe.

He was totally unprepared for the strength of her response.

When they drew apart, Julian stared down into her face, totally at sea with her as well as his own emotions.

"I do not feel the least like sneezing," Chloe murmured for no apparent reason Julian could see.

"I ought to apologize," he began.

"Why? I found it utterly delightful and if you dare apologize I daresay I might kick you in the shins," she said with charming candor, marveling that she dared to be so bold with him.

"I must say I had not expected to hear a rejoinder like that," Julian said with a laugh.

She leaned against him for a moment, then withdrew from his arms, walking toward the door with head held high, hands clasped before her. At the door she paused, then said, "I also daresay we ought to leave this room, charming though it might be. What stood regarding the danger with Sir Augustus holds true for you as well. You might not need the money but you most certainly do not wish a wife."

Before she could open the door, it flew wide, admitting the Dowager Lady Dancy in high dudgeon. When she saw St. Aubyn instead of whoever she expected she was thrown off stride, but only for a moment.

"St. Aubyn, this is unpardonable, to find one like you secreted with my granddaughter. I demand satisfaction."

"Lady Dancy," Julian replied with sinking heart, "I was about to come to you with the request for Lady Chloe's hand in marriage."

"Oh no!" Lady Chloe whispered.

Chapter 11

"*I*ndeed, ma'am." Julian felt his heart sink to his toes. Lady Chloe appeared to be horrified at the mere thought of being married to him. While he knew he had a reputation as a scoundrel and perhaps a bit of a rake, he did not think he was *that* dreadful.

Elinor Hadlow and Lord Twisdale pushed forward from where they had been standing behind Lady Dancy. Laura Spayne and Theo followed them into the room, and Julian wondered if everyone attending the Sefton ball would come following after them.

"Where is the cavalry?" he murmured to Chloe, who had drawn close to his side.

"Perhaps the Horse Guards?" she shot back in a strained whisper.

"Why, Mr. St. Aubyn," Elinor purred, giving him a look of loathing, "I fear you find yourself in a slight dilemma."

"Gone too far this time," Lord Twisdale pronounced in his most pompous manner. "No man would have a young gel once she had been compromised by *you*."

"He did nothing, I tell you," Lady Chloe said in a shaken voice, taking a step in her grandmother's direction and quite overlooking the sweet kiss she had shared with St. Aubyn. "Mr. St. Aubyn has always behaved with the utmost propriety toward me. Of course, he views me in a different light from more available females," she concluded somewhat recklessly, Julian thought. It did not help matters that Chloe glanced pointedly at Elinor.

"Chloe!" Lady Dancy declared, looking even more scandalized at her granddaughter, if that were possible.

Laura hurried across the room to stand by Chloe's side, turning to face the others with a defiant glare. "I know my dearest friend. She may execute wicked little sketches, but she would never do anything so bold as to meet with a gentleman in a sequestered situation. I think she must have been . . ."

"Your defense of your little friend is admirable," Julian inserted before Laura could finish her challenge. He had just caught sight of Mrs. Robynhod entering the room, and he did not wish the worst sort of gossip to circulate through the ton.

Laura frowned at him, but subsided, putting a protective arm about Chloe.

"I will confess to you all that I have found Lady Chloe to be a delightful and most charming young woman," Julian said with a slight bow in her direction. "She is everything my father asks in my wife and certainly meets my criteria as well. And, although it is not the least fashionable, I also confess that I am quite taken with her. You may as well know that the marriage will be an affair of the heart."

Julian took immediate note of the expressions on those in the room. Theo looked skeptical; Laura appeared willing to believe what he said if Chloe concurred. Grandmother Dancy looked fit to be tied. Mrs. Robynhod's protuberant eyes gleamed with the thought of the choice gossip that she alone could pass along. Chloe had sketched her as a predatory cat; now Julian could see why.

Elinor and Twisdale had drawn together as enemies uniting forces. The beautiful Elinor could well explode if someone did not remove her from the room. Her face had alternately turned pale and purple with anger and fury. He would not bet on her stability at the moment.

Twisdale was another matter entirely. He was furious, yes, but he was giving Laura a thoughtful stare that quite chilled Julian. There could be nothing to come of any interest from him, for surely Laura's mother would forbid such a match for her only daughter. And then maybe not, he considered when he thought of Twisdale's fortune, homes, and title. That was a difficult position to deny to an eager mother bent on seeing her child well established.

Julian moved to Lady Chloe's side, gathering her trembling hand into his own firm grip. With another glance at his reluctant bride-to-be, Julian turned to Lady Dancy and said, "I imagine you will wish a private ceremony. I will notify my father at once, and procure a special license as soon as may be, if that is your wish."

"Not at all," the dowager said with a sniff, surprising Julian. "I wish nothing havey-cavey thought about this marriage. It will be done with a proper calling of the banns and you will be married in church. Anyone"—and this she said with a glance toward an enthralled Mrs. Robynhod—"may attend the ceremony. I trust this will also be more agreeable with your father, for it will allow him time to come down to London in style."

"As you wish," Julian answered. At his side he could sense a lessening of tension in the slender body of his betrothed. Not quite certain what could be the cause for this, Julian continued setting forth his plans. "We can be married in Lady Chloe's church. Fortunately, I believe I reside in the same parish, so that will simplify matters."

"The rest of the details can be worked out at a more appropriate time," the dowager said. With an imperious wave of her hand, she commanded, "Come, Chloe."

"Yes, Grandmama," Lady Chloe said with proper respect. As she took a step toward her now departing grandmother, Chloe whispered to Julian, "I must see you. Meet me in the morning for a ride, same place."

Julian gave a faint nod of his head to let her know he would be at the Stanhope Gate awaiting her arrival.

Chloe trailed down the hall after her grandmother, then nearly bumped into that grand lady when she abruptly came to a halt.

"St. Aubyn," she said, turning to face the man who sauntered from the library at his own pace, "you had best lead my granddaughter out in a dance. No one will believe the betrothal otherwise."

Chloe did not point out that St. Aubyn had already danced with her that evening. She well knew the importance of appearances—she had it drummed into her often enough.

"With pleasure, my lady," St. Aubyn said with a bow.

Chloe accepted his escort, placing her hand on his proferred arm with good grace. What a dilemma to be in, to be certain. She had just been ordered to marry the man she had tumbled into love with and knew he had not the least desire to marry her. He had said so when he sought her assistance to escape Aunt Elinor's clutches.

He wanted time to be on the town, time for amusements, and he had no intention of becoming married for some years, or so he had thought. How ironic, Aunt Elinor had succeeded in pushing him right into her detested niece's arms. Or would he . . . be in her arms, that is. Chloe chanced a look at St. Aubyn and wondered what sort of marriage they might have. Judging from his kiss, it had a wealth of potential. But, oh, Chloe felt so guilty, as though her unspoken wishes had brought about their entrapment.

She could hear Laura behind her muttering to Theo, and suspected that Laura was not convinced about the proposal as a genuine desire to marry. What a challenge to convince not only Laura and Theo, but all in attendance this evening and the rest of the ton.

Chloe's dance card was in utter chaos; gentlemen were most likely denouncing her left and right for failing to appear when it came time for their dance. Perhaps the announcement of her betrothal would amend their opinion? At any rate, it removed one more girl from the marriage mart. One eligible gentleman as well. The hopeful mothers would not thank her for that.

While her grandmother marched regally over to where Maria Sefton kept an eye on the unmarried damsels in need of partners, Chloe stood by St. Aubyn, waiting for the present dance to conclude.

"The next will be a waltz, I believe. We shall have our dance after all. You disappeared for the other."

"Aunt Elinor's doing. I must say," Chloe murmured. "She looked as cross as crabs when you announced our betrothal. I wish it were not necessary," she added, commiserating with what must be his desire to be anywhere but at her side.

"There are some who would find fault with a fat goose. Just look at me as though you actually feel enthused about our forthcoming marriage," he said with a snap.

"Very well," she said quietly, suspecting that his patience was as tried as could be. Then she realized he also needed a slight reprimand and said, "You might try to look affectionate as well, you know, instead of looking as though you were going to a funeral." She culminated that remark with what she hoped was an adoring gaze at him accompanied by stepping a bit closer to his formidable form. What fun to be openly flirting with this proclaimed scoundrel. It was a bit like playing with fire, she supposed.

He made no comment, but gave her an exceedingly thoughtful look.

Chloe watched the promenade of dancers after the conclusion of the country dance, feeling very much as though she were about to make a performance on a theatrical stage.

"Now," he muttered, guiding her into the center of the floor with a hand firmly at the small of her back.

What followed was a dance like none Chloe had ever performed before. That scoundrel St. Aubyn gazed down into her face as though he wished to consume her. He held her closer to him than was proper, and he spoke soft words of romance every minute of the waltz. In short, he was making her feel deliciously confused, delightfully coveted, and delectably cherished . . . the scoundrel.

This must be what Aunt Elinor had found so entrancing. Chloe had to admit she would have been captivated as well, had she not known the true circumstances of the betrothal.

"Sir," she pleaded when she could find her breath, "we will find a way out, I promise. I doubt it is necessary to convince them all."

He appeared to be hurt by her words. She felt guilty. When he whirled her about in a spin that again deprived her of her breath she tried to make amends by beaming a worshipful smile at him.

"Never say so. We will deal famously together," he declared in a husky voice that did the strangest things to her nerves. Her power of speech flew out the window.

His effective method of persuasion and the intoxicating nearness of his highly masculine figure combined to erase her doubts for the moment. She smiled up at him, fluttering her lashes and in general using every one of the little tricks he had taught her in the art of flirting.

"Oh ho," he whispered, pulling her against him for one wicked moment, "two can play at *that* game."

She glanced off to see Aunt Elinor batting her eyelashes

at one of the older gentlemen, then back to St. Aubyn. "I thought you *were* playing a game."

"Not with you."

He spoke with such sincerity she could almost believe him. Except he was a scoundrel and who believed a scoundrel?

When they left the ballroom dance floor, Chloe could see heads bent in gossip, with Mrs. Robynhod holding forth behind the protection of her fan. The group of ladies clustered about her appeared most enthralled with her tale.

"It has begun," Chloe observed striving for composure after the assault on her senses by that wicked waltz. "But as I said before," she added once sanity returned, "I will find you a way out of this."

St. Aubyn gave her a puzzled look before being caught up in conversation with several of his friends who pounced on them, Theo joining along. St. Aubyn puzzled Chloe by keeping her firmly close to his side. It was quite as though he felt a genuine regard for her. But, she thought with an inward sigh, he was a consummate actor.

She was not sorry when it came time to depart.

Before she left the ballroom, she had time to press Laura's hand and insist, "Come see me tomorrow—late in the morning. I must talk with you." It was important to warn Laura. Lord Twisdale had a decidedly predatory gleam in his eyes when he looked at her.

Clearly intrigued, Laura said, "I will come if at all possible. Mama has been in one of her moods again."

Suspecting that those moods were the sort that came on while in the midst of the Season, Chloe nodded, then followed the dowager out of the room and down the grand staircase to the entrance.

"I made your farewells and planted the information with Maria." The dowager gave her coachman an impatient look for being slow, then accepted the groom's assistance into the carriage. Chloe climbed in behind her, sitting facing the imposing figure in cream satin and plumes.

She did not have to ask what information had been given to Lady Sefton. When the scoundrel married, it was news.

"At least this has given Lord Twisdale a disgust of me," Chloe offered hesitantly.

"I noticed that he was casting looks at Laura Spayne."

"I did as well. I must warn her about him," Chloe murmured.

"There is nothing irregular in his behavior. He is a peer of the realm, wealthy, with splendid properties. In fact, one of them is not far from St. Aubyn's home—or one of them," the dowager amended when she seemed to recall that the St. Aubyn family owned a number of stately homes and manor houses scattered about England.

"I should think that the St. Aubyn family would have a peerage, what with their wealth and properties," Chloe challenged, quite fed up with her grandmother's obsession in that direction.

"His grandfather was offered one many years ago. Turned it down. Told me that it came at too high a price. I suspect the king wanted more than St. Aubyn was willing to pay," Lady Dancy mused.

"You make it sound as though a peerage can be bought," Chloe exclaimed in dismay.

"And so they can," the dowager replied, leaning back against the squabs and offering no more on the subject, much to Chloe's disgust.

In the morning Chloe crawled from her bed at first light, unable to attempt sleep any longer. She had mulled over her dilemma for hours and was no closer to finding a workable solution. She chanced to glance at yesterday's newspaper. An article had caught her eye yesterday and she had wanted to study it more, so she'd whisked it up to her room when she was sure her grandmother had finished with it.

There was an item about an annulment that had been granted. The circumstances did not apply to her situation, but it stirred up memories. The Pouget case returned to mind. The details were fuzzy, but she seemed to recall reading that young William Pouget had married a highly unsuitable female and the marriage was nullified because of some discrepancy in calling of the banns. His name . . . that was it! His name had been incomplete, and even Chloe knew that all names were given at the reading of the banns.

When Ellen entered the room bearing the customary tray

with hot chocolate and scones, Chloe was partly dressed. At least she had donned her chemise, hose, and riding skirt.

"I think I have the solution," she cried to Ellen, a jubilant expression on her face. "I shan't compel St. Aubyn to remain married to me. I have found a way out."

"A way out of what, miss?" the puzzled abigail said.

"My marriage," Chloe replied between sips of chocolate.

"And I did not know you were wed!" Ellen said with sparkling eyes, obviously thinking her mistress was joking.

"I will be, but then I will not be," Chloe said with impatience, for she had no wish to explain the situation numerous times and she wanted to mull it over some more before presenting it to St. Aubyn this morning.

"I see," Ellen said dubiously, making it clear that she did not see in the least.

Once Chloe was dressed in her pretty new green habit trimmed in black braid, the jaunty hat with the clutch of black feathers tucked in the brim perched atop her head, she grabbed her crop and gloves and ran lightly down the stairs and around to the mews.

Her groom saluted her with a grin, then followed closely behind her as she anxiously rode off toward the park. When they reached the Stanhope Gate, Chloe turned to the groom.

"You may fall back a trifle. I am meeting my betrothed and we have many things to discuss."

Looking surprised at this news, for Ellen had said nothing to him, the groom gave a skeptical nod and fell back, though not very far.

"St. Aubyn, you came," Chloe softly declared, glad to see him again when he moved forward out of the shadows.

"Julian, please," he said with a wry grin. "I think we are safely into that state where first names may be permitted. After last evening it is generally held that I have paid you particular attentions."

"Julian, then, and I must say it seems odd to use your first name, even if I heard my aunt do so," Chloe said frankly. Ignoring his look of annoyance, she plunged on, "I have a famous scheme for us."

"Why do I not like the sound of that?" he queried, studying her eager face while they rose beneath the gentle dappled light of the trees.

"Listen," she said with a touch of her grandmother's imperious manner. "Do you recall the Pouget case sometime past? Well, remember that young William Pouget married a brazen woman of no account? His father sued to have the marriage nullified on the grounds that the banns had not been correctly read—William failed to use one of his names."

"That was a part of the case, true," Julian agreed. He also knew there was more to it than the omission of a name.

"Do you not see? I have a scandalous number of names. I shall simply omit one of them when it comes time to call the banns and we are saved. When my dearest mama returns home she can sue to have the marriage nullified on the grounds that the banns were not read properly."

"Your name?" Julian asked before he decided what to say in reply.

"Chloe Elizabeth Mary Susan Harriet Maitland," she cried with triumph. "Grandmama is Harriet, the rest are for all the rich old ladies in the family—those who lived at the time I was born. It was my papa's notion," she explained. "And it was frightfully effective, for most of them left me enormous sums of money in their wills."

Julian could not suppress the laugh that burst out at this revelation. Who would have thought Chloe could be so delightfully absurd.

"My dear Chloe," he began patiently at last, "there is little likelihood that an annulment might be granted."

Julian did not tell his betrothed that he, like many other young men of his position, had studied law. Not that he ever intended to assume the capacity of a lawyer or solicitor. The Inns of Court were much like a gentlemen's club and he enjoyed the company of intelligent friends while there. He had even bothered to write his exam, which most of those he knew had not.

It had been something to do to occupy his hours, and it had amused him as well as helped him to understand what was and was not permissible. He highly doubted this was permissible. Even Judge Sir William Scott was not likely to look favorably on this case, should it become one.

But, Julian considered with a thoughtful look at his charming bride-to-be, if Chloe continued to believe that it was possible she would also perpetuate the myth of their marriage, which he had decided would be a permanent one.

He admitted that he needed a wife—his father had been after him for some time and Julian had just learned that his parent was not in the best of health. That bothered him.

Also, Chloe was a delightful, rather special baggage, far from the plain child he had first thought her to be. Indeed, since he had been teaching her to flirt—something she did all too well now, considering her behavior last evening— she had blossomed into a truly charming and lovely young woman. She would most likely never have the raving beauty her aunt possessed. But she had integrity and a caring heart, both of which mattered far more to Julian.

"Well," he said in a considering way, "it is something to think about, certainly." He would have to find some way to allow Chloe to proceed with her scheme, yet make sure that their marriage was legal. It would not do to have problems later on—how the gossips would enjoy that! "Come, enjoy the morning and do not ruin our ride with such serious and depressing ideas."

"Oh, that reminds me," Chloe burst forth. "Speaking about depressing topics, I will be seeing Laura later this morning. I am most concerned with the way Lord Twisdale looks at her. He used to look at me just like that. Did you perchance notice?"

"Indeed," Julian said with a frown. "I cannot like the thought that Twisdale would pursue the lively Laura. No young woman should be subject to that threat," he added at the curious glance from Chloe that he did not miss. Could there be a spark of proprietary feeling there? He hoped so.

"We must do something," she declared firmly.

"I cannot see what," he replied with a grimace. "Lord Twisdale is not well liked, but one can hardly convict him of a crime when there has been no witness."

"That is it," Chloe cried, looking at Julian with great admiration. "How clever you are."

"I am?" Julian was thoroughly confused.

"Of course you are," she confirmed with a nod. The jaunty feathers in her little green hat quivered with about the same alarm that Julian felt.

"And that means?"

"We shall embark on a course of detection. If we can prove that Lord Twisdale *did* murder his wife, Laura and all other girls will be free of his threat. I could never stand idly by and see my dearest friend consigned to a brief life with him before a possible early demise."

"How do you propose to accomplish this?" Julian inquired, beginning to think that marriage with this delightful girl would not be dull at any rate.

"Well, we will have to think about that, naturally, but you are so clever, I have faith you will find a way," she concluded, beaming a trusting smile at him that made Julian feel quite ten feet tall.

"First you must warn Laura to be on her guard."

"Oh, she cannot abide the man, so there is little chance of his success as long as her mother does not take a notion that Lord Twisdale is an acceptable suitor." Chloe grimaced, feeling oddly in charity with the man she vowed to free of an unwanted marriage, even if it was to her.

"There is every likelihood of that, I fear," Julian said as they drew up alongside the Stanhope gate. He glanced to where the groom waited at a respectful distance. "I shall ride home with you, then perhaps seek an audience with your grandmother."

Chloe glanced at his riding clothes, then shook her head. "Later, perhaps after noontime. And dressed to impress her, please. There are all the other conditions of the marriage that she wishes to discuss with you."

"My solicitor will handle all those details," Julian said with a dismissive air.

"You do not know my grandmother very well, do you? She will also have her man of business there, so you had best be prepared." There was a note of warning in her voice that Julian did not miss.

"And where will you be, pray tell?" Julian knew it was not customary for the bride-to-be to have anything to do with the settlements. Indeed, even most grooms left it to their fathers and the solicitors to handle. He had been in charge of his own affairs too long to seek his father's help, but he wondered how Chloe viewed the matter.

"Between Grandmama and her lawyer, you will not find it easy going. I intend to do a bit of shopping, as is proper for a newly betrothed girl. Perhaps I may take Laura with me." Chloe flashed a gleam of sympathy at Julian as they drew to a halt before Dancy House.

"Remember that Grandmama is a dragon, and act accordingly." With that gentle hint, Chloe dismounted, then handed her mount to the groom.

"Oh," Julian said, bending down from his saddle to add one important bit of information, "I will instruct the jeweler to clean up the family engagement and wedding rings. I think they ought to fit your finger, for you are of a size with my late mother. I shall present the engagement ring to you at the first appropriate moment." He enjoyed the blush that bloomed across her face, adding a needed touch of color in the pale morning light.

"As you wish, Julian," she said, ducking her head so he lost sight of her expression. Drat, was she hiding her dismay? Or showing pleasure? He wished he knew.

Julian watched her enter the house with a bemused gaze. So much had happened in the last day he scarcely knew if he stood on his head or his heels. But one thing was certain, he had fallen into no bad situation through the maneuvering of two who sought to sow disaster. They may even have done him a favor.

Turning his horse in the direction of his modest city dwelling, he decided his first action would be to write his father. That done, he could confer with his solicitor, having sent off a message to that worthy gentleman first thing this morning.

While mounting the steps to his house, then strolling into his study he considered how pleased his father would be and grinned. Why, the old man might increase his funds even before the wedding. Not that Julian was anywhere near to being below the hatches. No, he'd invested his quarterly payments wisely, if discreetly, on the 'change. In fact, he was a wealthy young man if you added in the properties bequeathed to him by his mother and grandmother.

He did not need to marry for money, as did Sir Augustus Dabney. Which brought to mind another matter Julian wished to settle. Dabney ought to be made to see the error of his ways. His attempt to compromise Chloe had been a near thing. Although, Julian reflected, he supposed that any chap hard put for money needed to find an heiress if possible. On second thought, perhaps one could be found for him, a plain but worthy girl.

"I cannot fathom why Mr. St. Aubyn asked you to marry him, just like that," Laura said. "You are not plain—indeed, you have blossomed greatly as of late—but you are not a diamond of the first water, either. And you must know that he usually courts those fashionable widows."

"But gentlemen rarely marry those fashionable—and available—widows," Chloe reminded her friend.

"If you mean they are too available, I confess I do not know what that means. I heard Mama say that once, but it is Greek to me," Laura complained, then sipped her tea.

"Well, I suppose we will someday." Unable to conceal the truth from her dearest friend Chloe set her teacup on its saucer, then folded her hands in her lap. "You most likely wish to know the whole of it."

Not bothering to ask what "it" was, Laura nodded eagerly.

So Chloe quickly detailed the tale of how first Aunt Elinor tried to trap Chloe into marriage with Sir Augustus. Then, when St. Aubyn prevented that from taking place, he had found himself trapped instead.

"How dreadful," cried the romantic Laura. "I should not like to marry a man who is so reluctantly my groom."

Chloe did not say a word about the tender kiss, for that was far too precious to be bantered about, even to her best friend.

"Well, we have a plan, you see. If all goes well, we will be able to get an annulment once my mama comes back from her wedding trip."

"I think it is amusing . . . your mother and you both on wedding trips at the same time."

"Well," Chloe confided, "Julian and I plan to spend our time hunting for evidence of a murder."

Chapter 12

"*W*ith a scoundrel?" Laura shrieked.

"He will be my husband by then," Chloe gently reminded, settling on a comfortable chair near the window. She picked up a shawl to place about her shoulders when the wind outside caused a draft from the window.

"But who . . . why . . . how?" a confused Laura demanded.

"You know how I feared Lord Twisdale? Well, Julian and I feel strongly that he murdered his wife." Ignoring Laura's horrified gasp, Chloe forged on. "That is why you must do all you can to depress his interest—and you might try sneezing," Chloe inserted thoughtfully. "At any rate, there is absolutely no way of knowing unless we investigate. And what better to keep us occupied while in the country?"

"On your honeymoon?" Laura gave her friend a wryly skeptical look. "I was given to believe that a young couple had little difficulty in keeping occupied. Somehow, Mr. St. Aubyn seems rather inventive."

"Yes, well, perhaps. But you must have guessed that Julian does not truly wish to be married to me." Chloe nervously pleated the skirt of her fine green-print muslin gown. "He was excessively gallant when Grandmama confronted him in the Sefton library."

"He had no choice!" Laura exclaimed.

"Well, I must confess that I had far rather marry Julian than Sir Augustus, who was Aunt Elinor's choice," Chloe said in a vast understatement of the truth. Then she reflected, "Did you see how utterly furious she was when she discovered that Julian St. Aubyn stood at my side instead of the peacock?"

"Fancy being wed to that preening creature. I hope,"

Laura began, then hesitated. "That is, I trust you will be happy being married to Mr. St. Aubyn."

"As to that, time will tell, I suppose." Chloe rose from her chair to pace about the room. "Now that I am settled, as Grandmama is fond of saying, I am to have a splendid wedding gown. I will select something simple, for I have no wish to look silly. You well know what Society will say— that I have trapped a fine gentleman and that they expect him to plop me in the country while he gallivants about town. Why should I parade about in finery?"

"You want to look well."

"Julian," Chloe's cheeks turned a trifle pinker at the mere thought of him, "is coming over later to discuss the settlements, my jointure, and the like. He also said something about a family betrothal ring that I am to wear. Oh, Laura, it all seems so final."

"Soon you will be a wife and before long a mother," Laura said with a hint of envy in her voice.

At that bit of plain speaking, Chloe turned away, certain she must be as pink as a damask rose. However there truly was no need for blushing, for she would free St. Aubyn to go where he pleased. She would not be the mother of St. Aubyn's children.

The girls continued to discuss the wedding arrangements for some time, debating on what Chloe's grandmother might plan, for they both knew the old dragon would wish to foil gossip and do things up right.

"Thanks to Mrs. Robynhod I doubt we need to make an announcement," Chloe concluded sometime later.

"Mama said it was in the morning paper," Laura revealed. "St. Aubyn must have sent it over."

Chloe shook her head. "Not on your life. I fancy he keeps hoping something will happen to prevent the occasion from arising. Grandmama sent a notice off last night— even at that late hour. She wanted to get a march on the gossips." She exchanged a knowing look with her friend.

After promising to keep all they had discussed a deep secret—especially the part about Lord Twisdale murdering his wife—Laura slipped from the house. They had agreed to shop together if possible. One never knew about Mrs. Spayne.

Left alone with her unwelcome thoughts, Chloe wandered down to the ground floor, peeking out of the window at the passing carriages and wondering what the coming days might bring. When a carriage she recognized halted before Dancy House, she stiffened. Since it would not do to be found peering out at the passing scene, she quickly found her needlework and seated herself on a chair near the window so to take advantage of the light.

Scroggins ushered him in shortly.

"St. Aubyn," Chloe said in a soft cry. Her needlework forgotten, she rose to greet him.

"I thought we had agreed on Julian and Chloe," he retorted, striding across the room to reach her side. The heels of his Hessians made clicking sounds until he reached the soft plush of the Turkey carpet. Dressed in his customary gray coat, deep gray pantaloons, with a wine-and-gray weave waistcoat, he was all elegance and polish. And he looked rather formidable, promising to keep her grandmother in line. At least Chloe hoped so.

"It is difficult to be so informal when I have had otherwise drummed into my head for years. Julian. Is that better?" She could not resist his smile and looked at him with more affection than she had intended.

"I like the way you say my name," he said by way of reply. He bent over her hand, lingering close to her side as though he wished to do something more. "And I like your scent of heliotrope. I shall buy you gallons of it so you may bathe in the stuff."

"Sir, you put me to the blush." Chloe tugged at her hand, confused by his warm look and flustered at his mention of so intimate a subject as bathing.

"Ah, my little maiden," he said with a chuckle. Then he dug into his pocket to pull out a small velvet box. "The ring," he explained unnecessarily.

Chloe bit her lip, wondering why she felt so strange. Normally this would be a binding act, putting on the betrothal ring. Yet, in spite of the fact she intended to set him free, a part of her wished that she would truly be his wife. What a pity she loved him so dearly.

He removed from the box a simple gold ring ablaze with a fine emerald in its setting. "A ring has no beginning and no end, it represents eternity, perfection, and unity," he said quietly, as though making a vow. Slipping it onto her finger and seeming satisfied with the fit, he then tilted up her chin with one finger. "And we shall seal that with a kiss of promise."

There was no way that Chloe could have joked her way out of this predicament if she had wanted to. Before she chanced to reply, he had gently touched her vulnerable mouth with his warm lips. Chloe was sunk without firing a shot.

She could not prevent her trembling, for he had that effect on her. She acknowledged that it might not be so bad a thing to have a husband as skilled in kissing as Julian. Then, forgetting all about her resolves to the contrary, she abandoned herself to his delicious expertise, wrapping her arms about him, threading the fingers of one hand into his hair, so she might not disgrace herself with revealing her weakening knees. And she would consign all thought of odious Aunt Elinor to the refuse heap.

Julian reveled in the innocent response of his little bride-to-be. How different her eager kisses were from Elinor's practiced wiles. When he sensed a faint withdrawal in Chloe, he pulled away to study her flushed, rosy face.

"What happened just now? What thought came into your head?" he gently demanded, not releasing her, for who knew what notions she had, or when someone might come to interrupt them.

"Are you a mind reader in addition to all your other abilities?" she blurted out.

He gave her a little shake. "I would know this. Humor me?"

She looked away from him, withdrawing from his light clasp. He watched her walk across to stare out of the window and his heart sank a trifle.

"You were very close to my Aunt Elinor, I know." With a glance back at him she shook her head, adding, "I do not wish to know precisely how close, sir, but . . . she is very beautiful and no doubt skilled in the art of lovemaking. Whereas I am a rather green girl and do not know how to please an experienced man such as you."

He made an effort to deny her words, taking a step in her direction, but she stopped him with a wave of her hand.

"Perhaps—if we are to plan for an annulment—we had best leave off such delightful things as kissing. Once the omission in the banns is revealed, you will be free—free to go your way as you please." She gave him a frank smile, one a trifle sad at the corners. Her lovely greenish blue eyes met his gaze briefly before skittering away to focus on the blank wall.

Julian froze in his steps, deeply touched. She was the first woman he had known who was willing to place him before herself and her wants. All the others had made seemingly insatiable demands on him—for his gifts, his time, and most of all, himself. All Chloe desired was to set him free to be and do what he wished. And he found that he knew not the least desire to be free of this charming girl.

But, how to convince her of that?

"Your Aunt Elinor is beautiful, I'll admit. However I have no desire to spend the rest of my life with her. I think you and I might rub along tolerably well together." He wanted to express his true feelings for Chloe, but how on earth could she accept what he said when he had been with her aunt not so very long ago? And she well knew it!

No, they would proceed with the wedding and he could take his time convincing Chloe that he loved her quite madly. Why, he would have all the time he needed at his disposal and she would then be his.

"Speaking of that, I thought perhaps we could go to my estate in the country for our honeymoon," he ventured to offer.

The sight of her pretty pink cheeks amused him when she replied, "I thought that was what we had agreed we might do—so as to hunt down the clues to the real reason Lord Twisdale's wife died," Chloe said with an obvious attempt at being serious.

Julian was about to reject that idea when the thought suddenly struck him that it would be a clever way to disarm Chloe, to keep her so occupied that she would have no idea what he was up to—namely persuading her to fall in love with him.

"Ah, you think he killed her. How?"

Diverted from her forthcoming marriage for a moment, she took a step closer to Julian. "Well, how does one go about eliminating an unwanted wife?"

"How should I know? I don't have one," Julian teased.

"You will," she reminded him. "What about arsenic—is it not called inheritance powder for good reason?"

"As to that there are a number of herbs I have read about that are most effective poisons and leave little trace of their presence." Julian considered the idea she presented. "Although if he were cruel, he would not worry overmuch about that, would he?"

"Remind me not to displease you, sir," she said with a lift of her brows.

"You brought the subject up, if you recall," he reminded.

"Well, it is something to keep us busy while away."

Julian was about to inform the pert Lady Chloe that he had more interesting ideas about how to occupy their time when Scroggins entered the room, coughing discreetly against his gloved hand.

"If you please, sir, the Dowager Lady Dancy will see you now. She wished to know if your solicitor is to be with you."

Julian glanced at the long-case clock by the door. "He ought to be here any minute. Show him to me when he arrives." When Scroggins had bowed his way from the room, Julian turned to Chloe.

"I will protect you well, although I daresay your grandmother, being the dragon she is, will make that effort quite unnecessary." He took her hand, raised it to his lips to place a lingering kiss on her palm, then strode from the room.

Chloe stood where he left her, unable to move if she tried. Her nerves felt as though she might shatter if the slightest breeze touched her.

"Oh blast!" she declared, then fled from the room to the entry hall.

"I require the carriage, Scroggins," she rashly declared in spite of her grandmother's injunctions against her use of the same. She hoped to arrive at Laura's house before they could leave. Mrs. Spayne was always slow to depart for shopping, what with making list after list. Of course that was in the event Laura had persuaded her mama to go shopping in the first place.

They could go to Madame Clotilde's to order Chloe's wedding gown. There was much to do and her grandmother showed little inclination to help her, at least with her clothing and all the other little things desirable for a wedding.

At the Spaynes', Laura expressed her eagerness to go with Chloe. Her mother offered to join the girls when Chloe explained that Lady Dancy met with the lawyers over the settlements. She did so in lieu of a father, which Chloe didn't have at the moment.

"If you please, ma'am," Chloe said with gratitude. It would have been nice to have her own mama, and since Grandmama was a dragon she would accept help from Mrs. Spayne.

Madame Clotilde did not appear to be surprised in the least when Chloe made her request for a simple wedding gown. No doubt Mrs. Robynhod had been busy, or perhaps the mantuamaker read the announcement in the morning paper.

By the end of the afternoon Chloe had ordered her gown, found a lovely pair of satin slippers with tiny white bows on them, and a fragile white bonnet tied with pale blue satin ribbon just perfect for a wedding. New gloves, a lace reticule, and a soft satin sleeveless pelisse in heliotrope lined with delicate gold completed her preparations.

After depositing Mrs. Spayne and Laura at their home, she sank into a reflection. How had Julian managed with her grandmother and the lawyer? He would give as good as he got, she decided with satisfaction. Even if it meant a diminishing of her own interests, she wanted him to assert himself.

Surely he would take care to see that the annulment would not tangle their affairs for ages, would he not? She wondered at the gleam she sometimes caught in his eyes. Or was that usual for a scoundrel? She had once told him he was no such thing. But in her heart she confessed not only that he most likely was a scoundrel, but she found she had a decided weakness for a scoundrel. And that he must never know.

* * *

On the first Sunday of the reading of the banns Chloe sat in the family pew and listened with a trembling heart. "Lady Chloe Elizabeth Susan Harriet Maitland" rang ominously in her ears. Was there anyone who knew the truth? Could anyone guess she omitted one of her names so as to create a charge of fraud? This would result in a scandal, she supposed, but one could overcome that. Surely it was preferable to being married to one who disliked you.

Grandmama had grumbled in confusion, wondering aloud if that was correct, and why her daughter had given so many names to a chit in the first place.

It sounded so official, like a prophet of doom. She glanced across to where she knew the St. Aubyn pew was located, but did not see Julian there. The sermon dealt with the importance of truth and the danger of listening to false teachers. When the bishop who delivered the message said, "If you can persuade someone to doubt you, it will lead to unbelief," Chloe stirred on her cushioned pew.

Her mind had wandered off to the country and the peculiar death of young Lady Twisdale. Perhaps if they might plant doubt regarding the veracity of his lordship they might also be led to the truth of the matter, namely who assisted Lord Twisdale in eliminating his wife.

Chloe doubted he had done the deed alone, he seemed too lofty for that incriminating task. Which meant he had to have an accomplice. And, knowing full well that in the small country village little goes on that is missed by at least one of the inhabitants, the clue could be there—just waiting.

Whenever her thoughts went to what might have been—and the knowledge that it could have been Lord Twisdale's name linked with hers this morning when the curate read the banns—she felt chilled.

When Julian had discovered that Lady Twisdale had tried to run away, Chloe knew more than ever before that not only must she avoid marrying this man, but she must try to save her dearest friend from the same fate. Laura might have her hands full fending off his lordship, for he was a persistent man. Chloe wondered if either he or Aunt

Elinor would attend her wedding and decided it made little difference.

That afternoon, St. Aubyn came to call.

Chloe rose from where she was resigned to doing her needlework—a chair seat done in Hungarian stitch using deep greens and blues. One did nothing much on a Sunday in her grandmother's house. It was tediously boring but had the benefit that she had accomplished more needlework since arriving in London than in a long time back in Wiltshire.

"Julian," she exclaimed with pleasure when he entered the room, Scroggins having retreated to his customary place somewhere near the front door. "I did not see you this morning and decided you had left town." Or something equally serious, her tone implied.

"I arrived late and stood in the back. Are you more accepting of our coming marriage now that the first of the banns have been called?" he inquired with an intent study of her face. He reached out to touch an errant curl that had somehow managed to stand up and was quite out of place.

"Accepting?" Chloe met his look of regard with a wary gaze. "I made a promise to you, sir. I will not back out of that. I feel certain my mama will assist us, when she learns the entire story. There is no accepting involved, is there?" She gave him a candid look, wondering if the coming marriage was very dreadful for him. Acquiring the annulment might not be a simple task—cases could take a frightfully long time to be heard and decided in the Consistory Court. Of course, if he knew someone . . .

He gave her an odd look, then drew her along to sit on the sofa. Chloe perched as far from him as possible, uncomfortably aware of him and his intense maleness. He exuded a raw sort of power over her that frightened as well as fascinated her. For all that he was gentle and tender in his actions and words, she detected something that lay beneath his manner—something compelling. She dared not come too close to him or his attraction could lead her to behaving like an utter peagoose.

"Nice weather," she chirped.

"If one considers a day turned dreary and misty as nice,

then it is," he said with an amused expression. He reached out to pick up her hand, touching the ring on her finger.

"Sirrah," she cautioned, "it is not seemly for us to sit here like this, even if we are betrothed."

"Call your maid to sit by the door," he said, unsettling her completely with that smoldering look of his.

"I believe you are excessively mischievous," she cried, jumping up as though his touch singed her. "And I suspect you enjoy teasing me." .

"I still believe we will rub together tolerably well once married," he said, easing back against the sofa and looking far too enticing for Chloe's peace of mind.

When the dowager walked into the room Chloe gave mental thanks, for she had discovered that she was far and away too susceptible to Julian St. Aubyn.

"Well, St. Aubyn, I heard you had come to call," the dowager announced with definite disapproval in her voice.

"Yes, ma'am." He politely rose from the sofa and bowed to Lady Dancy with utter correctness.

"Cancel the horse race, did they?" The dowager settled on the sofa where Chloe had perched not long before. Julian looked distinctly ill at ease, a reaction Chloe would not have thought possible.

"Race on a Sunday, ma'am? Hardly."

"If you are trying to convince me that you are a saint in nature as well as name, you may as well forget it. Anyone who dallies with Elinor Hadlow cannot lay claim to any such thing."

Chloe felt a warmth creep over her face and neck. Why did her grandmother harp on that subject? Was she perhaps trying to push Chloe into crying off, of handing the mitten to St. Aubyn so she could compel Chloe to marry Lord Twisdale? She had no illusions about her dear grandmother. The old lady was entirely too fond of having her own way.

Well, she would find that Chloe was now made of sterner stuff. "Grandmama, I feel certain that Julian would rather not discuss Aunt Elinor. Indeed, I am not fond of that topic, either. She is scarcely my favorite relative."

Chloe sensed, rather than saw, the look of surprise Julian gave her.

The afternoon call went downhill from there. When Julian left, Chloe saw him to the door, then returned to face her grandmother.

"He wishes to take me for a drive if the weather improves."

"I doubt it will. But if you desire to drive out with that scoundrel, who am I to deny you."

"I should not wish to displease you," Chloe retorted, much goaded by her grandmother's wicked behavior.

"Ha! If you wished to please me, you would have accepted Lord Twisdale in the first place."

Vexed and unable to denounce Lord Twisdale to a woman who had set her mind in a particular direction, Chloe returned to her needlework, stabbing the canvas with her needle in her frustration.

"I believe I shall make up a theater party for Tuesday. I will invite Lord Twisdale and Miss Spayne. Even if you are a foolish girl, Mrs. Spayne seems to have sufficient influence on her daughter so that Miss Spayne will do as told." The dowager picked up her book of improving sermons and commenced to read.

Left to her thoughts, Chloe knew she must warn Laura about the added menace of Lady Dancy's involvement. It was too bad that most every girl must marry where her parents ordered.

The clock ticked away the minutes into the silence of the room, disturbed only by the turning of pages and the rustle of the canvas while Chloe stitched. She glanced out from time to time to see the mist still swirling about the street, moisture dripping from the trees. She would not drive out with St. Aubyn today.

"Best go to your room and prepare for the evening. You have not forgotten that we go to supper at Lady Edgecumbe's this evening?"

Chloe's heart sank, for her grandmother belonged to a Bluestocking set which met all too frequently, it seemed to Chloe.

She obediently left the room, but vowed that first thing in the morning she would be off to see Laura. It was small comfort that she had a friend in whom to confide. It would be terrible if her grandmother were instrumental in the ultimate death of her friend—as Lord Twisdale's second wife.

It was not to be that easy. Since her grandmother refused to discuss business on Sunday—and that included the plans for the upcoming wedding—she summoned Chloe at an early hour on Monday morning for her decree.

After revealing her plans for the intimate ball and supper party she intended to give Chloe—paid for out of Chloe's funds, naturally—she stared at her granddaughter.

"You seem to accept your fate."

"It is well I do, for there is no choice, is there?" Chloe said meekly before leaving the room.

Within fewer days than she would have believed, the moment for her betrothal supper and ball had arrived.

St. Aubyn's father arrived early with him and Chloe could see that Julian's charm was most assuredly inherited.

"Lady Chloe, I am well pleased with my son's choice of bride," he said, studying her from eyes quite like Julian's. With a twinkle creeping into them, he added, "It is about time he settled down. By his age I had a fine son."

"St. Aubyn, you put her to the blush," Grandmother said, for once speaking quietly.

After that bit of teasing, nothing could upset her in the least, not even when Julian took her by her hand to lead her out in the first dance following the agreeable supper party.

The strains of the prerequisite minuet began to drift over the modestly filled room. Julian took her properly gloved hand into his and led her through the figures of the dance, gracefully bowing and twirling about in stately decorum. She fluttered her lashes at him when she thought her grandmother was not watching.

"Baggage," he whispered as he drew her close in one of the figures.

"You would not wish me to use my fan, surely," she countered with a smile.

"I shall make a point to win on the score of flirting," he shot back when next he came close to her.

Chloe shivered with delighted anticipation.

Once the dance was over, Chloe was besieged with partners, all mostly friends of Julian's. Theo was first and when they joined in a rousing reel, he commented, "I daresay you will be a good influence on him."

"Never say so." Chloe could not help but laugh at the image of her schooling St. Aubyn into a model husband. Yet there was a little ache in her heart for she knew that all this fuss was really for nothing. As soon as her mama returned . . .

And then she was bidding her guests farewell.

Grandmother had cornered the elder St. Aubyn in the corner—no doubt complaining of his son's shrewd bargaining at the settlement table. They were still chatting when the last guest left the house. Chloe debated on whether to say anything, then turned to Julian.

"I will go up to my room now, for I am tired—as you must be. I trust you can convince your father and my grandmother that the hour is late. Our wedding is tomorrow and I would look well for it." She avoided meeting his gaze, for he had said nothing about how they were to resolve the matter of the annulment. She had done her part, and set the stage for a charge of fraud.

"You may be certain that you will look as pretty as any flower blooming," Julian said with charm and grace.

"Well, as to that, I hope I do not sneeze. Would that not be dreadful? I, Chloe, take thee, sneeze?"

Julian murmured something in agreement, then watched his bride-to-be resolutely march up the stairs.

Hours, she had said. *Today,* he knew, after a glance at the longcase clock in the entry hall. He slowly made his way down the stairs from the drawing room to the front door after nudging his father into making his adieus. Candles were being snuffed, oil lamps put out, and servants preparing for the night.

"It will not be long now, my boy. I cannot deny it pleases me to see you settled with such a modest girl, who comes not only from a fine family but with a fine fortune as well. I must confess, you surprised me," the elder St. Aubyn declared. "I had heard of your attention to Mrs. Hadlow and feared she might dig her claws into you. Instead you produce a wonder."

"Who also happens to be Mrs. Hadlow's niece," Julian added quietly with a look at his father.

"Oh, ho!" St. Aubyn senior said in bemusement.

And, Julian added to himself, I will have a wife who cannot wait to be rid of me.

Chapter 13

*L*ord Twisdale thought he might be forgiven if his smile was a trifle smug. Oh, what exquisite retribution for the young woman who had rejected him to be forced to wed a man who must detest her in every way. Although, Twisdale admitted, she looked rather well today. Couldn't put his finger on it, but she seemed to have acquired a sort of glow about her. Most likely the light in the church. He shifted about to see a trifle better and noted the bored expression on St. Aubyn's face. The man appeared ready to bolt.

Well, she deserved a fellow like St. Aubyn, one who'd go haring off after another woman as soon as the ink was dry on the church register. Little to detain the scoundrel at the side of that dab of a girl who had the nerve to draw a man of his own stature as a serpent.

A twinge of unease flickered through him at the notion that some protective parent might snoop around his past. Then he dismissed the thought as stupid.

Oh, no, Lady Chloe would receive precisely what she deserved. But, Twisdale admitted ruefully, he would have liked the taming of the girl. He would have relished subduing that spirit that had dared to ridicule Society with those wicked sketches.

However, and his gaze shifted to the sparkling girl dressed in pale pink who stood attendant to Lady Chloe, the little friend showed possibilities. Lucky for him that his title, wealth, and those convenient country homes could most likely win him what he wanted. Anne, that worthless girl he had married, had been weak and foolish. Laura Spayne looked to be a spirited survivor, and that seemed most promising. He found a woman of spirit intriguing.

Elinor Hadlow glanced at the man on the other side of

the church and shivered at the evil smile that had settled on his face. Twisdale, the old bore, must be giving rein to some particularly nasty thoughts at the moment.

Well, she had a few of her own. Her hands clenched as she considered how her carefully laid plans had gone awry. Who would have thought that St. Aubyn would have been caught in the trap she set for Lady Chloe and that idiot Sir Augustus! Fury swept through Elinor when she considered that Chloe would be wearing the St. Aubyn jewels, gracing the St. Aubyn tables, and worst of all, sharing St. Aubyn's bed.

He looked far too handsome in those biscuit breeches, white hose that clung to well-formed legs, and the deep gray coat that needed no padding to appear impressive. His only touch of color was a rich gold waistcoat from which hung a single fob of discreet dull gold. He would be utterly wasted on her niece, poor innocent.

Well, Elinor soothed herself, it would not be long before Julian would deposit that young thing at one of his estates in the country and return to more mature pleasures in the city. Although, she decided, it would not be to her.

She must consider her future. Glancing about the church, she contemplated the potential of a half dozen of Julian's cronies. There were one or two who looked to be promising. She must begin immediately. Her looking glass was reflecting more wrinkles every week, it seemed.

Julian stood uneasily before the altar, assuming a bland expression. He had thought he would be sleepy, given the late hour he went to bed. He was wide awake, and fully aware of the fraud he was perpetrating with the pretty girl at his side. Fraud! What would she say and do when he finally had the nerve to tell her the truth?

Chloe shifted nervously while repeating her vows. She had not expected to feel so guilty about this all. Repeating her names—minus the one—had seemed a simple ruse when she first thought about it. Now there were grave undertones. She was declaring before God and the assembled people—particularly her grandmother—her vow to remain with this man for the rest of her life. And she had not the least intention of keeping that vow.

How wicked she was. Yet, in spite of her love for Julian,

she could not tie him to her when it was all a ghastly mistake, a vicious scheme gone awry. She vividly recalled his denouncement of Aunt Elinor, how he would do anything to avoid falling into her trap. He had not figured on the supreme escape—marrying someone else.

Merely standing at his side made her weak with longing. How would she survive weeks—months—close to him? She had to plan something. Perhaps the investigation of the murder would serve as the needed diversion. She could only hope so.

Julian repeated his vows with a strong desire that both he and Chloe meant their pledge. That is to say, he did, but he knew the dear girl at his side was contemplating just how long it could be before she instigated the annulment. Did she have someone else in mind? He considered all the chaps he knew who had dangled after her and could only think of Theo.

Could it be Theo? He turned his head slightly to catch a glimpse of his groomsman. No way to tell, unfortunately. But he would keep a sharp eye on any and all who sought her side. He needed time—time to convince her that his love was genuine and that life with him would not be so very bad.

And then the ceremony was over and done. They left the altar to enter the chamber where the church register was kept. Julian signed his name with a flourish and then studied her signature. Lady Chloe Elizabeth Susan Harriet Maitland. Was that the same group of names that had been announced during the reading of the banns? It would be ironic if she omitted the wrong name this time.

The bishop beamed a fatherly smile at them and said, "Julian St. Aubyn and Lady Chloe St. Aubyn, I wish you many years of wedded happiness. May you be blessed with children to cheer your old age."

Chloe swallowed carefully at the mention of children. She had avoided that topic in all conversations with her grandmother, figuring that it was quite pointless. Now, darting a sideways look at a very virile Julian, she was wondering if she would have been well to ask a few trenchant questions. Silly, she rebuked herself. He no doubt is panting at the thought of leaving me in the country and returning to the pleasures of the city.

So, she placed her prettily gloved hand trustingly on his arm and together they left the vestry where the church register was kept. Her lie—the incomplete signature and her knowledge that the banns had been incorrectly called—left behind them. The deed had been done.

The Dowager Lady Dancy grimly noted the angelic expression on her granddaughter's face and wondered. Well, her mind was at ease. She had accomplished what her daughter wished—namely that a fine husband be found for Chloe so that when Isobel and her new husband returned from their honeymoon there would be nothing to mar their peace and comfort. Silly woman. Isobel could have had much pleasure from seeing her only daughter married and happily settled.

As to happy, the dowager amended her thoughts slightly. One never knew with a scoundrel like St. Aubyn. It might be heaven and it might be the opposite. For Chloe's sake, she hoped it would be tolerable.

Chloe and Julian exited the church into the morning sunshine, smiling at the cluster of women and children who lurked about the porch and steps. Some of the children threw flower petals at Chloe while she waited to enter the carriage and she flashed an amused look up at Julian.

Her husband.

There was no turning back now. Keeping a cool head might not be easy, but it was imperative for the success of their plan.

They both settled onto the cushions, as wary as a pair of strange dogs in new territory. Julian rubbed his hands together, then studied Chloe. He began his strategy, one planned with the carefulness of a general.

He fussed about her, tucking a pillow behind her, seeing that she was comfortable, all the while touching her here and there and taking notice that it seemed to fluster her greatly. "Our kiss at the church was most proper, would you not agree?"

Aware that if he had kissed her as he had other times all her resolve would have washed down the drain, Chloe gave him a hesitant smile. "Indeed, it is a private matter, and ought not be done while in public."

Since this is what Julian had expected she might say, he repressed a smile, then swiftly and very smoothly drew her into his arms. In short order he expertly kissed his bride to his own satisfaction—and he hoped hers. When he drew back, he looked down at her bemused expression and felt he had achieved a measure of success. His first step in correcting matters as they stood.

"Goodness, my bonnet," she squeaked in a breathless little voice.

He adjusted her dainty little head covering, noting the touch of blue ribbon under the brim. "Something blue?"

"Laura brought it for me to use. She is very sentimental."

"Seems a shame that Twisdale has his eye on her."

As the carriage drew up before the Dancy house, Chloe placed a hand on Julian's arm, a frown creasing her brow. "We must not allow this. Once we are in the country we will hunt for clues—although if he poisoned her it may be impossible to discover the truth of her death."

"Later, my dear. For now we must portray the happy bride and groom."

Chloe nodded and accepted his hand after he had climbed down from the carriage. When he tucked her little hand close to his body, she wished she might bolt and run off, or perhaps merely be brave enough to walk on her own, without his assistance over the cobbles.

Lady Dancy had surprised both Chloe and Julian by offering to provide a reception for the invited guests. Scroggins stood by the door, his sour-lemon face for once looking halfway agreeable as he ushered in the bride the groom, then those who followed.

Laura and Theo entered immediately after Chloe and Julian and looked to be in complete charity with each other. Lady Dancy chatted with the senior St. Aubyn, quizzing him about the condition of the country estate where Chloe and St. Aubyn would retreat for their honeymoon.

"Honeymoon! Such a ridiculous term," she declared while casting a skeptical gaze on the pair in question.

"A time of tenderness and adjustment to one another, or so I thought," the elder St. Aubyn said. "You have doubts?"

"Actually they may do well enough together, if they can overcome the first few hurdles." She exchanged a look full of meaning with the gentleman, leaving him slightly perplexed. When she sailed off to tend to a newly arrived guest his curiosity was left unsatisfied.

Since it was an early morning wedding, the reception did not last much past noon. Before she knew it Chloe found it was time to change into her traveling dress. Laura came up to assist her, although Ellen did the actual work. Laura was more inclined to chatter.

Once dressed, Chloe turned to her friend, "Do I look well enough? I am such a plain little thing. I do not know how St. Aubyn will adjust to me on his arm when he has had my gorgeous aunt there."

"Does it bother you to know that he was so close to your aunt?" Laura said with a delicate hesitancy. Had the girls not been such very dear friends, the words would not have been spoken at all.

Chloe fixed her gaze on her gloved hands, fidgeting with the reticule she had picked up at the very last. "Of course it does. I cannot help but wonder if he compares me to her when he looks at me. My kiss cannot be as practiced as hers, nor do I have her skills—whatever they might be. However, she proved unacceptable, so much so that he turned to me in many ways before that disastrous confrontation in the Seftons' library. If I do not do anything stupid, we may rub along together tolerably well for the time required."

"I do not envy you, dear Chloe, and I so wanted to," Laura said, dabbing her eyes with her handkerchief.

"Well, perhaps I will be cheering at your wedding one of these days," Chloe replied with a heartiness obviously not felt.

"Indeed," Laura said with a watery chuckle. "But know this, my best of all friends, there is nothing about you that is plain. I must say, you look quite delicious in that dark green with the pale blue trim. What an interesting combination of colors and such a dashing design. I vow, Madame Clotilde is worth every penny you pay her."

With that happy thought, Chloe lightly walked down the

stairs to greet Julian, who waited with more patience than she would have expected.

The ride from London and out through the country was tension-filled. Chloe kept wondering if Julian was again going to kiss her, or touch her as he had before the reception. When he did not do either, she wondered what had happened to change him.

Julian was all courtesy to her when they came to halt for the night at a comfortable-looking inn on the road north. He helped her from the traveling coach and into the inn, where they were given the best of rooms to be had, or so the landlord proclaimed.

They mounted the stairs together. Chloe wondered what would follow and little fears began to dance through her mind.

While there had been nothing said about consummating the marriage—for it was her understanding that it made no difference whether consummation (how frightening that sounded) occurred or not when it came to the annulment, which seemed quite odd to her—he had not indicated he intended to proceed with it. Whatever *it* involved. Chloe had not the least notion of married life, for her papa had died so very long ago and her mama had showed no interest in another man until the earl came along.

Chloe was indeed a green girl.

When Julian entered the neat little sitting room from the bedroom he adopted as his, Chloe turned to him and brought matters to a head. "How vexing this must be for you, Julian. Saddled with an inexperienced girl who does not know the first thing about married life or what is entailed." She twisted her hands together, the only sign of her unease.

He gave her a surprised look. Crossing the room to her side, he studied her anxious face for a few moments, then gestured to a nearby chair.

"Sit down. I expect the sooner we discuss this the better you will sleep at night."

After a look at his face, Chloe abruptly sank on the chair without more than a glance at it. "Well?" Her hopeful gaze was nearly his undoing.

"Ours is a most unusual marriage," Julian began, starting

to walk back and forth with his hands behind his back. "I appreciate your sensitivity to the circumstances and would not for the world upset you. I must say," he added in an aside, pausing to look at her again, "I am surprised that you wish to discuss it at all, considering that you are intent upon an annulment."

Chloe made little noises that could have been anything, but made not the least sense. Finally, her gaze fixed on the floor, she blurted, "I read that it does not make any difference to an annulment whether consummation occurs or not. I wished to know what to expect." She could feel the heat in her face at this bit of plain speaking. Where the nerve to say such words came from she did not know.

"I see. And what do you wish?" he said with grave courtesy.

Chloe looked up at him with wide eyes and bravely said, "I should like to spend time with you, if I may. Perhaps we might be friends for the time we are together?" The matter of consummation was left suspended.

Julian fought the urge to laugh. She wanted to spend time with him? Be friends? He cleared his throat of a sudden obstruction and said, "I think that is a very excellent idea. What a wise young woman you are." He was rewarded by a brilliant smile and an instantly relaxed girl.

"So, I will order us up a fine supper and we can spend time visiting. Tell me, what sort of books do you enjoy? We never seemed to find the time to discuss our reading habits in all that has gone on to date."

Julian plunked himself on a matching chair that also faced the fireplace, turning so that he faced her. When he saw she fingered the buttons of the lightweight pelisse she still wore, he was up again and at her side.

"Let me help you, my dear. Ellen is busy sorting out your things in the next room, is she not? This room is very warm, even with the windows open. Shall I call for lemonade?" He slid his hands over her shoulders to ease off the garment, taking note of her heightened color at his touch.

"Lemonade? That sounds lovely," she stammered. Chloe half rose to assist in removing her offending pelisse, then abruptly sat down again once it had been whisked away.

Julian went to tug at the bellpull, then gave orders for not only the lemonade but a fine supper as well. When he returned, he found her smiling. "Pleased?"

"Yes, well, I think we may do well enough."

"Indeed." Julian sat down, relaxed against his chair, and smiled.

And it did go well enough. They managed tolerably well through dinner and when they retired for the night Chloe paused long enough to thank Julian for his indulgence of her whims.

"Never fear," she said in a confiding manner, "we shall find our way out of this predicament one way or another."

As the door closed behind her, Julian stood musing on her words. And then he grinned. Indeed they would find their way—but perhaps not quite as she envisioned.

The following day was all amity between them, although the weather turned nasty. A mist fell, making the road a sea of water-filled holes and muddy ruts. When they straggled through the gates of a well-tended avenue Chloe exclaimed with relief.

"We are at Aubynwood. This is to be our home, my dear," Julian said, opening his window to look over the fields they passed. Things looked to be in fair condition, better than he expected after his stay in London. His father had been reluctant to allow Julian a say in managing the estates until Julian had badgered him to permit the control of one of the minor estates to be his own.

"You said this is your own house, not your father's?"

"He has deeded the place to me—it is not entailed."

"That means?"

"That if I have no heir, my widow could remain here as long as she wished. I have a distant cousin who is my heir at present. Fortunately he is in good health and pocket, so I need not fear him."

Chloe shivered at the thought of death, for it lurked about them all too often. "Well, it will be interesting to see what we may learn about Lord Twisdale's first wife. It is very hard to prove a poisoning in court?"

"Next to impossible." Julian had decided to confide the information about his reading law to Chloe, with the hope it might prepare her to better accept the coming news. He knew that sooner or later he must tell her.

The traveling coach came to a halt before the main entrance to the house. There was no sign of life, most likely because of the weather being what it was. The house sat on a rise with a view of a lake on the far side. Today the wind whipped at the branches of the oaks and birch and the rain nearly obscured the lake.

"It must be a pretty place when the sun shines."

"I like it," he said with clear satisfaction in his voice.

Chloe was surprised that the scoundrel of London should care about his estate other than as a source of ready money to use for gambling and high living.

The door swung open and a spare, tall man bowed to them. "Sir and my lady. Welcome to Aubynwood."

"What a lovely name," Chloe exclaimed with delight, quite capturing the hearts of all in the room.

The entry seemed vast to Chloe, with columns marching around the edge of the room and niches holding statues that appeared to be bronzes. Delicate plasterwork and a fine fireplace surround that looked to be the work of Robert Adam caught her eye. Shades of rose and gray contrasting with the white marble pleased the eye, and she liked her first glimpse of her new home.

"This is Godfrey, my dear. He presides over the house when I am absent," Julian said at her side.

Chloe shook hands with suitable gravity, murmuring her "I am pleased to meet you" with proper restraint.

Around the entry room ranged the smallish staff. Housekeeper, cook, footmen, housemaids, grooms, and a few others who could be anything stood at attention while Julian introduced them to Chloe. Again he surprised her by knowing each and every name.

"Rogers will be here later on this week. He is my agent and oversees operations of the land."

Chloe began to suspect there was a great deal more to the estate than she had been told.

They left the assembled servants and walked up the stairs. They paused outside the third door.

"This will be your room." He showed her inside, placing a casual arm about her shoulders while pointing out the beautiful—and vast—bed, and pretty cherrywood dressing table in front of the window, and the large armoire for her clothes.

Through an open doorway Chloe caught sight of a charming sitting room with more of the delicate plaster-work done in white with blue walls and a rich carpet. The furniture looked comfortable, the sort in which one might truly relax. On one wall hung a painting of a boy and Chloe guessed it to be of her husband. It was a handsome, wistful boy with beautiful eyes and a beguiling smile.

"We will share this room for our quiet moments," Julian said, trailing his fingers down her arm.

Chloe trembled at his light caress. The days ahead looked to be quite intriguing.

The following week passed most agreeably. Ellen settled into the new house and staff with scarcely a ripple.

The tensions that Chloe had felt the day of their wedding dissipated somewhat. Nevertheless it remained to some degree, lingering in the air, haunting her when her husband touched her—which he seemed to do very frequently. At first these little touches had disturbed her, sending her pulse racing and color rising.

Now—well, Chloe admitted that she still remained acutely conscious of his presence and even more of his touch. But she was becoming accustomed to it.

One day about a week after their arrival Chloe came down to breakfast with a purposeful stride. She entered the family dining room, concentrating on the man who sat at the linen-covered table.

"And what do you plan that lures you so strongly, my dear," Julian inquired from behind the newspaper that had arrived the evening before.

Chloe sank onto the chair closest to him, propping her chin on her hands. "I think it is time we go detecting. I had a letter from Laura and it is clear to me that she is being pursued by Lord Twisdale even as I was. Could we begin today? The weather is pleasant, there is nothing pressing, for I asked Godfrey."

"Covered all bases, I see."

Chloe gave him a confused look, not understanding his slang, but persisted. "I think it important. After all, I could have been his wife by now and I shudder at the thought. I would not have Laura trapped into that state."

"Do you feel trapped, my dear? It would not be surprising considering the nature of our betrothal and marriage." He looked concerned, perhaps angry.

She glanced at him in alarm. "I may have felt trapped at first," she said carefully, "but no longer. Were Lord Twisdale as considerate as you, there would be no dilemma. Somehow I do not believe he would be a caring person."

"I doubt few men would accept our situation, if truth be told," he murmured. At least that was what Chloe thought he said but was unwilling to ask for a repetition of his words. They brought back that heart-pounding sensation again and she licked her lips nervously.

"Eat some breakfast while I make arrangements."

Left to herself Chloe managed to eat a respectable meal. By the time Julian rejoined her she felt ready to face anything. Almost anything, she amended when she looked up from her teacup to see him standing in the doorway.

His handsome good looks still had the power to take her breath away. That he should prove so considerate almost unnerved her, for she had not expected the scoundrel to treat her thus.

"Coming." She set down her cup with a clink on the pretty china she enjoyed so much. Then with a whirl of skirts, she slipped past Julian into the entry hall where Godfrey waited with her pelisse.

Julian drove in the gig, that useful little carriage that most country folk employed to dash about the lanes. Chloe clung to the sides when he feathered a corner.

"I do hope we may arrive in the village in one piece," she said at last.

Julian slowed their pace, then settled back on the cushion. "What shall we do? Where do we begin?"

"I think we should separate. You can inquire most casually about Lord Twisdale at the local inn while I will nose about in the shops that the village has to offer. I imagine they will be curious about me, having heard of your marriage."

"Why do I feel there is an 'at last' in that sentence?" he said with a hint of complaint.

Chloe smiled but did not argue with him about it. She had managed to survive this long week by holding tightly to her emotions and avoiding confrontations of any sort. It took all night to soothe and restore her composure after a day spent in his company. And then she listened to his footfalls in the next room, waiting for precisely what she was not sure. Only when all was silent did she drift off to sleep.

When Julian drew to a halt before a likely-looking bow-fronted village shop, Chloe climbed down, peering up at him with a conspiratorial look. "I shall meet you later by the village green."

He nodded, then went on to the Three Crowns Inn, where he could leave the gig while he explored one way or another.

Inside the pretty little shop Chloe discovered about the same sort of merchandise she had seen back at home. The proprietor was a Mrs. Baxter according to a neatly lettered sign. Chloe chatted with her in an agreeable, disarming manner for some while, then mentioned she had met a gentleman from this area while in London. "A Lord Twisdale. Have you heard of the man?" She carefully called him a man, not a gentleman, a distinction she hoped would be noticed.

The friendly face became shuttered. "Aye, we all do. Not many girls from around here willing to work at the Hall," the woman reported after a curious look at Chloe.

"He is said to be looking for a second wife. I wonder . . . " Chloe mused aloud, then continued, "He seems respectable enough, but there are those who will not speak to the man, and a girl I know recently refused to marry him."

"You don't say," said an enthralled Mrs. Baxter, easing her demeanor considerably at this revelation from Town. "Well, I had little to do with his wife, poor dear."

"Poor dear?" Chloe said promptly, perking up her ears at the tone of voice.

"'Tis said all was not as it should be up at the Hall. She rarely came to the village, not unless he was with her. And as he often left her alone there, she spent most days wandering through the gardens, such as they are."

"The gardens are not to be remarked, then?"

"Shrubbery and weeds, mostly. My husband used to be the gardener there."

"Used to be?"

"Aye. He was fired when Lady Twisdale died. They claimed he brought in poison berries, but no gardener would do such a thing and we both know it."

"Indeed," Chloe murmured.

Chapter 14

*J*ulian stared across the village green, wondering if his wife sensed his growing regard. A shard of sunlight captured the gleam of her auburn curls where they peeped from beneath her small chip bonnet as she walked toward where he waited. In her green sprigged mull she resembled a summer sprite, a very precious sprite. A gentle breeze blowing her muslin gown against her slim form revealed the slender body veiled beneath. And Julian felt the tension within him increase as he surveyed her perfect little form.

Slim legs, a slender body—a comely shape, all in all. She was his—yet not his—and his sense of frustration grew day by day. Did she experience any of these sensations, he wondered, irritated at his inability to withstand her innocent charms. His patience wore thin.

Come night he paced the sitting room, tossing glances at the connecting door that led to where she slept. Or did she sleep? He hoped not, in a way, for it was only just that she feel something of what he endured.

He had read and heard that a proper lady did not have such emotions as passion, yet he wondered about that as well. It had been his experience—particularly with the beauteous Elinor Hadwell—that certain of those ladies possessed most passionate of natures. Perhaps it was a disgruntled and impatient, possibly obtuse husband who reached that particular conclusion.

"Did you have any luck?" she asked in a breathless voice as she reached his side, for she had hurried when she observed that he waited for her, leaning on his blackthorn cane for ease.

Julian caught a drift of heliotrope and felt a tightening in his loins. Blast it all, the very scent of her aroused him.

With superb control Julian took his wife's elbow in a gentle clasp, guiding her along the flagged path in a leisurely stroll. The effect of the feel of her delicate bones on his fingers he preferred to ignore.

"I learned that Lord Twisdale came here now and again, mostly to visit his wife. He was not one for bothering about the workings of his estate, leaving all that to his agent. Few seem to know much about him, nor have the least liking for the man—which is not unusual for a peer of his rank," he said, acknowledging a truism.

"Well," she offered with a demure show of triumph, "I had very good fortune indeed. The shopkeeper said her husband had served as the gardener to Lord Twisdale for many years, his father before him, giving good service. He was abruptly fired immediately following her ladyship's death. It was claimed that the gardener had brought in a basket of spoiled berries which the cook made into a tart for Anne." Chloe looked at Julian with a pleased expression at her information.

"And you think this significant?" he asked, more to absorb her eager little face than to acquire knowledge, which he might surmise on his own—given a clear head.

"No cook worth her salt would use spoiled berries in a tart for her mistress. Unless, perhaps," Chloe reflected, "she had been ordered to do so, or perhaps hated her mistress and wished her harm."

"I had not considered that possibility; I was so intent upon proving Twisdale's guilt." Julian frowned at the introduction of this new angle.

"There have been numerous cases, or so I have heard, where a servant has tried to murder his or her employer," Chloe said in a thoughtful way. "I fancy were one to receive horrible treatment for a long period it might happen. It would be as though goaded for so long, the person lost control."

"Remind me to stop beating my valet." He gazed at her earnest little face with amusement, thinking her friend Laura was lucky to have Chloe as champion.

"You tease, sir, but I think that has merit as a motive." She gave him a playful tap on his arm, and Julian felt progress made at her sign of familiarity. She so rarely touched him of her own accord.

"We will continue to search, my dear. I will not consign the threat from Lord Twisdale to a heap so quickly."

"I would not have Laura marry the man if it could be helped. But how can we prove anything?" Chloe turned a trusting face up to Julian, as though looking for guidance. He found her complete confidence in his ability to supply answers quite stirring.

"You could try nosing about the kitchen servants. Gossip being what it is, there might be something found there."

"That I will do," she said with a little nod. "Do you recall helping to send my grandmother's scullery maid from the city? I found she is very happy here and most grateful to us for her removal from that house. I will wager that she would be pleased to snoop about for us if I ask."

Chloe gave a happy skip as they approached the carriage that awaited them by the village inn. How fortunate she was that Julian was willing to help prove Lord Twisdale an unsuitable husband for Laura.

"While you interrogate the little scullery maid, I shall nose about on my own. Perhaps our gardener knows a thing or two he can impart." Julian was thankful they had something of this magnitude to occupy a number of hours in the day or this honeymoon would prove unbearable.

He placed his hands firmly about her little waist to lift her up into the carriage rather than permit that dainty foot to use the step provided. The sight of so much leg was his alone, not to be shared with any village lad lurking about the place. It was a decidedly mixed pleasure to feel her body in his hands.

Once again, he experienced the frustration that came from his near-intolerable position. Perhaps if he could solve this crime they felt certain had been committed Chloe would turn to Julian with gratitude and something more? He grasped at any straw that came his way.

They rode back to the estate in companionable, if uncomfortable on Julian's part, agreement. He pointed out where Lord Twisdale's estate began, commenting on the austere house that could be viewed for a few minutes before they made a turning in the lane.

"I could see why Lady Twisdale might have run away from so dreary a place, if the exterior is anything to go by," Chloe said with a concerned look at Julian.

"And if she feared for her life, would she not be more driven?" he added, persuaded that this might be the case.

"I believe I should," Chloe said in a sad little voice.

Julian gave her a quick glance before returning his attention to the lane. The bend into the avenue that led to their home required care to negotiate and he had no wish to upset the carriage or cause Chloe harm.

Once in the house Chloe parted from Julian in the entryway, conscious of his gaze following her as she carefully marched up the stairs to go to her room. When she had turned the corner she relaxed a trifle. How difficult it was to restrain herself when he touched her so often. It had to be accidental, for surely he was not truly interested in her. But how it affected her. Why, when he picked her up to set her in the carriage she had felt as though she might just go up in flames. It was most disconcerting, for she had never known anything like this before.

When they had discovered the truth of the matter involving Lord Twisdale and his wife now gone aloft, Chloe intended to distance herself from Julian. Perhaps he would at last grow bored with rural life and take himself back to the city? While she longed for his company she was not so foolish as to think he cared for her—in spite of his tender regard. Most likely he was merely putting on a show for whoever happened to be in sight. Or perhaps it was second nature for a scoundrel to be solicitous to a woman. Even his wife—such as it was.

She changed into a proper day gown, completely shutting from her mind the knowledge that it was not necessary that he put on any sort of display when they were alone or otherwise, for that matter. Nor would she permit his enormous appeal to swerve her from her determined path.

Chloe's entrance into the kitchen caused a small stir, for the servants were not accustomed to a mistress around, let alone one who made frequent appearances. She soon found her quarry.

"Rose," Chloe said gently, so as to not alarm the girl, "I

have a puzzle. Could you help me find out something for a dear friend of mine? 'Tis very important."

Rose was speechless for a few moments while she absorbed the idea that her adored mistress would actually seek her help in anything, then she nodded eagerly. The girl had never been so happy in her short life as since she came to this country home. She would do anything possible to help the good lady who had made it possible.

"I need to know something about the people in the house on the next property," Chloe began after checking to see that no one was about. "I suspect there was something a trifle havey-cavey about the death of his lordship's late wife. Could you poke about and listen or ask a question or two about the matter? Someone said something about a spoiled berry tart. I want to know when it was served and by whom. I also want to know what sort of berries were used in the tart," Chloe concluded.

"Well," Rose said after some thought, "I be friendlylike with the kitchen maid. I kin ask her first." From the dubious tone of Rose's voice it was clear to Chloe that the girl felt her mission would not be very successful.

"Please tell me anything that you are able to find out. I will come again tomorrow."

Chloe gave the girl an encouraging smile, then walked back through the kitchen to the hall where she met Mrs. Beeman. The housekeeper bobbed a curtsy when she saw her new mistress.

"Tell me, do you know any of the servants on Lord Twisdale's estate?" Chloe ventured.

"That I do, ma'am. Or did," the lady amended. "I had occasion to meet his housekeeper while in the village from time to time. Fine lady. I was sorry to see her leave."

"He fired her?" Chloe guessed.

"Aye, and no referral, either. Why he did not send that miserable cook of his packing I'll never know." Mrs. Beeman firmed her mouth, an outraged look on her face.

"The cook who made the berry tart that her ladyship ate before she died?" Chloe said with growing excitement.

"You know about that?" the housekeeper asked in amazement.

"That I do and am desirous of any details you could offer," Chloe said in a coaxing way.

"I do not know much other than that, but it was mighty odd if you ask me." Then Mrs. Beeman seemed to realize that she was actually gossiping with her new mistress and ought not, even if encouraged. She curtsied again and murmured something about the stillroom.

Chloe felt that in spite of the lack of information at this moment she had made a small and promising beginning.

Julian crossed the lawn to where the head gardener, Watcock, supervised the cleaning up of a flower bed. Plants past their prime were being removed to make way for others. It took some time to work around to the topic Julian wished to know more about.

At last the questions that had poured forth from Watcock were answered to the man's apparent satisfaction and Julian found his chance.

"Understand that the gardener on Twisdale's estate was accused of picking spoiled berries for the cook. Know anything about it? I have a need to know."

Watcock gave Julian a shrewd look before replying, then said with slow deliberation, "Aye. As though a man of his experience would do a thing so stupid as that." The gardener made a derisive spit at the ground. "Pollard—for that was his name—was a good man and knew his work. Never would ha' picked spoiled berries."

"What sort of berries were they?" Julian said, ignoring for the moment the use of the past tense in regard to Pollard.

"Berries? I suspect they were whortleberries."

"What happened to the gardener?" Julian ventured.

"Pollard was accused with offering spoiled fruit to the cook, but naught could be proven one way or the other. So his high-and-mighty lordship sent off the best gardener he could find. Not long after that Pollard was run down by a coach while walking home from the Hare and Hart in the village. Never recovered." Watcock shook his head and sighed.

With that the gardener clamped his mouth shut and said nothing more on the matter, although Julian patiently prodded him for additional details. It appeared that Twisdale's effect on the servants extended beyond his land.

Julian sauntered off across the grounds after finding out the location of the bushes on his land that bore those small blue berries. Once he located the patch, he hunted until he found a few, then picked them for perusal. Two were past ripe and had that dull, wilted look of a berry about to go bad. He doubted anyone who knew a thing about the fruit could make a mistake. And if they were spoiled a trifle, could they cause death? He thought they could give one a stomach ache, but scarcely death.

Puzzled, for he suspected that he had consumed a few of such berries in his lifetime and suffered no serious effects, Julian wandered back to the house. Godfrey directed him to the library, where he found Chloe, her nose in a large book.

"What ho?" he inquired. He crossed the room until he reached her side. She stiffened as he drew near—which he found blasted annoying at this point. How was he ever to persuade her to accept his deception if she was as prickly as a hedgehog whenever he came near her?

"I am hunting through this excellent herbal to see if there is any clue in here," she said in polite reply. Then, recalling where he had most likely been, she turned to eagerly ask, "Did you learn anything?"

"Not much," he admitted. He casually reached out to brush a curl from her cheek, then rested his hand lightly upon her shoulder.

"Nor did I," she confessed with equal vexation. She gave an uneasy glance at his hand, but said not a word about his touch.

"We will have to hope that someone will decide to come forth with the vital information. I did discover that the gardener accused of presenting those berries was later run down while walking home from the Hare and Hart."

"Do you suppose it was deliberate?" she asked, alarm clear in her voice.

"Who could prove it?" He exchanged concerned looks with her.

"How dreadful." She shivered, wrapping her arms about herself as though chilled. He patted her shoulder in an attempt to offer comfort and felt a tremor vibrate through her. Well . . . he fancied she reacted to him, but how?

"I suppose I might disguise myself and investigate over there firsthand," she said with forced enthusiasm. "I could pretend to be a maid . . . or something."

"Do you think you might be believed?" He picked up one of her slim, dainty hands that were delicately soft and smooth, ostensibly to peruse it.

"Oh!" Chloe tugged her hand away from his grasp with a charming blush and ruefully shook her head. "What a goosecap I am. Of course I would be suspect. I can only hope that Rose will learn a tidbit of use."

Julian stood still while Chloe slipped from her chair, shrugging off his hand with a dip of her shoulder.

She crossed the room, then turned to face him, her hands clasped before her.

"You look as though you have more on your mind than the problem of the spoiled berry tart and Twisdale. Is it your friend?" Julian poked at the Turkey carpet with the end of his cane for something to do while awaiting her answer. The longer she deliberated, the more concerned he grew.

"It is our marriage, you know," she said at last.

Julian did not know how to reply. If he said something encouraging she might bolt. On the other hand he wondered if this was the right moment to confess his deception. She might be furious with him and all the ground he had hoped he had gained would be lost. He did not relish starting anew.

"What about our marriage," he said at last, taking fully as long to reply as she had taken to make the remark.

"We must decide when to arrange the annulment," she continued without looking at him. She studied the carpet at his feet, watching him poke at it as though he did something important.

"We could try to work things out, you know." He paused for a moment before daring to add, "Have you considered that were you to be granted an annulment you might be ostracized by Society? How would you find a husband then? Remember, although we have not shared a bed, they do not know that." This was a part of his argument, albeit not one he relished. But he felt the truth of it and he suspected even she must admit he was right.

When she turned pale, he realized she had not considered this aspect of her scheme.

"You had *not* calculated on such a thing, had you," he gently stated.

"No," she replied in a choked voice, some of her color returning as she spoke. "I had thought that we could institute the nullity procedure and be done with it. What will Mama say," she wondered aloud.

Julian had not said anything about Lady Montmorcy, now Lady Crompton, as the earl's new wife. In his opinion she ought to have remained in London to supervise her daughter's come-out, not gone haring across the Continent on her honeymoon. The thought of her basking in the pleasures to be found somewhere in Switzerland or Italy while Chloe struggled with this dratted problem—which might have been totally avoided had her grandmother not been so insistent on the poor girl marrying that Twisdale—made him long to scold the woman.

Yet at the time he had been grateful to escape from Elinor Hadlow, delectable though she might appear. There were a lot of poisonous plants that looked luscious, too. Which brought him to a sudden notion.

"We shall discuss this more at another time when you have had a chance to reflect on it. Had you thought Twisdale might find a poisonous berry?" He glanced at the herbal, then back to where Chloe stood.

Looking quite relieved at the chance to turn from a difficult subject, Chloe shook her head in a considering way. "No, but perhaps there is something of help in that book of herbals."

They joined in perusing the book until they came upon the *atropa belladonna*.

"It says here to use care that you not mistake it for another, an edible berry, for the belladona is deadly poisonous," Chloe said with an anxious look at Julian. "It blooms from June to August, so fruit would be available for a long period."

"The deadly nightshade, it is called," Julian said, recalling something he had read about the plant long ago. "I will ask Watcock if it grows locally."

"Do that at once," Chloe urged. "And if it does, perhaps we ought to destroy them all."

"The herbal indicates it has useful purposes. Like many things, it is the overuse that is fatal." Julian grasped his cane firmly in his hand, then left the room before he said anything more. He wanted to return to the topic of their marriage but sensed that she perhaps needed to come to terms with what had been revealed.

Chloe watched her husband leave the library, then turned back to the table where she had sat while turning the pages of the book. Placing her hand on the herbal, she stared off into space, deep in thought.

He was undoubtedly right about the marriage business. The chance of their obtaining Sir William Scott as their judge was problematical. He had served as judge in the case she'd read about. But she could not recall the details of the case involving the young Pouget and wondered if Julian kept accounts of such matters, if he was interested in the law. And why was he interested in the law, pray tell? He was a wealthy landowner, accepted everywhere, even if he had been a scoundrel.

She returned the herbal to the shelf, then hurried up to her room before Julian could return. He had left her to learn more about the berries, but she suspected that perhaps her husband wished to give her time alone as well.

Time? She gave a doleful chuckle. Once in her room she set about writing a letter to Laura. Chloe had decided she would say nothing about how her marriage to Julian went along. Rather she sought to offer hope to Laura by telling her that it was plain Lord Twisdale had wanted his wife out of the way and had found a clever way to eliminate the poor woman.

A scratching on her door halted her task. Chloe rose from the pretty little rosewood desk she had found so delightful and called out, "Enter."

"Ma'am?" A shy Rose crept into the elegant room looking clearly intimidated by the splendid surroundings.

"Rose, have you learned something?"

"'Deed I have," the maid said proudly. "'Twas whortleberry tarts her ladyship liked. The cook ordered berries from the garden near every day when they was ripe. That cook, well, she be a dragon, she be. They have trouble keeping help over there cuz of her, or so says Kate." It was clear that Rose found the older kitchen maid an object of great admiration. "And it was the cook who took the berry tart up to her ladyship to tempt her appey-tite. She was poorly afore she died. Though she tried to run away. They said not, but Kate said she believed it."

"Thank you, Rose. We suspected that might be the case."

The little scullery maid bobbed a wobbly curtsy, then scooted from the room as though afraid to remain.

Chloe wandered back to look out of the window at the gardens below. She could see Julian striding across the lawn, and Watcock standing where he must have been when confronted by his employer.

Again his words returned to her. If she pursued the matter of her annulment to Julian she would most likely not easily find a husband again. Why had she not thought of this? Was it because she had grown so fond of Julian even before the episode in the Seftons' library?

Within a brief time Chloe heard a sharp rap on her door and this time she merely called for the person to enter, for she suspected that Julian sought her.

"Well, I found out that there is an abundance of deadly nightshade growing in these parts. Seems they grow along the lane, in the grove, in fact found most anywhere. I have ordered that the ones on our land be destroyed." He paced about the room, thrusting his left hand through his hair while gesturing with his cane.

"Rose informed me that Lady Twisdale had a special fondness for whortleberry tarts. If the drawing in that herbal book is anything to go by, they look fairly similar. Could it be that the cook could have substituted one for the other? But would she not know it?"

"Perhaps she did and was paid well to do her work," Julian suggested with a pause in his steps. He shook his head in dismay at the thought of his neighbor doing anything so horrible.

"It was the cook who carried the final tart up to Anne, or so Rose informed me—which is a bit odd if you think on it.

Normally a maid would perform that task, not the cook. If we believe that Lord Twisdale murdered his wife with deadly nightshade—in the form of that tart—what can we do about it? Who would believe us? And how can we possibly prevent Laura from marrying the man?" Chloe cried.

Julian walked over to look down at Chloe, frowning in thought. "We might plant suspicion among the villagers. It would be easy, for none of them like him. Once we convince them to doubt his innocence, it will be but a step to persuade them of his guilt."

"I believe that might actually work," Chloe said upon a small reflection. She toyed with the pen she had been using to write to Laura. "On another topic altogether I have had an inspiration of a sorts."

She could see him tense and his look was highly cautious.

"And that is?" He took a step toward her. Chloe refused to back away from him even though he intimidated her with his size and the attraction he held for her.

"Why, you could sell me."

"Ye gods!" he exclaimed. "I had not thought you that scatterbrained."

"It is done, is it not?" she said, ignoring the fluttering in her heart when he towered over her.

"True," he admitted. "For those who cannot afford a bill of divorcement, selling a wife is a way out of an intolerable situation."

"They agree to part, and that is it?"

"But, my dear wife, it is customary to have a purchaser provided beforehand. You would not wish to be paraded in public indignity . . . would you? And who would you choose for a husband?" Julian said with a slight frown settling on his brow.

Chloe sank down upon the little chair at the desk, utterly aghast. She had not thought beyond freeing Julian of his unwanted wife. "There is no one else I would care to marry."

"No one?" Julian said quietly.

"None I can think of," Chloe replied woefully. How could she have forgotten such an obvious matter as a husband to buy her? Stupid! This proved that Julian turned her brain to mush.

"There is also a possibility of a deed of separation," Julian said, walking over to stand by the window as Chloe had done not long before. "It is a very private arrangement."

"And that involves what?" Chloe said, rising from her little chair to confront Julian.

"My attorney draws up a contract that grants you an annual maintenance allowance—including your pin money—but disallowing any future debts. You would be in all respects a single woman, free of me, to live where you please."

"Except that in the eyes of the church we would still legally be man and wife," she countered.

"True."

"Oh dear," she murmured, sinking down on her little chair once again. "Well, then, since you must wish to be completely free of a wife, we must rely on the incorrect banns. There is no other way for you. And me," she added hastily at his peculiar expression.

He looked about to say something when there was a sharp rap on the door to her sitting room.

"Squire Hopgood to see you, sir," the maid said with a curtsy.

Chloe exchanged a look with Julian before he strode to the door.

"What do you suppose he wants?" she wondered aloud.

"He is a local Justice of the Peace. I sent for him. Perhaps he can advise us on what may be done about Twisdale. Were you aware that I am the local Lord Lieutenant? I seldom occupy myself with the business hereabouts, but I believe I must now. And Hopgood will be the one to help us find a way to be rid of Twisdale if one can be found."

Chapter 15

"Get rid of Twisdale!" Chloe echoed after her husband strode from the room. How ominous he sounded.

She followed Julian from the room and along the hall to look down to the entryway while he lightly ran down the stairs to greet the gentleman who awaited him.

Squire Hopgood was only slightly portly and wore his hair neatly tied at the nape of his neck. He garbed himself in the clothes of a country gentleman—a tailless brown coat suitable for hunting, tan breeches with leather spatter-dashes buttoned up to his knees, and a moderate cravat above a simple blue waistcoat. In his hands he carried a round hat and a riding crop. He reminded Chloe of an eager hound on the trail and so she would sketch him. He looked intent on his business. Chloe wondered what he would have to say to Julian's disclosures.

Julian greeted his neighbor with a firm handshake, then walked at his side to the library, where he offered the squire some liquid refreshment before settling down to business. He had been aware of Chloe's watchful gaze as he met Hopgood and wondered if he ought to have invited her to join them.

After appointing Hopgood as the justice Julian had been very pleased with his diligence in office. He had tended to the poor with a shrewd eye, kept a keen watch on the main-tenance of the local highways and roads, and wasted no time in bringing petty criminals to trial. In short, he was a good man and proved an able administrator. If he felt it an insult to have a Lord Lieutenant who was labeled a scoundrel by those in London, he never gave a sign of it.

They chatted briefly before the squire gave Julian a per-ceptive look. "Rumor says you are interested in your neighbor's activities. Lord Twisdale do something I don't know about?"

"Perhaps." Julian strolled about until he reached his desk, then settled onto the chair behind it, knowing that it offered him an appearance of command. "I became acquainted with a problem involving him while last in London. There are stories circulating about Town, not widely, only a few. But they greatly disturb me."

"Involving his late wife?" the squire hazarded.

"What makes you deduce that?" Julian said, surprised at this assumption from his justice.

"I was never easy about the death of the late Lady Twisdale. Eating a whortleberry tart does not seem to me to be just cause for going aloft. Even if the berries were spoiled, would it not cause a stomach ache rather than her demise?"

"Precisely my thinking," Julian agreed. "My wife was to have married Twisdale as his second bride—her grandmother's doing, I might add. He frightened her with his oily manners and it was fortunate indeed—for us both—that she accepted my hand instead." Julian thought he glossed over that particular news rather well. He continued, "Now her dearest friend is threatened with marriage to Twisdale and Lady Chloe takes a dim view of that much-esteemed girl going to an early grave."

"Your wife suspects that Lord Twisdale intends to—shall we say—do away with his bride?" Hopgood leaned forward in his chair, intent and alert.

"In short, murder," Julian confirmed.

The squire rubbed his jaw for a few minutes, subsiding into a meditative silence. At last he spoke. "I truly do not see what we can do about it. If the man takes a bride to his country home, there is no way we may interfere. Suspicion of intent to do bodily harm is no cause to pry or force entry. A man has a lawful right to chastise his wife, even punish her severely if he feels 'tis required. Our hands are tied." The squire exchanged a look with Julian, one of concern and uncertainty.

"I have ordered the destruction of all the deadly nightshade in this area. My men will convey the message to Twisdale's help as well. I feel strongly that the *atropa belladonna*, commonly known as deadly nightshade, was responsible for Lady Twisdale's death. It somewhat resembles the whortleberry—being a dark blue berry of similar size. It is possible the belladonna berries might have been mistaken for the others." Julian placed an emphasis, a skeptical one, on the word "mistaken."

"But you do not believe this, do you?" The squire compressed his lips into a grimace. "What then? How do you prevent Twisdale from taking this innocent girl to her death—supposing that is what he intends." The squire laced his fingers together, awaiting a pronouncement from Julian.

And Julian did not know what to tell him.

When a gentle rapping on the door disturbed their conference Julian was glad for the momentary respite.

Chloe hesitantly entered the room, pausing by the door and offering a pleading look.

"If you please, sirs, I would not disturb you but for the letter just come from London." She stepped forward and turned to face Julian. "Laura has written that her mother presses her to accept Lord Twisdale. She fears her only hope is to run away. That could be dangerous, particularly if that serpent catches her. He might well elope to Scotland with her."

Squire Hopgood gave a start at Lady Chloe's name for Twisdale, then nodded. "Aye, the man is a serpent, a regular snake in the grass."

Chloe whirled about to look at the squire, a hopeful expression on her face. "Then you agree that my dearest friend must not face the prospect of death at his hands, for I know that must be what happened to the late Lady Twisdale."

"Why would he do such a thing?" Julian mused aloud.

"Money," the squire shot back. "Lady Twisdale came well dowered. It seems he gambles heavily and lately has lost on some investments. I was suspicious and did a bit of investigating on my own some time ago. Didn't call the runners up from London, not sufficient evidence. The remains of that pie disappeared mighty quickly." The squire gave them a knowing nod, then added, "One of the maids noted that her ladyship seemed to have unusually dilated eyes, but that girl disappeared and has not been seen around here since. Word has it that she was kidnapped but there again, no proof exists. There were rumors of slavers, but . . . "

Chloe gasped and sought a chair upon which to sit. "It would seem that Lord Twisdale has the power and influence to further his evil scheme."

"We thought to spread a few rumors about Twisdale in the village—the sort to thoroughly discredit the man," Julian said, wondering what the squire thought of such a notion.

"Good. It would be well to drop hints that anyone who offers information will be kept safe, the identity of that person not revealed," the squire added.

"My gardener said Twisdale's man—Pollard was his name—was run down by a coach as he walked home from the village inn. No clue there?"

"None," the squire said, shaking his head with obvious disgust. "It were a plain black traveling coach of the sort you see fairly often. No decoration on the sides, nondescript horses from what I can make out. Ordinary. Everything was ordinary, except a man was killed."

"And the driver did not stop?" Julian asked.

"No. It is possible the driver didn't know Pollard had fallen beneath his wheels when he drove that coach thundering through the village. But I doubt it. Pollard looked to be run clean down, no accidental hit, pardon my blunt speaking, Lady Chloe," he added when he observed how she paled.

Julian exchanged a look with Chloe, then turned back to the squire. "I would appreciate any help you can give us on this, Hopgood."

"I'll do my best, sir, make no mistake on it. I have no love for Lord Twisdale, nor do many hereabouts."

"I will write to Laura and other friends in London, dropping more hints about Lord Twisdale's late wife, if you think that might help," Chloe said, her color coming back nicely at the thought of the man reaping his just rewards.

"You hope to draw him into the country?" the squire inquired, alert and reminding Chloe again of an eager hound on the scent of a vixen.

"Yes," Julian said, thoughtfully rubbing the handle of his cane while he leaned back against his chair. "I should like to meet him out here." Then a thought struck him. "What luck would we have with the cook? Suppose we confronted her, concoct some manner of tale?"

"Might be frowned upon by some purist, but I'd not say a word against it. Come to think of it, you are the supreme official in the county—at least you have the regulating of the militia. I fancy there are few who will argue with your methods in ridding of us a blackguard like Twisdale." The squire rose from his chair and saluted Julian with one hand as might a soldier. "I think we may just know success in this endeavor."

"If Twisdale will only fall into our trap, once we have it set," Julian concluded with a cautious smile.

Chloe joined Julian while they sauntered to the front door to bid the squire farewell. They chatted about the weather, the squire observing that the harvest looked to be a fair one if the weather continued good.

He paused before leaving to turn to Chloe. "I know you two are on your honeymoon—and surely this must be the strangest one on record, but my wife and I would deem it a pleasure to welcome you for dinner and a bit of conversation. Mrs. Hopgood would be pleased to hear of London fashions, you see, as well as to meet you."

Chloe blushed prettily and said all that was proper. They arranged to attend a dinner at the Hopgoods' home the following Friday.

If she was in a muddle it was all Julian's fault, Chloe decided once the front door had closed and she watched Julian retreat to his library. The dratted man turned her brain into a jumble and disordered her senses so she scarcely knew whether she was on her head or heels. While they had chatted with the squire, Julian had lightly rested his arm about her shoulders, drawing her close to his side. 'Twas a wonder she could make a coherent reply.

All he had to do was to touch her. That was it. And as she had noted before, he seemed to do that quite often.

"Chloe," he called, beckoning her to follow him.

"What is it?" she said when she joined him at the door where he waited for her.

He leaned against the polished wood, staring down at her

as though debating something. At last, reaching some conclusion he spoke.

"About the cook. How did your little scullery maid obtain her information on the goings on next door? I wondered if we might use that same connection again." Julian again placed an arm about Chloe's shoulders, guiding her along into the library with him to the window that looked toward the Twisdale estate and house.

"Rose?" Chloe said, reflecting on the maid and struggling to remain sensible. "No, I scarcely believe she would ask Kate to snoop. I rather think that you and I will have to pay a call on the Twisdale house. You in your capacity as Lord Lieutenant and I as a witness to the call and the interrogation."

"By Jove, do you think it might work?" He tightened his clasp on her shoulders, disturbing Chloe's nerves.

"If we present the image of people who know the truth of what happened, perhaps offer her clemency if she will confess to what Lord Twisdale ordered her to do. For the more I think on it, the more I am convinced the cook was his pawn in all of this. Why else would the very one who prepared that deathly tart be still employed and the others dismissed?" Chloe reasoned, trying to ignore the enticing warmth of his arm about her, the masculine scent of him, his very nearness.

"Excellent reasoning. I suggest there is no time like the present. Ready yourself in your most intimidating garments, my dear wife. We are paying a call on a cook." He grinned down at her, drawing closer and closer to her until Chloe thought she would expire from sheer longing right then and there. It was wicked for a man to have such long lashes and dark eyes that were beautifully rich in color. Wicked.

Chloe gladly fled the library to dash up the stairs to the security of her room.

Within short order she was dressed in London style, prepared to call on a duchess at the very least. Her garments were rich and elegant and designed to impress. The evening primrose pelisse had a skirt trimmed with tiers of exquisite vandyking and a wide collar edged in rows of lace. It covered a gown of ivory-and-green striped poplin that peeped out when she walked. A matching parasol was tied with green ribbons—the same green that embellished her straw bonnet. Evening primrose silk roses were tucked beside the green ribbons in the very latest London charm.

She clasped the parasol with hands covered in yellow limerick gloves and her yellow kid slippers peeked out from beneath her gown with each step she took down the stairs.

"Well, you look splendid, my good wife," Julian said while reaching out to adjust a ribbon on her bonnet when she reached his side.

Chloe wanted to beg him to cease calling her his wife so often. Why did he persist in this, reminding her of what ought not be? Did he think to taunt her? Or perhaps he tested her?

"Come, I requested that the gig be brought around for us. It is a homely little vehicle but much used by the country folk."

When she saw his notion of a homely little vehicle Chloe wanted to laugh. True, it was a gig, but its elegance and style proclaimed it to be from the finest carriage builder in London. She suffered him to lift her onto the seat, then waited, acutely aware of him when he climbed in at her side.

He took the reins and they set off along the avenue and the lane that came from the village.

At the Twisdale gate Julian drew to a halt, then jumped down after handing the reins for Chloe to hold. There was no evidence of anyone about to tend the approach. "Dratted gate is shut tight against possible invaders. I shall change all that," he declared with a sharp push of the heavy wrought-iron entry gate. It creaked open and within minutes they bowled along a weedy, overgrown avenue.

"What a difference between his estate and yours. He has a poor agent, for the place looks uncared for and nothing is as it ought to be," Chloe remarked while searching the grounds they drove past.

"How did you become so knowledgeable?"

"With my brother John off to the Continent, Mama and I were left alone. It was necessary at times for me to take charge when Mama was absent or not feeling quite the thing."

"It is well she has someone to look after her now," was Julian's thoughtful reply.

"Mama was not intended to live alone," Chloe agreed.

The main house was quite as gloomy as the glimpse from the road implied. They drew to a halt before the front entrance and sat in the gig for a minute or two to study the place. No servant came to tend them, nor to open the front door in greeting.

"Perhaps if some of that ivy was cleaned away it might appear a trifle more cheerful," Chloe suggested.

"Trim needs painting, lawn needs trimming, indeed the whole place needs a freshening up. Sign of a lack of money or interest and in Twisdale's case, I fancy it must be both."

He climbed down from the gig, then looped the reins over a post before coming around to assist Chloe from the little carriage.

Their wait before the dull, ornate oak door proved long. Julian tried the door pull without success. The rap of the knocker echoed through the house loud enough for them to hear.

"I wonder if there is anyone at home?" Chloe mused just before the door was thrown open and a man with a severe expression confronted them.

"Lord Twisdale is not in residence. I have no notion as to when he plans to come here again," the man announced with proper dignity.

"I am the Lord Lieutenant for the shire, Julian St. Aubyn. I insist upon questioning your cook."

"The cook, sir?" the butler echoed, turning several degrees paler. He backed away from where Julian and Chloe stood just inside the door and looked as though he would most gladly flee if he could bring himself to abandon his post.

"We shall await her presence in the library. Direct her to us immediately."

"Indeed, sir. At once, sir. I shall fetch her directly, sir," the butler gabbled in his haste to be gone, then he fled down the long hall toward what was presumably the kitchen, for all that there was no green baize on the door.

"You have been here before? Else how would you know how to find the library?" Chloe wondered, trotting along at his side while traversing the entry hall.

"Once, years ago. We met in the library and it was the previous Lord Twisdale we met. He was quite different from his son, who seems to have taken after his mother." At the far side of the hall Julian gestured toward their left, the right corridor heading off where the butler had disappeared.

The walk down this hall revealed a few spaces on the wall where pictures had obviously been removed. Otherwise the house appeared in surprisingly good condition. Unlike the exterior, the rooms were neat and clean, smelled of lemon and lavender, and showed that someone cared.

At the far end of the corridor, Julian paused, then opened the door leading to a splendid library. Beautiful paneling adorned the walls into which bookshelves had been built at one end of the room. Deep red draperies flanked the many-paned windows. Above the bookcases a row of classical busts frowned down upon them and Chloe shivered when she glanced up to catch sight of them.

"I feel much the intruder," she said after finding a seat to one side of the enormous mahogany desk.

"You are Lady Chloe St. Aubyn and look to be a duchess at the very least," Julian said. He gave her a considering look, then added, "I shall have to consider loaning the Prince Regent a vast sum of money so I may acquire a peerage, so as to join your rank. I think Lord and Lady St. Aubyn has a nice ring to it."

"Julian, it is hideously expensive and you need not do so to please me," she cried softly. "Think of the money, and would it not be better spent elsewhere?"

"What? A good wife who seeks value for money spent? I am indeed a fortunate man." Julian felt his first ray of hope, for all unknowingly Chloe had spoken of a life *together* in the future.

When she met his intense gaze Chloe found her breath had taken leave of her, for she could not breathe for a moment or two. Then she drew in a ragged bit of air and thanked the cook for her timely intervention when a sound came from the hall.

The woman who charged into the room was tall, spare, and well-muscled for a female. She confronted them with a narrow-eyed stare, coming to a halt a few feet from where Julian now sat at ease behind the desk.

"Ye want to see me?" she demanded—and not in a timorous way. Rather she seemed aggressive, unlike most servants who might fear dismissal if they were overly bold in their speech or behavior.

"We have heard troubling things about the death of Lady Twisdale and seek the truth. You have been charged with replacing the whortleberries that Pollard brought you with berries from the deadly nightshade." Julian also narrowed his gaze and Chloe was extremely glad she was not the recipient of that forbidding stare.

"Me, sir?" the cook said with a bit less bravado and seemed to shrink a trifle in size.

"Evidence on the case that has been suppressed before has recently come to my attention. Consider . . . Lady Twisdale had a fondness for whortleberries, but an excess of that delectable fruit would cause no more than a stomach ache—even if a trifle overripe. Pollard was an honorable man, a gardener who had served his lordship's father before him. Unlikely that a chap with that sort of record would poison the wife of a man he served so capably and for so long."

The cook stood in silence, her bosom heaving with suppressed emotion of some sort.

Julian continued in his decisive recitation. "However, it is known that you were not only the cook who prepared that deadly tart, but you also served it to her ladyship, something highly unusual. Is it not?" he said in a quiet, menacing voice. When she made no reply he went on.

"The maid who tended Lady Twisdale has since disappeared—without a trace, I might add. Pollard has been run down, murdered, some say." Julian toyed with the pen that had been in the inkstand on the desk, waiting for a reaction of some kind, it seemed to Chloe.

"I had naught to do with that," Cook burst forth, then clamped her mouth shut again.

"How much were you paid to switch the whortleberries for the deadly nightshade that was brought to you?"

The shocking words fell into the awesome silence of the room with visible effect. The cook fell back a step and her reddened face paled some. Her mouth worked just as though she would speak, but no words came forth.

"For you see," Julian continued, "we know you have been paid to remain silent. Only we are not going to permit justice to miscarry. Lord Twisdale is to be punished for his crime. When he is called to account, he will most likely place all blame on you, for it was you who baked the poisonous tart and brought it to Lady Twisdale, not him. You are in effect the murderer."

"Not me," she erupted into speech. "I baked the tart, then I took it to his lordship. 'Twere him what fed it to her ledyship. I jus' baked the blasted thing." She took another step back toward the door.

Chloe rose from her chair and darted across to prevent the cook from decamping. She took a position by the door and felt the cook sufficiently intimidated that she would not dare shove Chloe aside to flee the room.

"Do you wish to face charges of murder, hanging until you are dead?" Julian emphasized each word, sending shivers up Chloe's spine with the dreadful picture they painted.

"No! I hain't going to let them kill me fer that!" the woman shouted. "'Twere his lordship who did all but bake the tart and I did that or be turned off without a reference."

"Will you sign a statement to that effect?"

"I cain't read," she whined, all hint of her previous bravado vanished.

"You must trust my husband to do what is right," Chloe inserted. "He is a good man and wants what is best to be done."

The cook glanced at Chloe, then back to the man behind the desk, who now wrote on the piece of fine vellum he had found in one of the drawers.

"I will." She crossed to make her mark where Julian pointed his finger, then stepped away. "What now?"

"By all rights you should be hung and you know it. You were an accomplice to a murder. However, in signing this paper you have helped us to nab the true criminal and for that you perhaps deserve a second chance."

The woman looked nigh unto fainting and Chloe moved to stand at her side. "And?"

"There will be a space for you on a boat to Canada this very week. You will find a situation easily enough, for English cooks are not plentiful there. I would suggest that you resist any temptation to repeat this crime, however," Julian concluded, rising from the desk so he towered over the now-intimidated cook.

"No, sir, never, sir. I'll go this very minute."

Chloe followed the woman to the hall where the butler hovered in suspicious proximity.

"Cook is to pack her things and leave immediately," Julian said from behind Chloe.

Such was Julian's air of authority that the butler said not a word but merely nodded his head.

The wait was not long before the cook reappeared with her belongings—a pitiful canvas satchel only half full. She had not bothered to remove her apron or her white cap.

Chloe looked at Julian but he said nothing, apparently deciding any kindness to the woman would be interpreted as weakness.

"Have a groom drive her to Squire Hopgood. He will see to her travel," Julian commanded.

They watched the pair leave the house, then Julian escorted Chloe to where the gig still stood, the horse calmly nibbling on the plants close by.

"We ought to tether him here, 'tis a dashed sight better-looking than before," Julian quipped as he lifted Chloe to the seat.

"Julian, it was utterly dreadful. What if she had demanded to see the proof you claimed to have unearthed? All you had were the suppositions and reports from the squire." Chloe stared ahead to the gate that still stood ajar, permitting them access to freedom from the gloomy place.

"A servant would rarely take such a step. They are conditioned to receive orders from their employer, not make challenges. I banked on the cook turning tail when she was accused of murder, or an accomplice in one. There is no out for a servant accused of such a crime. She would be tried and hung before she knew it."

"It was a dreadful scene and I am relieved it is over,"

Chloe said in a soft voice, almost trembling in her reaction to the raw sensations of the past hour.

"For the remainder of the day I decree that we shall enjoy ourselves," Julian declared, placing a hand over hers. What do you say to a drive to the village. We could inform Mrs. Pollard of the new turn of events. I trust she will be heartened to learn that justice will ultimately prevail."

"That means you believe that Lord Twisdale will learn of what has happened and come up here. Oh, Julian, I am very afraid of that man." Chloe stared off at the passing scenery with unseeing eyes, lost in reflection of what Twisdale might do when he confronted Julian, as he most likely would.

"And you are concerned for my safety? I am touched," Julian said the words lightly, but he truly was affected. A scoundrel rarely had anyone shed a tear over him, unless it was one of vexation for his departure.

The day went as he had ordered. Mrs. Pollard said little, but Chloe felt the woman would spread the news of what had happened. Squire Hopgood sent the cook off on the next coach that went to Liverpool, along with his most trusted deputy.

By the end of the day Chloe had begun to feel as though the entire episode had been a frightening dream.

"Dare I write Laura that she need not fear his lordship anymore?" Chloe inquired before retiring for the night.

"Best wait another few days. I would know the results of our interference first."

Chloe paused before her door, wondering what Julian would do if she chanced to invite him inside with her. Something had to change, she knew that for certain. But what? And how?

Chapter 16

*I*t was several days later that Lord Twisdale presented himself at the Aubynwood front door, demanding to see Julian.

When ushered into the library and then forced to cool his heels until Julian was found, Twisdale was in a most foul humor by the time Julian entered the room.

Offering a nod that barely managed to pass that which was civil, Julian strode over to his desk, standing beside it while fingering the paper he had kept to hand in the expectation of this call.

"I want you to know that I intend to sue you, St. Aubyn," the beleaguered gentleman challenged.

"On what grounds, pray tell?" Julian calmly inquired, bestowing a look of utter indifference on his guest.

"First of all, you drove off the best cook I have had in years." Twisdale began to pace back and forth, hands at his back and looking quite distracted.

"Dutiful, so I hear," Julian inserted in a snide, but subtle voice.

"What's that? Dutiful? Well, and all my servants are that, or I'll know why." Twisdale scowled fiercely at Julian as though he might in so doing intimidate the younger man.

"What do you do if they are not? Run them down with a coach or sell them to the slavers?" Julian took a threatening step toward Twisdale and the man paled.

"Those are damnable accusations. I'll sue you for those as well," he snarled. "There is no connection between what has happened and me."

"Pity about that, but it is your word against mine, and at the moment I daresay I have the more credit in my account," Julian countered.

"You made unjust accusations against me," Twisdale said in his most blustery manner.

"I gather you operate on the theory that the best defense is an offense," Julian said with a shrug. He again took a step toward Twisdale. "I made charges because your cook confessed to everything—that you gave her deadly nightshade berries to substitute for the whortleberries your wife so loved. And that instead of a maid or the cook, it was *you* who carried that fatal tart up to Lady Twisdale. Rather than join you in the hanging, Cook elected to take the next ship to Canada. I believe she must be at sea by this time," Julian added with a glance at the calendar on his desk.

"No proof of anything without the cook," Twisdale said with a triumphant sneer.

"Ah," Chloe added in a velvety soft voice from the open doorway, "but I was present and heard everything, and besides, the cook made her mark on a statement admitting all."

"The woman cannot read a word, it was collusion," his lordship bluffed.

"And," Julian said in a soft, dangerous voice, "one of my men just now informed me that he observed you out picking berries the day of Lady Twisdale's death. You were not near whortleberry bushes, Twisdale. You were stripping berries from a plant of deadly nightshade. So we *do* have a witness to your intent who does not have to fear for his life.

"Squire Hopgood accepted the cook's statement when he viewed it. And he will accept the word of a man the village has known and respected all his life as well," Julian added. "You see, he has had suspicions all along—you apparently were not too successful at covering your tracks. As the Lord Lieutenant for this shire and ultimately responsible for the keeping of the peace, I charge you with the poisoning of your wife."

"The rumor has found its way around London by now," Chloe inserted in her gentle voice. "I made sure to write everyone I know and urged them to pass it along. Were you to return to Town at this point, you would find it most uncomfortable for you."

Lord Twisdale looked from Chloe to Julian, then away. "She was not a dutiful wife," he said at last.

"That was no reason to do her in, Twisdale," came a voice from behind them all. When they turned, they found Justice of the Peace Hopgood standing at the open doorway, one of his beadles right behind him. "As a peer you will be brought before the House of Lords for your trial. Until then, you will be confined on suspicion of murdering your wife."

"Nonsense, you cannot prove a thing!" Then Twisdale collected himself and gave Hopgood a sly, twisted smile. "I shall claim that I picked the fruit with my own hands to satisfy her demands for a berry tart and that I mistook the berries. It was an unfortunate case of a well-intentioned mistake, gentlemen and Lady Chloe." He bowed slightly in her direction. "Just a mistake."

"In the event that you are freed"—and Julian knew that this was highly possible, given Twisdale's rank—"I suggest that you commence a long journey to the Continent. Even if you achieve your freedom, you will not be allowed to enjoy it in England. We will see to that."

Twisdale went along with Squire Hopgood and his beadle, unbowed and defiant.

"That is shocking. To think a man who has murdered his wife should be allowed his freedom," Chloe whispered, drawing closer to Julian.

"We do not know for certain that this will be so, but you are probably right and I agree that something ought to be done to the laws, so that this is not permitted. At least," he offered as a crumb of comfort, "you need not fear that Laura will be compelled to marry Twisdale now. No mother of sensibility would think of such a thing."

"A title is a powerful inducement to overlook anything and everything about a man," Chloe mused. "Think of how Grandmama was about to give me to Twisdale, even when we had some doubts about his character."

In an attempt to lighten the atmosphere Julian put his arm about Chloe and drew her along with him to the window overlooking the gardens. "I vow I shall make that large loan to Prinney. He should make me an earl at the very least. Would you not wish to be my countess?"

He turned to face her, tilting up her face so he might judge her reaction better.

That disturbing gleam appeared in his eyes again. Chloe wanted to cry out that she would be quite happy just to be his wife, but did not know just how to phrase it properly. For she wished to be his wife in more than name only and *that* was a most delicate subject to bring up. She would no doubt blush herself clear into Tuesday should she venture to say such a thing.

"I told you that would be hideously expensive," she temporized. "You ought not to waste your money on such a frivolous scheme, for you know he will never acquire the money to pay you back." Chloe dared to meet his gaze and wondered at the expression she found there. He looked more than pensive, he almost looked sad. She attributed it to the recent altercation with Twisdale and patted Julian on the arm, forcing her other desires to the back of her mind. "I feel certain you will find something else to spend your gold on. A new horse, perhaps?"

"I have all the horses I require at the moment," he said with a sort of defeated expression on his face.

Chloe disentangled herself from his clasp and moved toward the door. "At least you can cease worrying about my aunt. Elinor has become betrothed to Sir Augustus."

"I thought he needed money," Julian said. He sounded rather amused and Chloe glanced back to see he was now smiling.

"It seems that her stepson offered her a vast sum of money if she would marry and remove herself from London. She and Sir Augustus are to travel on the Continent, or so Laura writes."

"Perhaps they will meet Twisdale while there."

"Please excuse me, Julian, I have a few things to attend," Chloe blurted out, unable to stand being so close to him in such an intimate situation.

Julian watched his wife hurry from the room with a wry expression on his face. Odd, when he had checked his reflection in the looking glass this morning, it had seemed the same one that had charmed the ladies in London. Yet his own little wife who he adored ran from him at every turn.

He picked up the confession the cook had signed and placed it in a folder to be sent to London along with the statement he would obtain from his undergardener. It seemed a futile exercise, but he felt constrained to do what he might to punish Twisdale.

That Friday Chloe reminded Julian they were to dine with the Hopgoods that evening. Since the atmosphere at St. Aubyn's Court was becoming more tense by the day, both occupants were only too happy to seek the company of others.

All was going well until Chloe began to dress. She had sent Ellen off to press her silk shawl and then decided she'd not wait for her return to slip on her gown. It had seemed such a simple affair, with a back that hooked up, then tied with a bow. Surely she could manage it.

She could not. Twisting about and trying this way and that, she decided that women's gowns were designed to require a maid.

"Oh," she cried in frustration, ready to remove the dratted thing and fling it to a corner.

"Are you having a problem, dear wife?" came an amused drawl from the door that led to the sitting room.

"Julian!" she gasped, whirling about to stare at her husband while clutching her gown to her bosom. This portion of her anatomy was decently covered in a sheer white linen shift over her stays. Feet clad in white stockings peeped from beneath the dragging hem of the dress, but she felt horridly uncovered.

"Your maid?" he said, slowly crossing the room, coming closer and closer.

"Pressing my silk shawl. It was frightfully wrinkled and I wished to have it this evening. I thought to dress myself, but find most gowns are impossible to manage on one's own." Chloe babbled, she knew it. But the sight of Julian in his shirtsleeves had a strange effect on her ability to think straight.

"Perhaps I could assist you." Without waiting for her to tell him to depart at once, Julian walked around her to calmly take the fabric from her hands and began to hook up the back. His fingers felt cool against the heat of her skin when he came to the upper part of the dress. Even through the sheer lace and silk sarcenet of her gown, her thin linen shift, and the stays she had been exquisitely conscious of his touch. On her bare skin it was a delicious sensation, something of the sort that ought to be forbidden.

"Are you cold?" he inquired, all solicitous. "You shivered when I did up your gown." He placed warm hands on her bare shoulders as though to test her temperature. She didn't know what he found, but was certain that she must be feverish.

He walked around her as though to study the gown and Chloe wondered if he knew the difference between a shiver from cold and a trembling from desire. She would wager he did.

"That is a very lovely gown and becomes you well," he said in that sensuously husky voice she had heard on occasion before. It was that tone that prompted her knees to turn weak, her voice to fail, and her heart to do curious flip-flops.

"I . . . I like it," she stammered at last, knowing she must sound like the veriest fool.

"As do I, not to mention the delightful package it wraps." He ran a finger across her shoulder, then followed that light, seductive touch with his lips, caressing her with the most erotic whisper against her skin.

Chloe shut her eyes, reveling for a moment in his attentions. If only he had not been forced to marry her. If only he were not so skilled. Or perhaps she ought to be thankful for that small mercy, for he would soon tire of her and take himself off. If he failed to do that, she must escape from him.

He would be her undoing. One of these days she would throw herself into that scoundrel's arms and demand he ravish her, or whatever it was that husbands did to their wives. All she knew of the matter was that she wanted most desperately to explore the world that Julian revealed to her in tantalizing glimpses.

Then he kissed her closed lids, and at last her mouth.

Oh, Chloe wanted to forget about that dinner, the world, and above all the promise she had made to Julian that she would free him. She wanted nothing more than to remain by his side. Only she was honorable and kept her word.

But, oh, it was hard. His kiss was enticing, alluring, and madly wonderful.

When he released her, she said the first thing that popped into her bemused brain. "No wonder you were such a successful scoundrel. You do that beautifully."

Had she tossed a bowl of iced water in his face she could not have shocked him more, it seemed. He pulled away from her, giving her a look compounded of hurt and anger—or so it appeared to her.

"That is not the correct thing to say to your husband when he kisses you, dear wife," he snapped, then turned from her and marched from the room, slamming the door behind him.

"Well," she replied to the closed door, "*I* was not the one who was a scoundrel, after all."

The door to the hallway opened and Ellen slipped in bearing the silk shawl, now nicely pressed.

"Sorry, miss, nothing seemed to go right in the laundry room this afternoon. Just one thing after another."

While she bustled about adjusting the ribbons on Chloe's gown and other little attentions, Chloe could not help but reflect that the sentiment could well cover the situation in the bedroom as well.

The evening went well, she supposed later when driving back to Aubynwood. If the Squire and Mrs. Hopgood noticed the particular strain that existed between the newlyweds, they gave no indication of it.

Mrs. Hopgood proved to be a charming, intelligent lady and quite fascinated with London fashions. She prompted Chloe into revealing every current mode that existed before her retirement to the country upon her marriage to Julian.

Across the room Julian and the squire had sat in comfortable conversation discussing the coming fall season and the likelihood of excellent hunting. Twisdale was not mentioned by an unspoken mutual agreement.

Chloe marveled that the man who had been the toast of the ton could sit so at ease with the squire. She knew better than to say anything, however. She had decided that Julian was a trifle touchy about his past as a scoundrel. She couldn't think why, since he had behaved in that manner for so long and apparently enjoyed it.

Julian drove through the moonlit night at a rapid pace, whisking them around the corners at such speed that Chloe slid across the seat until she was pressed tightly against his body. She felt it necessary to cling to him, but refused to utter a word of rebuke, for he seemed in an odd mood.

When they reached Aubynwood, Chloe felt the tension between her and Julian intensify. They entered the house and walked up the stairs in silence. At the door to her room, Julian paused, staring down at her with a frown.

"Good night," she ventured to offer. "It was a very pleasant evening. And, Julian, please remember that I will do my very best to keep my promises to you."

He shook his head as though puzzled by her remark but said nothing about it. "I wish to speak with you in the morning. There are certain things we must discuss."

Chloe knew what they were. He wanted to tell her that he was returning to London and his old life. He refused to see her way of dissolving their marriage and would try no other. Now he would leave her in the country so he might pursue his old ways—chasing elegant women and living the life of a scoundrel.

Well, she would not have it that way. Annoyed with everyone in the world, especially Julian, she did not want him to be able to hide behind her skirts when a lady became too insistent. He should be free to pull himself out of any predicaments!

Maybe that was why he had kissed her, so to turn her up sweet and she'd not mind his leaving. Well, she would go first and *now,* without telling him a word about it.

Deeply incensed, Chloe quietly agreed to meet in the morning, then entered her room.

Frustrated to distraction, Julian did not go to his room, but turned and ran down the steps and out to the stables, where he saddled his horse and tore off across the countryside for a midnight ride.

Ellen entered Chloe's bedroom from where she slept. The maid was still alert and neatly dressed. "Ma'am?"

"Pack what you can of my things, enough to see me for several days until the rest of my belongings can be sent to me. I have had a sudden message from my Cousin Elizabeth. I must go to her at once." Chloe was sorry for the fabrication, but knew she needed a powerful excuse so to convince her maid.

"Indeed, ma'am," the maid softly replied, then swiftly commenced to pack the basic requirements for a Lady of Quality. Chloe slipped down to send a request for a carriage to take her to the village. Here she could hire a post chaise for the reminder of the trip.

When ready, Chloe cautioned the maid, "Ellen, I do not wish to disturb my husband. We exchanged a few words about . . . my going to see my cousin. She needs me and I will go." Chloe could almost believe her tale, so convincing she sounded.

They slipped from the room and down the stairs, out a side door, and around to the stables with no one the wiser. The groom silently drove them to the village, too mindful of the ways of his betters to question any mad behavior.

At the inn, Chloe managed to convince the innkeeper that she wished to travel by post chaise rather than the St. Aubyn coach, claiming she did not want to take the coach away when her husband needed it himself.

Since most men came before women, the innkeeper was satisfied and made the arrangements.

Chloe perched uneasily on a chair while she waited for the post chaise to be brought forward. What if Julian decided to invade her room again and found her missing? He would come after her and be utterly furious, although why, Chloe could not understand. She had made her promise and the sooner she kept it the better. Indeed, it would have been far wiser if she had taken herself off to visit some cousin immediately after the wedding instead of going along with him and falling more and more in love with the man. Oh, he was a dreadful scoundrel, make no mistake about it.

At last she was summoned to the post chaise and with a suspicious Ellen trailing behind her, they entered the carriage and took off in the vague direction of Cousin Elizabeth's country home. Chloe had been most careful to confide her direction to the driver, afraid the innkeeper would pass the information along to Julian in the odd event he did come searching for her.

"You left Mr. St. Aubyn a note, did you not?" her drowsy maid inquired.

"I did, you may be certain." Chloe had been most careful as to what she had put down in that note, too.

"He will not like this in the least," the maid predicted before dropping off to sleep.

"Hell's bells," Julian ranted when he found his wife had decamped. He had slept late following his ride, then decided to check on her come morning. Her room had been oddly silent. He had become accustomed to her gentle murmuring to her maid. Instead he found the note.

"I have gone to keep my promise. Your Chloe." Promise!

Julian searched her closet and drawers, discovering that quite a few items were missing—at least he presumed she must have packed enough for several days before departing.

It wasn't until he queried the groom that he found his first clue.

"Took her to the village. She said it were a matter of emergency, something to do with a cousin."

Julian thanked the groom, then fumed all the way back to the house. His dear wife had cousins ranging from one end of England to the other. How he was to find her before she discovered the truth and hated him for his deception he didn't know. But he had to try. Last evening had revealed another delightfully responsive side to his beloved wife that he fully intended to explore, the sooner the better. Before he totally lost what mind he had left at this point.

"I think we are lost," Chloe said to Ellen after a searching gaze out of the post chaise window.

"Can't see a thing from here. If you were to ask me, that last driver were more than a trifle tipsy," Ellen replied, her nose glued to the window on the other side of the chrome yellow post chaise, also searching through the fog.

"I cannot recall a fog this dense. Whatever shall we do?" When Chloe had decided to leave Aubynwood she had not figured on becoming lost in a fog with a tipsy driver and her maid.

"We could just sit here," Ellen offered hesitantly and most reluctantly. "But that fog gets cold and damp and we could both come down with a case of galloping consumption and be dead before anyone finds us."

"Nonsense," Chloe said but not sounding convinced at this diagnosis from her normally silent maid, "the color yellow alone should alert anyone that there is trouble here, what with the coach standing idle and all."

"That fellow should have stayed with us, not gone haring off into the gloom, I says," Ellen replied testily.

"I suspect he needed another glass of restorative for his cold," Chloe said, still not sounding convinced.

"Cold? More likely he wanted another pint of gin and ale."

"Gin *and* ale? Goodness," Chloe said in amazed reply. "Small wonder he could scarcely walk if that is what he's been consuming."

"Best strike out from here and follow the road," the usually taciturn Ellen advised. "In this fog, who would be fool enough to venture forth?" Her tone implied that her mistress easily qualified for that term with no trouble.

"Very well," Chloe said meekly, feeling terrible that she had fallen into such a stupid situation just because of her most noble intent to free Julian from his unwanted marriage to her—a marriage that ought not have taken place if he had just listened to her in the first place.

"At least he will not have to worry about my Aunt Elinor now," Chloe mumbled to no one in particular, which was fortunate because her maid was busy gathering the portmanteau, the bonnet box, and the other bundles—thrusting a few of the smaller ones into Chloe's numb hands.

They set off down the road, which was little better than a track, stumbling and struggling with their burdens as best they could.

It must have been an hour of fog and cold and a miserable road full of holes where one least expected them when they at last reached a village. There was one inn, a surprisingly respectable one, and Chloe headed for it like a hungry horse to the stables.

While the innkeeper would normally have turned away anyone who arrived on foot, there was something about this pair of women that captured his attention. The one was obviously a maid, and the other—well, she seemed to be a lady.

"Innkeeper," Chloe said, then she sneezed, totally spoiling her attempt to appear lofty. "Kachoo!" she repeated, giving up her pretense at once. "Please, I need a room for my maid and me. That wretched driver abandoned us in our post chaise some distance down the road in this dreadful fog and chill. If I ever find that dratted man I shall order him dumped into the sea!" Her sniff somewhat spoiled the threat of dire retribution.

Convinced that this was indeed Quality—who else would behave this way—the innkeeper bowed low and ushered Chloe and Ellen up the stairs to rooms. He proudly displayed a neat sitting room, a bedroom, and a closet with a cot where Ellen might be as cosy as a hen on her nest.

"Kachoo," Chloe burst forth once again when the innkeeper had left them with the promise to send pails of steaming water for a bath.

"If we don't catch galloping consumption it will be a miracle," Ellen grumbled while helping Chloe out of her wet garments. Chloe had fallen into at least two of those nasty holes in the road and taken quite a wetting. Ellen, being the cautious type who looks before leaping, had fared better. She was damp and chilly, but a hot drink, dry clothes, and a blazing fire soon cured that.

It wasn't long before Chloe had soaked in a hot tub, drunk a posset sent by the innkeeper's wife that was guaranteed to cure practically anything, and was popped into bed. The posset made her a trifle woozy, but otherwise she felt amazingly splendid, except her woeful tendency to sneeze, that is.

It was after noon of the following day that she finally woke up. A shaft of sunshine filtered through crisp curtains and touched her crumpled linen pillow. Outside birds sung in the trees and leaves danced in a light breeze. No hint of fog lingered and the air was summery again.

She saw Ellen sitting by the window and said, "I feel surprisingly well. I suppose we had best be on our way." She made a halfhearted attempt to get out of bed and was discouraged by her weakness.

"Nay, not with the fever and shakes and all you have had, my lady," Ellen proclaimed, rising from her chair to nudge Chloe under the covers again. "You need more beef broth and posset before you attempt to go anywhere."

"I do believe there is something odd in that posset, Ellen. It certainly does put me to sleep." Chloe sank back against the pillow and gave said posset a suspicious look.

"You stopped sneezing and that's a blessing. I thought for certain you'd be taken from me with a nasty case of galloping consumption." Ellen smoothed Chloe's hair back from her forehead, also noting the resumption of normal temperature at the same time. She saw to it that Chloe drank her posset and consumed a few bites of custard.

"Well, I cannot stay here forever. Not but what I cannot pay for the excellent services, for I took all I had saved for just such an event."

"You expected your cousin to have need of you, my lady?" Ellen said with a skeptical look.

"Indeed," Chloe said with a serious face. "I have known for some time that I would have to make this trip."

Then she burst into tears and allowed Ellen to stroke her hair until she drifted off to sleep once again.

The maid stared down at the tear-streaked face of her dear mistress and resolved to do anything about affairs as they stood. Once she was certain her mistress was sound asleep—for the posset did indeed have something odd in it, she left the bedroom.

Belowstairs she consulted with the innkeeper, who was most impressed with the superior lady's maid. He hastened to assist her, and before long a message was sent off to Aubynwood.

The pity of all this was that Julian had left long before the message informing him as to Chloe's whereabouts arrived.

He had tracked her down to the village, the first and second stages of her journey, by that time having a notion of which cousin she intended to visit. It was when he attempted the third stage of the post chaise run that he ran afoul. The man had decamped, the innkeeper informed him. The driver had known trouble before but this beat all. He had left the coach, passengers and all, in the middle of a road and headed off for a drink.

When informed of the direction, Julian took a chance and dashed off, following the innkeeper's muddled instructions the best he could.

It was late in the day when he drove into the quiet little village. He noted the pleasant inn, but felt no particular hope that he might know success. Even though the road had been rutted, most roads were like that. It proved nothing.

He entered the inn, found the genial host, then posed his question.

"I am looking for two women. One is a taciturn maid, the other is my wife, Lady Chloe St. Aubyn. She was on her way to visit her cousin and I had hoped to catch up with her."

The suspicious look on the innkeeper's face dissolved at the mention of Chloe's name and the visit to the cousin. Everyone in the inn knew about the cousin.

"Aye, she be up those stairs, first room on the right. Mind you, she might be asleep, for dreadful ill she's been. Maid was afraid she'd take to galloping consumption. M'wife sent up her special posset that did the trick, I'd say. She looked right as rain, or so says the maid, this afternoon."

Julian scarcely heard the last of these words. He raced across the common room and charged up the stairs. Once at the top he hurried to the first door on the right, tapping first before opening the door and entering the sitting room. Ellen was in the act of rising from a chair when he surprised her.

"Well, if you ain't the speedy one. She be in there. She's as well as can be, and I've had a frightful time of it, keeping her in bed when she's fine. If you had not come today, I'm afeared she would have demanded to go on." The maid picked up a shawl and prepared to leave the room.

At this outburst Julian gave Ellen an amazed look, then entered the bedroom, his mind awhirl. Ellen had *conspired* to keep Chloe here for him?

"Julian? Is that you, dear? Or am I imagining your voice again," murmured the slight figure in the bed.

Peeling off his coat, Julian tossed it aside, then advanced upon the bed while tearing his cravat from around his neck. "Indeed, dear wife, it is your loving husband."

At that Chloe sat bolt upright and shrieked, "Julian!" Then more softly, "What are you doing here . . . and in my room!"

He slid onto the bed, placing a hand down on either side of her so she could not escape from him again.

"I have found you and now intend to tell you what I should have told you weeks ago. It would have saved a great deal of anguish . . . on my part at any rate." He leaned forward and placed a highly satisfactory kiss on her surprised lips. Then he continued with business.

"You kept insisting on eliminating one of your names in the calling of the banns, as though that would invalidate the marriage. Sweetheart, unless we were able to find a judge that was both blind and deaf, we wouldn't have a chance with that ruse."

"But the Pouget case . . . " she began.

"Slightly different, my love. The Pouget marriage was annulled by reason of false publication of the banns in connection with the minority of the husband and failure to obtain the father's consent. It was not just the banns, dear. It was fraud on several counts. He was only sixteen." Julian kicked off his shoes while he tenderly traced the lace that edged his wife's neckline of a deliciously sheer lawn nightgown.

"Julian, am I truly your love?" she whispered, quite forgetting her promise, and the Pouget case, and that Julian must have known all this the entire time, and, indeed, forgetting everything else in the world but her beloved husband.

By this point Julian had managed to divest himself of his clothing and climbed in bed beside his wife. "Indeed, my love, you most certainly are. And shall I show you the many ways in which I love you?"

"Please do," she whispered back at him, quite willing to be taught by her scoundrel husband.

And so he began.